𝕹eural Surveillance

by

Zsoall Robi

Copyright © Zsoall Robi 2015

The right of Zsoall Robi to be identified as the author of this work (Neural Surveillance) has been asserted by him under the *Copyright Amendment (Moral Rights) act 2000*.

This work is copyright.
Apart from any use as permitted under the *Copyright Act 1968*, no part may be reproduced, copied, scanned, stored in a retrieval system, recorded or transmitted in any form or by any means, without the prior written permission of the author.

This book is a work of fiction. Names, characters, places and incidents are either a product of the author's imagination or are used fictitiously. Any resemblance to actual people living or dead, events or locales is entirely coincidental.

Birology Books.
birologybooks.com.au
enquiry@birologybooks.com.au

Chapters

Death Certificate
A New Day
Breakfast
Lunch
Afternoon Tea
Post Natal Counselling
Dream
Parents
Weekend ride
Happy Time Trip
Trivial Pursuit
The Sleep Disorder Doctor
Trip 4 – Back in the air
PDad
NITS
Recruited
Daydream
The Deck and History Strings
Greeog
Trip Five
SDD Assignment
The Commission
Death Dates – 2173
New recruit for TC-S

Days of the week

Dominica - Sunday
Pir - Monday
Tyr - Tuesday
Woden - Wednesday
Thor - Thursday
Faith - Friday
Sabt – Saturday

                    Zsoall Robi

Prologue

n a society where freedom is so vigorously curtailed that people are even afraid to speak to one another, life can quickly become meaningless. Most turn to the pursuit of pleasure, Hedonism, as a life's goal. A few who are not driven to excess still pursue pleasure, but in a less self-destructive manner. Their aim is to enjoy the simple renewable pleasures of everyday life; a refuge from the oppressive control of The Church-State.

Zallo, an artist, is such a person. He believes the global oppression of people is unacceptable. He is susceptible to other forces in operation in the society other than the compulsion to create. These forces are personified in the form of the Ghosts.

These people have managed to free themselves from the shackles of neural surveillance and are dedicated to the overthrow of the global government. Zallo, because of his sleeping disorders, seeks the help of an organisation called the Sleep Disorder Doctor.

He has always dreamt that one day he could contribute to the freeing of society from The Church-State. That opportunity presents itself when he is commissioned to create a special piece of sculpture for the Supreme Ruler. Problems arise that he is not equipped to handle.

Nevertheless, Zallo is able to pursue the simple pleasurable moments of his existence, to the very end.

Zsoall Robi

Death Certificate

<u>*Hospital-Cathedral of President-Saint Sutsugua*</u>
<u>*2105 – Sabt, April 25th*</u>
<u>*Code: 2359599942APR252105ZALLO-LIOAN-CALI*</u>

 ime: 23:59:59.92942. That's the actual time when my artificial Neural Network Transmitter (NNET) was encoded and activated. My code defines me. There is no escaping it.

I am, at age sixty-seven, a reasonably healthy albeit balding man. Shorter than average and not as obese as the average. The snow white cover had slipped from the top of my head to gather in untidy clumps under my nose and around my chin. But that is not how I would be 'officially' described. My code is the definitive descriptor. If I knew what was going to happen after the neural implant I would never have come out into the light of day. This is my first trip through Playback. I wouldn't recommend it to anyone who wishes to delve into their past unless they happen to have masochistic tendencies.
'For Gods' sake what now!'

I've just spent the last hour getting squeezed, starved of oxygen, pushed through a warm, wet, slippery passage and grabbed by the head and pulled. And I didn't like it! Now I'm cold and wet and some sadistic idiot is trying to talk to me while he's holding me upside down. Obstetrician-Father Sicnarf was in the process of winding up his prayers while holding me in that undignified position, just after he'd belted me on the bum.

As I re-live the experience some details become clearer, like my first feeling of revulsion towards the man. His basset hound eyes are bloodshot and tired. A slightly bulbous red nose assaulting the space between those tortured eyes attests to a deep dissatisfaction with his own life, which he attempts to escape through drink. Maybe that's one thing in his favour - maybe. Blotches of discoloured reddish skin crawl from

Zsoall Robi

his drooping jowls and make their way up on either side of his face to patches of baldness on his scalp. The remnants of hair have no sense of decorum.

It wasn't a good introduction to a life which was supposed to be dedicated to the pursuit of pleasure. Apart from being painful, the substantial whack frightened the crap out of me. Obviously the man didn't want to waste time getting me to breathe.

"… and may President-Saint Sutsugua grant this child a platinum-gold access to all his desires … blah … blah … blah …"

The birthing liturgy was all drivel as far as I was concerned. The blood gravitated to my head making the rest of me feel colder by the second. Finally, finally he put me down into a cold stainless steel bowl! I couldn't see very well yet, but there wasn't anything wrong with my hearing. Maybe that's why the ugly idiot in the lab coat and pointed hat carried on. Perhaps he wasn't talking to me, because I heard his voice turn away from me. Three other individuals must have been there. I heard them responding one after the other to the end of the loathsome idiot's prayers,

"So unlimited credit be it."

Gods know what they were jabbering about, but what I do know is the next thing the demented idiot said was simply not natural. It confirmed my initial diagnosis that the man was indeed a deviant imbecile.

"… and here is his Death Certificate …"

Why on earth would you give a newborn child his death certificate clipped to the back of his birth certificate? I didn't like the sound of that at all. It wasn't the only thing I didn't like.

"… and over here, fill out his name, 'Zallo' … we will fill out the cause of death as soon as it decided, but I can give you the death-date-code now if you wish."

Australia
Births, Deaths and Marriages Registration Act 2015

𝕯𝕰𝕬𝕿𝕳 𝕮𝕰𝕽𝕿𝕴𝕱𝕴𝕮𝕬𝕿𝕰

Code: 23595992942APR252105ZALLO-LIOAN-CALI

Surname ……….. *Bori*

Given name ……. *Zallo*

Date of death …... *To be advised*

Date of birth …... 2105 Nov 29

Activation ..……. *2105 April 25th 23:59:59.92942*

𝔐𝔄𝔯𝔯𝔦𝔞𝔤𝔢𝔰

Spouse 1 ……….. *Ulie Stosie Bori*

Spouse 2 ………. *Nil*

𝔠𝔥𝔦𝔩𝔡𝔯𝔢𝔫

Child 1 …………. *Nil*

Child 2 …………. *Nil*

𝔭𝔞𝔯𝔢𝔫𝔱𝔰

BMother ………... *Lioan Bori*

PFather …………. *Ical Bori*

PMother ………... *Asiil Ponsien-Bori*

𝔇𝔢𝔞𝔱𝔥

Cause …………... *To be advised*

Issuing Officer …. *Sicnarf Notes (ObF)*

𝔇𝔦𝔰𝔭𝔬𝔰𝔞𝔩

Recycle ………... *Yes/~~No~~*

Cremate ………... *~~Yes~~/No*

𝔇𝔞𝔱𝔞

To be Erased …... *Yes/~~No~~*

𝔇𝔢𝔞𝔱𝔥 𝔇𝔞𝔱𝔢 𝔠𝔬𝔡𝔢 … *To Be Advised*

I hereby certify that this is the original document recorded and registered by me at time of birth,

At … *Hospital-Church of President-Saint Sutsugua*

On … *2105 Nov 29* … Obstetrician-Father … Sicnarf Notes

Zsoall Robi

Apparently parents didn't have the choice of having the death date code deciphered for their children. Some, actually most, preferred to remain ignorant anyway. Typical. Most people opted to remain ignorant of most things these days. The information revolution had come and gone, and with it a great deal of paranoia. But what I really hated was my name. By the time I was old enough to change it by law, I'd gotten so used to it there was no point really.

As the birthing, naming and death defining ceremony progressed, my adult sensory inputs began to function more clearly and I was able to see a hazy picture of the room and its occupants through the eyes of the infant me.

I first recognised my BMother (birth mother), Lioan, by her smell. She didn't waste any time scooping me out of the bowl and clutching me to her breasts. Whatever I might have thought of her in the future, at least she warmed me up. Presently the other two came over making inane noises. Siila, my PMother (provider mother) at least smelt good although she seemed a bit business-like, not unlike Cali my PFather (provider father).

There were only a few minutes left of my Playback Trip and I was distracted by thoughts of why the sadistic idiot choose to pray to the State first, before he prayed to my parents' choice of deity on my behalf. Later I learnt the reason and it seemed perfectly logical. In fact, I had even considered a career as a priest-politician once, before realising my cat had a firmer grasp of reality than the esteemed practitioners of that particular vocational philosophy. It was inevitable that economic and population growth pressures would eventually force an amalgamation of the two driving forces of society; The Church and The State (TC-S). Both were essentially political organizations anyway, both relied on the population believing the unbelievable; like promises made by politicians, and 'salvation' promised by the disparate faiths of the over-crowded world.

Thus, being in a distracted state, I didn't notice my three parents had also chosen not to know my death-date-code. It was only a code, but a code that could, under special circumstances, be de-coded. I would have made a mental note to follow up on that, but again I was distracted by

Zsoall Robi

the cretinous idiot waving a strange rubbery thing around my head before actually putting it on me and pushing it tightly against my skull.

The scan only took a few minutes. The skullcap talked to my artificial Neural Network Transmitter, turning it on in the process, which in turn talked back to the skullcap and told it all its functions were working - even after the difficult tunnel passage. The skullcap then checked with the data storage units at Playback Inc. to ensure all sensory data was being received uncorrupted and stored with all the other data so far collected since the activation.

What you need to understand is, that now, in the year 2105, privacy is no longer an issue because it simply doesn't exist. Nobody is being monitored by hidden cameras, their purchasing patterns aren't being recorded and law enforcement personnel are hardly ever seen in the streets. There is no need. Data - that's all the global governing body needs. Every single minuscule item of sensory input received by our brain is being recorded at a mega-data storage and analysis facility. Privacy was a luxury of the past, as was personal freedom. A situation that weighed heavy on my mind.

Unlike the brain, the data storage complex doesn't make connections between sensory input data. It doesn't set up a 'knowledge' base and memory recycling system. It cannot formulate and store ideas. It just stores data. But it is data that can be interrogated by the powers controlling all of humanity on the planet. I was still pondering these things, while my baby body was being subjected to probing and prodding and measuring.

Much too soon my Playback time was up. Playback Inc. provided a comfortable departure lounge warm to ambient body temperature. There was no sound nor light nor smell of any kind. The suspension of a body in a gel nullified even the pressures of gravity. In effect it was a sensory depravation chamber. Without those sensory input safeguards a human brain could go into an un-reality loop and never find its way back to actual reality even after the Playback sequence had been terminated.

In one respect such a journey can be a profoundly disturbing re-experience. On the other hand, it can offer the unprecedented opportunity to re-live a pleasure and to gather new reactions and enjoy

　　　　　　　　　　　　　　　　　　Zsoall Robi

new emotions generated by it. They could either enrich one's life (which possibility is limited by TC-S anyway) or cause one to waste it on continuous sojourns into unreality if one became addicted to the process to the exclusion of enjoying one's simple renewable pleasures in empirical reality.

Playback Inc. offered a unique service both to individuals and to TC-S. For the individual it ensured privacy, but only from contamination from other individuals' data. TC-S had full access to all data, for reasons of security we were led to believe. Playback Inc. also provided medical support for the duration of the Trip. The other user friendly provision was the optional pick-up and delivery service. When I'd finally decided to go on a Trip, after years of uncertainty about the value of the process, they did everything for me. After inducing a deep sleep state at home, Playback Inc. picked me up from my bed and delivered me back to it at the end of the journey, still in a dream state.

It is from that dreaming state I'm now trying to awaken. As I lie here thinking about it, I'm not entirely certain whether I've been actually dreaming or 'tripping'. Perhaps after a few more events, the distinction will become clearer. My mind goes back to the idea of recording all of living humanity in the form of raw data. Perhaps it's only an extension of the evolution of DNA and its purpose. I can see the sense of knowing how many guests there are going to be in the hotel, and when they are going to leave. You can plan. There would never be a shortage of food, always enough accommodation and so on.

The world eventually achieved a stable population, albeit high at fourteen billion souls. With a five-unit family structure; two kids and three adults, two major issues had been resolved; housing and family support. The Provider Mother (PMother) and Provider Father (PFather) provided financially for the family while the Birth Mother's (BMother) essential role became the raising of the children. Sometimes it was a PFather who assumed the responsibility as he was strictly considered to be the sperm provider. Controlling birth rates (it was mandatory to have two children per household) and controlling death rates provided a workable balancing mechanism for the world population growth problem.

                                          Zsoall Robi

A New Day

Rural residence
2172 – Dominica, April 26th – time 06:35 approximately.

"Miaow … MIAOW … mew … MIAOWrrrr!"

As much as I enjoyed ruminating over those global issues, my three-legged cat Valisy decided I'd had enough cerebral pleasure for one morning, and began her wake-up concerto. As the seconds ticked by, her lament decibels increased to the point of waking up Bird. Bird, whom we call Ikik, is a South American Sun Conure parrot. He embodies all the extremes of the breed. He's the smartest, the most loving, the crankiest, the one with the sharpest beak for piercing ear lobes … and the most colourful with orange, red, yellow feathers highlighted by bands of green and blue. With both of them firmly incarcerated in the en-suite I had no choice but to shake off the lethargy and let the squawking Ikik and operatic Kitty out of their nightly prison.

The en-suite is a double security facility for Ikik. Oh the pleasures of family life! I don't need an alarm clock. At precisely between 6:30am and 6:37am Valisy begins. Ikik in his closed cage, which contains an internally woollen lined tube as his bed, joins Kitty to ensure their personal human provider doesn't neglect his duties. Maintenance of peace amongst the species determines the morning ritual. Because Bird controls and intimidates Kitty, attacking her whenever she's in my bedroom, Valisy has to be let out first. As soon as the door begins to open her great urgency magically disappears. Kitty looks up with a mew - mew escaping her whisker tousled face to turn those Mediterranean blue eyes at her human. The Mediterranean used to be blue once, I was taught at school. Kitty promenades out to the centre of the carpeted room to expertly roll herself exactly where the morning sun shines through the large picture window. Flat on her back, with her single front leg extended to its maximum reach, she waits patiently to bestow upon me her lioness purr, but only if I deign to stoop low enough to stroke her proffered white furry tummy.

Zsoall Robi

There is no sound like that purr, it contains within its cadences the secrets of the universe. My data bank must be full of it, for she's lavish with her affection. Let Playback Inc. and TC-S chew on that!

"No … No! Stop it!" I cry.

The daily admonition soon follows as Kitty proceeds to sharpen the claws of her single front foot on the corner of the carpet. I open the door. Kitty ejects herself into the hallway while Bird escalates his squawking. Valisy executes a dazzling ninety degree turn on the run at the end of the hallway to make her way towards the laundry door.

Kitty routine: Avoid Tober, the twelve-month old miniature party poodle, mostly black with a white tuft on his chest and chin, who has not yet learnt the morning Kitty etiquette. Kitty makes a mental note to herself, *Train dog in morning etiquette.* Exit house, check for cane toads. Proceed to studio door: if open go inside to finish off any unslept sleep: if closed, go under house and wait for Zallo to get up (he's always goes back to bed for half an hour after letting pterodactyl out of cage). Wait half an hour (exactly) then go to front door: Sit on edge of flower planter and call: if Zallo doesn't get out of bed proceed to vociferously wake him.

I walk to the bathroom to let Bird out. "Squawk, ktchtk, ktchtk – *Thank you but you could have come sooner! I would not have been able to hold it any longer!"* Ikik stops on the cage door for a moment before flying to his perch by the large bedroom window to evacuate his bowel.

"Splat-t."

There is only one place Bird finds suitable for defecating; on the newspaper under his perch. Nothing else will do. Even if flying around the rest of the house, an urgent squawk will announce his intention as he jets towards the open bedroom door. All the doors are open in the house. There is freedom in this house. Skinks and frogs and even snakes can come and go as they please, and *they* will not be punished for it. Ikik never wants to go out any more. He did once, and spent an entire night out in the open. Must have scared the tail feathers off him, because ever since then he doesn't even look at the 'outside' through an open door.

Freedom is an elusive concept for us to comprehend now. Once, 'time' and even 'reality' used to be considered as illusions. Freedom has graduated to that philosophical status. The NNET has ensured all

                                    Zsoall Robi

unauthorised activity is immediately notified to the Peace Corps. The intent of the perpetrator may not be known, but his location, heart beat, skin temperature and neural activity will all indicate that the prospective perpetrator is engaged in an activity which the perpetrator believes to be unauthorised.

Bird proceeds to greet the morning and his familiar friends with ever decreasing frequency of parrot squawks. I'm back in bed. The covers are drawn up to my chin. It's a cool morning. I close my eyes and begin to count down the squawks so I can get a few more minutes sleep …

Squawk! 1 - 2 - 3 - 3 - 4 − 5 - 6 - 7 - 8 - 9 -10 - 11-12 …..

Squawk! 1 -- 2 -- 3 -- 3 -- 4 -- 5 -- 6 -- 7 -- 8

Squawk! 1 --- 2 --- 3 --- 3 --- 4 --- 5

The gaps between squawks get longer and longer until silence allows me to drift off again.

"Hold the other end. I can't get the bottom of it through the door," I call out to Ffoge as we try to push a large fridge through the hole in the door.

"Wait, let me get the flowers," says Nyl.

"Wait, let me get the flowers," says Nyl.

"Wait, let me get the flowers," says Nyl.

"Hold the other end. I can't get the bottom through the door; the hole isn't big enough!" I call out to Ffoge as we try to get the … try to get the …

"Hold the other end. I can't get the bottom through the door,"

"Wait, let me get the flowers," says Nyl.

"Miaow … miaow … MIAOW."

The sound wafts through the open window to rouse me from the refrigerator obstruction problem.

"I'm coming Kitty, I'm coming." The calls stop. I crawl out of bed. It's harder this time. Toilet. Get changed.

"Miaow!"

"I can hear you Kitty. I'm coming!"

Slippers. Shuffle to the front door. Open door. Kitty darts inside. Wagging tail of dog greets me before Kitty distracts him.

　　　　　　　　　　　　　　　　　Zsoall Robi

Breakfast

Rural residence
2172 – Dominica, April 26th – time 08:30 approx.

 o back to bedroom. Forgot Kitty's bowl and Bird's bowl with the apples. He hadn't eaten much yesterday. Fill up large water bowl - large enough for Bird to have a bath. Bird Loves bath. It's best when we have a bath together. While I was letting Kitty out, Bird had a bath by himself. I'm standing in front of the cage looking at the puddle on the floor, thinking of the last bath we had together. It was the same then, water everywhere. What did Bird care? He was happy. A simple little pleasure that always made him happy.

The early morning cloudless sky promised a warm day. Maybe that's why Ikik wanted another bath in the hand basin. I sat on the toilet, he sat on the edge of the hand basin … waiting; not saying anything, just shuffling from side to side and looking at me. I know that message by now. He's trained me well. Soon I'm standing at the hand basin; he's flown to the top of his cage. It takes a couple of minutes to fill the basin. I turn the spout to the side to give him more room, but he doesn't come right away. It's a little fun game we play.

"Come on Ikik, come on pretty Bird." He sits on the perch with the sun on his orange, red and mango feathers. A magnificent festive prince to a backdrop of tropical green.

"Come on Pretty."

He's on my shoulder now, making his way down my sleeve, beak over foot. I open my palm just under the water and he steps close to the edge. Dip beak in first, shake to the left and to the right; test the wings with a bit of a flick; more beak. Temperature perfect apparently, because he's now standing in the middle of my palm doing the Birdy shake-shake. Chest wet, bottom of beak wet. Head still dry. I get the spray bottle. We love the spray bottle. First a little on the head and a bit on the tops of the wings.

Oh, "Not enough on the head," you say. Bird tilts his head to the left and puts his beak on my wrist while still standing in my palm. A good

                                    Zsoall Robi

sprinkling on this side, then Bird tilts head the other side. "More please." Certainly little one! Another big dunk of the body, and another squirt on the wings. Head goes down again, but this time left wing is fully extended into the air so I have a clear view of its underside.

"Armpits please!"

It took him a while to teach me that one. First squirt one armpit then the other. Just about done. One last shake of the head. Have to be careful not to get too water logged otherwise 'no-can-fly'. Back to the perch. Hard because the tail is saturated. Happy Bird!
Right, what was I doing?

"Miaow!"
Oh yes, breakfast. Everybody wants breakfast!

Ulie's still in bed. Valisy follows me to her bedroom, shared bedroom I should say. Two men and a woman. CC the tomcat lounges at the foot of the bed, beginning a stretch as I approach the door. Tober-boy is already on the pillow beside Ulie giving her the morning come-wake-up kisses.

Two cats, a dog and a parrot. That's our family. Plus, there's the two of us. We don't qualify as a suitable family to receive the benefits granted by TC-S. We are only a two-unit family. Neither of us would receive authorisation for the decoding of our death-date-codes as we have no licensed dependents. However, we do qualify as possible suspect dissidents. The way my thoughts for seditious action have been bubbling to the surface that may not be too far off the mark. It's not considered natural to have a lasting pair bond, let alone to be childless. It is our duty to The State and to The Church to procreate and so ensure the continuation of the economic-consumer cycle. With fourteen billion people on the planet everyone must be seen to contribute to the common good. People must have jobs; jobs produce goods, people buy goods, people have jobs to purchase goods and so on it goes.

Our artificial NNETs don't just transmit. They also receive. The purpose is to enable behaviour modification of an individual by transmitting sensory input directly into the recipient's neural mass. As non-conformist Hedonists we are both under suspicion. The activity of pursuing simple renewable pleasures isn't deemed to be an acceptable use of one's life-Time allocation.

Kitty thumps herself around the bedroom on three legs. She's hungry. First under the bed, then on top, flashing past dog. Out into the corridor, then back to the bedroom impatient for me to serve her.
Why isn't he following!
"MIAOWrrrr!"
Come on, get the mince out of the fridge and let's go!

Two small parcels of mince, enough to fill two fists, wait patiently in a small stainless steel bowl on the first shelf of the fridge. Half is for Kitty, the other half for the Butcher Birds.
Good, good, that's it. Now follow me.
Her psychically broadcast instructions are quite clear. Front door is already open and Valisy leads the way from the house to the side door of the studio.

The only reason we are permitted to have a rural domicile, with a tiny bit of land around is because we are artists. Subliminal messages can be most effectively delivered through the arts. The visual and performing arts are considered by TC-S to be the most efficient way of infiltrating the thought patterns of the masses. Advertising has evolved away from the Billboards and Social Media, and has infiltrated the decorative arts. Blatant in-your-face messages can be resisted. However, the human brain has limited defence mechanisms against subliminal messages. So Ulie and I produce Infiltration Art for TC-S in order to survive. It's the price of our limited freedom.

Kitty always decides whether to use the first or the second studio door. Sometimes it is a quick decision, sometimes it requires careful consideration. A quick clean of her bottom while I wait and watch is generally enough time to make the choice. It's the second door this time. She goes first, I follow. The rules are simple. Any human can learn them with a little concentrated application and a modicum of intelligence.
Now, listen and learn.

Cat jumps on chair, from chair onto table. Human has to keep up as best he can. If human gets to the end of the table first, which is unlikely, he has to wait. Cat walks, not runs but walks to the end of the table and points tail directly into the air. That is the flagpole signal for human to

Zsoall Robi

pick up cat and carry her, with gentleness and great affection, into the office. Please note - a show of affection by the human is not a request. It is mandatory to put cat in the right mood to accept the human's unworthy breakfast offering.

Human sits at desk and again awaits the arrival of cat, as she makes her way ever so elegantly across the desk top, furniture, papers and files. The human by this time will be getting impatient, so cat must exercise a bit of discretion as to how quickly and eagerly she accepts his humble, unsatisfactory offering.

Listen up all you kitties out there …

'Your human must be made to feel that what he has to give is never quite good enough. Don't, and I cannot emphasize this too strongly, don't immediately eat the first piece of mince he gives you. Look him in the eyes and express your disapproval with a reprimand, but not too loudly. After all, you are hungry and the mince is sooo nice. Let him try again. But only accept it if it isn't a large piece. Decorum is paramount when eating. Sometimes it is a good idea, if the human gets distracted and is not paying enough attention to you, to simply walk away. He will call after you. He will say your name, and say "puss, puss … come my pretty little girl … aren't you hungry this morning? … come on puss, puss." *After the second or third invocation you should return and reward him with your presence. When you've finished eating, always, Always leave a small piece behind. It will keep him on his feet. He will wonder whether you are ill, and he will make sure he has something else tasty for you later. It's a nice bit of insurance to leave a little piece uneaten.'*

"Well puss, puss. Are you not hungry this morning? You never eat all your food. Makes me think you're not well."

'See, I told you!'

"Come on, let's feed the Birds," suggests my human.

'Ambrosia to my soul! I love it when he feeds the Birds. There's always a chance, just a slight chance I'll get lucky.'

On my way out of the studio I almost trip on Kitty as she darts ahead of me to the bird feeding area. We go to the back veranda and I whistle my Butcher Bird call. No luck for Kitty this morning.

I glance at the kitchen clock on the wall. A lot to do today, and I have another Trip scheduled for later this afternoon. There are few things to sort out before the next big commission. A great deal depends on what I find out. PMother and PFather are coming tomorrow. BMother is at the gas mines and could not get away. Energy demand is particularly high this year. She occasionally takes on a job, partly for the credits and partly because she gets bored at home now that her two children are fully grown. Coal ran out fifty years ago and the oil is almost gone. Fracked Gas is the main source of energy now. Solar cannot provide enough for the demands of billions. There's talk of TC-S reducing family numbers down to one child. But that's not my problem. I don't really care. Politics and Religion created the problem, they can solve it. I'm just trying to stay in touch with reality.

Kitty is already under the monstera leaf that's hanging over the ground like a protective hand. It's directly under the bird feeder. She could never jump that high, but I can feel her excitement as her pupils dilate and tail begins to twitch. There are three King parrots on the feeder enjoying the seeds Ulie left for them earlier. I marvel at their colours and their peaceful natures.

I whistle again. There they are! All three of the Butcher birds. The parents always come first. Their ten-month old baby is still with them but is a lot more cautious and lands a little further away. One of the parent's grabs onto the trunk of the nearest tree, only three meters away from me. She calls to me like her baby used to call to her for food.
"Ulie! Did you hear that? She's asking for her breakfast!"

It is such a thrill to have the connection. I come back every morning to reaffirm our bond, every morning for the last four years. It's a perfect way of revisiting a past moment in time, without the dangers associated with Tripping.

I throw the piece of mince high in the air, and she hovers to catch it before flying over my head to the nearest branch. The father doesn't want to miss out and he repeats the performance. Baby cannot catch in the air yet. So I throw it a piece away from the lioness under the monstera leaf. After a few pieces for each of them, the ritual is over. Kitty doesn't move and continues to stare with hunting eyes. She's an optimist. It's hard to be upbeat when you only have three legs.

I think about that a lot: Optimism. It's a word that's gone out of fashion. Perhaps it will disappear from the English language altogether. It's not even a case of pessimism taking its place. Life isn't like that anymore. It's all about reality and dreams and Tripping and unreality.

It's about the pursuit of the moment and re-living the past moment. Everyone knows they have no freedom. We only have escape. We can only escape into yesterday and make that into today. That suits TC-S. People who have no aspirations, who have no plans for the future, those who don't think beyond the next Trip are generally easy to manage.

After the advent of neural data transmitters, an idea developed extrapolating on the concept of a closed time loop. It clashed with general String Theory, but it was an idea that liked the concept of a closed loop of energy. It became known as The String Theory of History, commonly referred to as the 'History String', where the two ends of the flexible loop of time were joined; the front bit representing one's conception, and the end bit representing one's death. Both of them happen to be at the same place in the string. Tripping became a practical application of the theory which enabled any recorded individual to revisit any point on their History String - A highly addictive and exceptionally dangerous activity. I was to learn it was particularly dangerous because of the possibility of data cross-contamination with other individuals' data, and because the data was susceptible to manipulation by TC-S; by design of course.

The mince is all gone. I'm getting hungry too. Time for breakfast toast. Whatever else happens during the day, if I get the toast ritual right then everything else will be right. It binds me to actual, empirical reality. In this reality, if I have a wound and it gets badly infected, I could actually die and have all my data erased. There is no way back from the ultimate Trip. In this reality my senses tell me things that have never been before; never exactly the same before. Tripping is only a replay. Dreams are only a replay. This morning, today, this very day and this very hour I will re-create the reality of breakfast toast: an actual pleasurable reality.

Take a loaf of rye bread, cut three slices to toast thickness, not sandwich thickness. Remove the butter from the butter tray. It shouldn't be necessary to make two trips to the refrigerator. Life is limited. I know it's been programmed to end at a certain time in the future, perhaps the near future, but I don't know when that is. So I try not to waste what has been allocated to me.

                                        Zsoall Robi

Place the butter on the kitchen bench, put the three slices of toast in the toaster. Don't forget to turn it on. Sometimes I do and then the sequence is lost. The whole day could be ruined. Retrieve a knife from the drawer, a special knife that has just the right balance for slicing and spreading butter, and prepare several slices of it ready for the toast.

Before removing the tea cups, fill the kettle with exactly enough water for two cups of tea. To achieve this simple measure first turn on the tap - place the kettle under it and count down ten seconds.
That's known as the 'Ten seconds of water', for two cups; one for Ulie and one for me.

The teacups should be the middle sized, also two large cups for cooling the tea. A simple technique, easy to learn. But first a little water in the smaller cup to help with the medication. Obtain said medication, and a 'green' tea bag from the pantry, not forgetting the honey and cinnamon. By this time, if the ritual is being carried out to the letter, one should be almost in a Zen-like meditative state. This can be, and is highly recommended as the best preparation for a serious day's work. Swallow the medication with a little water and place the tea bag in the cup ready for the boiling water.

If each action was carried out in the correct sequence the water should be boiling and the kettle whistling. Without the whistling kettle, Bird would not know the toast is almost ready. There is sufficient time to pour the water before the toast pops. It is imperative the toast be immediately buttered so the butter softens to a spreadable state on it.

Standing relaxed in front of the three slices of toast, consider the texture of the butter and how it permeates the fabric of the bread. Before it is totally melted sprinkle a little cinnamon and add a scoop of honey. Mix the butter, honey and cinnamon into a paste. As the palette prepares itself for the eating, remove the tea bag from the brew in the smaller cup. Pour the contents of the small cup into the first of the larger cups, and count to twenty. Pour its contents into the second cup. That's known as the 'Two cup temperature'; perfect for sipping without burning the lips or the beak.

It is time to snap out the Zen state. Bird has arrived on my shoulder, alerted by the whistling kettle and wants his almond jar opened. He

　　　　　　　　　　　　　　Zsoall Robi

drops down to the lip of the jar and picks up the first almond. Ulie is awake, already sitting at her desk. She's still checking her electronic correspondence. She doesn't do the Zen Toast Ceremony. She waits until I sit on the couch in front of the family room window before making her own breakfast. She's left-handed and I'm right-handed. The logistic relativity of motion of that configuration is such that our movements around the confines of the kitchen often intersect at the same coordinates, so the kitchen area isn't large enough for both of us to be moving and turning in it at the same time without clashing.

*

When going on a Trip one has to be precise and careful in defining the exact moment of entry onto the History String. One's exit is controlled by TC-S. The Zen Toast Ceremony assists greatly in training for precision in decision making. Ulie has not yet gone on a Trip. She has come to stand in front of the open fridge; she's thinking. She closes the fridge and goes to the pantry. She stands in front of the open pantry, thinking.

I've eaten one slice of toast. She's still thinking. I have finished my second slice of toast before I hear the small pot on the stove. She must have come to decision. Today she's making porridge. Selecting what to have for breakfast is often a hard choice for her. Perhaps she will never go on a Trip.

Bird is part of our breakfast reality. First he has some porridge from Ulie, then comes to me for a nibble of Zen Toast. It is a duty incumbent upon my humanity that I also provide Bird with Zen Tea to complete his breakfast. Can there be any greater pleasure in empirical reality than the contemplation of contented Bird sitting on the forefinger as he dips his beak, just to the edge of the tea to test its temperature. From my finger he climbs to the edge of the large teacup. It has a thick edge, most practical for a parrot's claws to grip with surety. Two stretches of the neck indicate his approval of the tea's perfect temperature.

I watch with fascination as he scoops up just enough to fill his lower beak. Then lifting his head, he lets the warm, soft fluid flow gently down his throat. He doesn't hurry, savouring the moment. He blinks several times before taking another sip. Looking at his face and his concentration I'm convinced he's not at all thirsty. He's just enjoying a simple pleasure, the company, the sharing - the Zen Tea moment.

 Zsoall Robi

The termination is abrupt. Bird flies back to his room, I perform a quick wash up, before plunging into the quagmire of daily complexities. I try not to think about the Trip later today. But there should be no danger. I'm going back a long time. The closer to the present the target point on the History String the greater the possibility that the human neural network will not recover from reality confusion. There have been rumours of cross contamination of data sets but nothing has been substantiated. There are multiple layers of safeguards against that happening, so I'm not particularly concerned. I'm more apprehensive about my Death Certificate and the outcome of the mandatory post-birthing counselling.

Zsoall Robi

Lunch

Studio
2172 – Dominica, April 26th – Lunch: 12:00 pm.

ortunately, it is a busy day in the studio today so there will not be much free time to think and get anxious. The feline studio manager is already in attendance as I walk in the side door. I'm late according to her, which she explains in a multi-syllable expletive as she sails comfortably from concrete floor to the large work bench. In spite of missing one front leg Kitty's height calculation is precise, accurate to three decimal points. She flies through the air with a trajectory that delivers her to the top of the bench with the accuracy of a bowling bowl as it softly lands on the green to hurtle towards the jack. She lands as a feather would, oblivious of the pull of gravity.

It is my responsibility, as studio labourer, to take instruction before doing any single thing. Said instructions are conveyed from a comfortable perch on my back. By my leaning forward and placing both my elbows on the bench Kitty is able to jump onto my back, settle comfortably with front paw tucked in across her chest and begin explaining the morning program. Not unlike a Gregorian Chant her rhythmic purring conveys much more than a set of instructions transmitted by vibrating air molecules. I close my eyes and clear my mind. Her purring begins as a low murmur deep within her soul. I contort one arm sufficiently to enable me to stroke her back. She turns so her nose is in the vicinity of my left ear. Her chest begins to vibrate as the volume of her chanting increases. I can feel her breathing into my ear, the vibrations passing from her being into my torso conducted by the warmth of her belly.

Our sessions generally end with my inability to comprehend the gravity of the intimacy and my sense of urgency to carry out her instructions. Rarely do I get it right. As I write these lines I'm only hazily aware of what she's telling me. They are not a set of commands for action of varying degrees of priority - she's trying to impart to my soul the art of 'being'.

*

As I don't have children of my own, it is only second hand information I receive about children's 'certificates' in undertones and guarded phrases from those who do. TC-S makes certain decisions at the birth of each individual. Those decisions are conveyed to the parents in the form of a contract. Any breach of the contract has unpleasant consequences for the children and for the parents. The PMother is also the enforcer of the contract within the family unit as well as being one of the providers. As I have come to suspect from my own course through life up to this point, The Church-State has little interest in matters of personal spiritual well-being. That responsibility, it seems, has been relegated by The Universal Consciousness to the critters that become part of our lives. It is the one area where TC-S has no jurisdiction.

My parents, in particular Siila my PMother, have clearly defined their wishes (ostensibly the wishes of all three of my parents, but more likely the contractual instructions of TC-S), regarding the things I should and should not be. It wasn't in the plan that I should be an artist, although with some reluctance TC-S accepted the role for me. There was a price to be paid for that concession.

*

I'm content with the ministrations of Bird and Kitty and of course Tober, the poodle. But he's still too young to take any serious responsibility for the welfare of his human. First item on the studio agenda; unload the kiln and clean the items fired overnight. Run water, splash about with sponge … oops … answer the comms … stack items in the rack and let them dry. Next, paint the orders. I'm hoping in the back of my mind the studio manager will let me get on with the job. As I make my way to the painting department, thoughts of the impending Trip break through my concentration. It's not the counselling really that's a worry. After all, life has not been altogether unsatisfactory. It's more about the death-date-code. Now don't get me wrong, I know the inevitability of life ending. Some days I think it would be good to know when it's going to happen. Other days, I don't give a rats. What gets me, really gets me, is that it's been predetermined by some person, some 'human' person who has absolutely no right to do such a thing. Forget Fate. Fate is impersonal. It doesn't know who you are, doesn't care what you want, whether you are happy or disgustingly healthy, or whether you are sick. Another meteor strikes a distant planet and makes a little hole in it. That's Fate. It is good.

What I cannot say aloud to my very best friend, even finding it hard to put into words on this page, is that … that … TC-S has no business deciding … why should It decide when a random meteor hits a random planet. It is fortunate, and one of the few blessings of life in this the 2172nd year, that TC-S cannot transmit our thoughts through the artificial neural net. Thoughts defy categorisation as data. They appear as white noise.

*

I'm standing in front of the painting bench. I can't remember when I arrived there. Too much white noise. Right … mix the pigments … done. Vermillion, special cobalt blue, ruby purple and canary yellow. I hope white furred Kitty doesn't … "Well, hello kitty-puss!" Valisy has jumped up onto the painting table and prostrated herself before me. The temptation is too great. Painting will have to wait. Nothing is so urgent that Kitty can't be given a cuddle. There goes her motor again…

… breath out - "Purrrrrrrrrrrrrrrrrrrrr … breath in - Hurrrrrrrrrrrrrrr … Out - Purrrrrrrrrrrrrrrrrrrr … In - Hurrrrrrrrrrrrrrrr …"

In and out her breathing orchestrates. For each of my strokes she responds with increased intensity until her body visibly oscillates left and right to her own vibrations. I let her stay while I apply colour to the sheets of glass. She sits up giving me Kitty-love-eyes while I work. It's getting close to lunch. Engrossed in the act of creation I don't notice Valisy leave, annoyed for not giving her one hundred percent of my time - of my life. Cats are like that. But this one gives a lot back.

Eleven fifty-eight am. I have two minutes to get to the kitchen. There is no particular reason to be so precise about it. But it's hard to break many years of precision. There is a time for all things, and all things must be attended to in their allocated time slot. There is flexibility allowed for the timing of birthing. None is allowed for the dying. I must do this next Trip. There are things I have to know; things I cannot remember, but it has all been recorded. Soon, soon.

Lunch. Just concentrate on lunch. "Time for lunch Ulie. Are you having some?"

Zsoall Robi

My partner and I like to have lunch together. Mostly together. Synchronisation can be a problem … sometimes. Today we'll have it together at the deck table outside. The day is warm, no wind, dappled shade. King parrots are already lunching on the bird feeder. Kitty's come along to join us. I think she's assessing her chances. Tail is swishing and ears are angled slightly backwards. She's calibrating heights from her favourite 'pounce' location.

I make my lunch first. It's a large kitchen, but the layout is tricky when both of us try to work in there. First, a large glass of water.
Our water is still clean, no chemicals. TC-S permits rainwater tanks. They are not much good in high density population areas … too much pollution and all the water has to be treated to make it potable. There are additives that are supposed to prevent various illnesses. Some people believe that. Some think more sinister thoughts, but it's dangerous to voice one's thoughts. Our water is still clean.

Fruit. Grown locally. Low kilometre fruit, all non Genetically Modified. On a white ceramic plate (white is best because it shows up the colours and textures of the fruit), first a peeled banana then a peeled mandarin. Sometimes arranged randomly, sometimes I set up a pattern, and eat the pattern in stages to keep it in balance. Next, a fifteen centimetre carrot cut into quarters, followed by an apple. The apple is cored and diced into six sections. The mandarin generally has an odd number of slices so it's nice to balance that with having an even number of apple and carrot slices. Lastly, but not always, a short stick of celery. The mind is already savouring the delicacies, even during the preparation. My body is readying itself for the nourishment, the flavours and textures. It is important to eat in order of least to the sweetest items. Occasionally I add a few almonds into the mix. The crunch of an almond orchestrates well with the melt of the banana and the juicy squash of the mandarin.

We sit opposite each other. Tober settles beside Ulie. He just wants to be near her. Conversation is sparse. What is there that needs to be said? What can be said to add to the moment? Why spoil it by sharing it with TC-S. All things said and heard are recorded. Rainbow Lorikeets arrive. They argue … about anything and everything … between themselves and with the King parrots. We watch and eat. Magpie turns up just as we are about to finish. He asks for his mince. Magpie catches my offering deftly in his beak. Dog is jealous … he wants all the attention

                                        Zsoall Robi

focused on himself … lunges at magpie. Maggie flaps away nonchalantly.

"Stop it! NO! Tober come here … sit … sit …. Sit Tober! … gooood puppy." Ulie and I smile at one another. Nice lunch.

It's one of those autumn days that should be bottled and sold to the folk in the cities. No doubt they would pay dearly for a breath of fresh air, molecules dancing the solar tango laced with the fragrances of late season sub-tropical flowers.

I turn at a noise behind me. It is Tober taking Ulie for a walk. She doesn't need much convincing. Tober decides when and where they go. He fetches his lead from the basket in the bedroom, together with the car keys. Ah … today he wants to take Ulie to the park in the village. Ulie holds the loop end of the lead. Tober has the other end in his mouth, a little past where its clipped to his collar. He likes to take his human for a walk.

All is being recorded. If only Ulie could see with my eyes. As the car winds down the driveway I turn back to the studio. There's a big blue sky above my balding patch. No clouds today. Too good a day to continue working, but I keep walking to the side door. Kitty bars my path. I must bend down to start her motor. It only takes one touch. Yes, it is too fine a day. Then I remember.

Afternoon Tea

Studio
2172 – Dominica, April 26th – Rest break at 3:00 pm.

layback Inc. are coming at 4:38pm. I'm having second thoughts. Do I really want to know? If I knew what was in the contract would it make any difference? What compromises did PMum have to make to let me diverge from my pre-ordained life trajectory? I'm sitting on the ground keeping Kitty's motor running. Too much to do before they come. I force myself to get up.

The morning's washed glass load is dry. Better pack that lot and get it out the door. Credits are not easy to come by these days. Kitty doesn't care about such banal matters. Her priorities seem to be governed by higher principles of existence. I begin unfolding newspapers for wrapping the glass. Newspapers still exist. The news, like the paper, is manufactured from recycled materials. There isn't much 'new' news. Life is fairly predicable now. But certain messages still need regular re-enforcing. The newspapers are good for that, and excellent for wrapping glass. When you buy one it gives the illusion you have made a choice by using your free Will. You tell yourself that's ok. Life is full of illusions. You even tell yourself it was your choice to read this or that article. But they are always the same. They are all engineered using data-cloud-psychoanalysis, your data and everybody else's data. You can only ever read what TC-S decides is to the benefit of the society. It is a comfortable illusion. I should learn to appreciate the care, but I can't. Something has to be done.

The stack of papers is ready. Kitty decides it is an exceptionally perfect stack of newspapers. What makes them particularly perfect is their location. Location is everything. It is directly in front of her human, and unfolded. It is at a height that will not require him to make an effort to give Kitty a cuddle. Barely has the last sheet settled into place on the stack before Valisy has claimed it by prostrating herself on her back on the stack, each of her three legs extended in a different direction. The temptress is extraordinarily skilful at distracting her human away from his work.

Zsoall Robi

I give in to her, yet again, but only for a moment. Gently I slide the stack to my left on the long packing bench, and begin a new stack. Kitty continues purring and watches my pathetic efforts. She waits. I smile because I already know what she's planning. There is time. There is always time for what matters, I kid myself. Stack number two is looking good, almost ready. It needs to be just the right height to make it soft. I don't need to concern myself with getting the height right. Kitty is monitoring progress. There! Now! A white purring blur has departed stack one and planted herself precisely in the middle of stack two.

Eventually we reach a compromise. Compromise. Always compromises. Evidently Kitty's bellows need a rest. She allows me to move stack two to position two (with her on it), and retrieve stack one to position one. Finally, I can begin the wrapping ritual, an activity that does provide the mind adequate space in which to contemplate, even to meditate in a fashion. Time moves quickly as I add more useless data to the already extensive collection recorded under my code. At least it will be on record that this particular activity promotes a regular heartbeat and a steady rhythm of breathing.

It's now three o'clock in the afternoon. My mind is too preoccupied to notice the quality of the afternoon light. This is my last refuge opportunity for another pleasant ritual before I have to prepare for the Trip. I try not to think about it. The first Trip wasn't really traumatic so I don't understand my current state of mind. Perhaps what makes me feel just a little uneasy is that people who have Tripped before tend not to speak about their experience. I sometimes wonder why that is. Perhaps it is too personal. I hope it's something like that and not something less savoury or perhaps unpleasant, or even … but TC-S wouldn't do that. Overt interference would undermine their control if people felt they were being manipulated in such an open fashion.

The kettle is boiling. How did I get into the house?

"Thanks for putting the kettle on," I say to Ulie.

"That's ok, but it wasn't me."

To the sound of the whistle Ikik makes his appearance. It gives me great pleasure to satisfy his craving. Maybe it's an addiction. I like a little sugar in my one coffee of the day. Bird also looks forward to his sugar hit. As soon as I move towards the pantry he begins his shuffle across my

Zsoall Robi

shoulder from left to right, right to left. First the sugar bowl, placed on the bench directly beside the pantry. He's already on his way down my arm. The lid is hardly off the bowl and Bird has perched himself on the edge and begins dipping and crunching. I think he likes the crunching as much as the sweetness. I leave him for just a few seconds, three to four dips, tops. Next, coffee jar and rye bread out onto the bench before going back to Bird.

"Come on sweetie pie, that's enough," and I hold out my right index finger to just below the rim of the sugar bowl. Such a good little bird. Even from the very beginning of his addiction he's always immediately reached out his left foot to search for my finger. He never complained, never wanted more unlike the people of our current society. Such a good little bird. Back onto the shoulder to enjoy the rest of the ritual. He also loves butter. Just a little nibble. He's truly a gourmand without ever taking his eating to excess. I sweep up the sugar he's dropped on the bench and put one spoonful in the cup to add to the spoonful of coffee.

The boiling kettle complains as the water steams its way up the funnel. It's almost as nice as the gurgling of a cappuccino machine. Add milk, not too much and stir. Toast is already in the toaster. I can't remember if I put them in before or after the water boiled. The toaster now controls my life; for the next forty-five seconds of life I have complete freedom. There is nothing I want to do, there is nothing I must do. I wait and watch the flashing lights of the toaster count down the seconds before the golden toast is ready. I wait … Oops … forgot the butter. Dive to the fridge, Bird flutters, grab the butter … toast pops. Perfect. Some things are hard to get wrong.

I place four slices of perfectly browned, crisp toast on a white plate. White is important in my life. I prefer white sheets on the bed, but Ulie likes colour. So we have coloured sheets. A white plate is also a perfect background for the orange, mango, red, green and blue colours of Bird. The three o'clock sun shines in through the kitchen window casting a diagonal ray across Bird's head and back. I'm lost in his beauty. I forget to butter the toast, until Bird takes a big chunk out of one of the slices and almost pulls it off the plate altogether.

There is some flexibility in the afternoon tea ritual. Depending on the quality of the day there are a number of location options available for

Zsoall Robi

consuming the petite meal. The porch table on a warm afternoon amongst the shadows of the palms; perhaps the courtyard if the wind is angry; or even the studio office if the sky is crying and shows no sign of being consolable. There is no need to hurry. Time enough to enjoy and still prepare for the Trip. Bird has to go back to his room. He's not allowed to come outside. I know he wouldn't fly away. He's proved it to us a couple of times before. But it's for his own protection. We know better what is good for him. Hmm, that has a familiar ring to it.

Zsoall Robi

Post Natal Counselling

*Hospital-Cathedral of President-Saint Sutsugua
2105 – Woden, April 25th – time 23:59:59.92942
Obstetrician-Father Sicnarf, BMother, PMother, PFather,
Child: 2359599942APR252105ZALLO-LIOAN-CALI*

y law, the signing of the contract had to be at as precisely a determined time as the activation time of the child's neural network transmitter. Counselling itself was scheduled for one hour beforehand, the actual date and time of birth being a minor detail.

The Playback Inc. couriers arrived on time at 4:38pm to pick up my body. By then I had been asleep for about an hour, induced by a preparation provided by Playback Inc. Asleep isn't quite the right term for it, more like comatose. Dreaming wasn't permitted prior to the Trip or during the event. Technology of the day wasn't able to distinguish internal sensory data, produced during sleep episodes, and externally received sensory input. The welfare of Trippers was a secondary concern. Data corruption, or more specifically, the corrupted results of interrogated data would not be tolerated. During normal sleep periods the neural net would automatically switch off transmission, triggered by a reduction of beta waves and an increase of alpha waves within the neural mass. Playback Inc. transport vehicles were set up to start the sensory depravation process while the Tripper was on the way to the isolation chamber.

*

I looked around the bare consulting room. There was a sense of unreality about it - the kind of room one would find oneself in when dreaming. The walls themselves provided the lighting; glowing with a soft, diffuse, cold, dead light, so dead even shadows felt uncomfortable in there. Everything was white; the walls, the single rectangular desk platform made of a white slab of material protruding from one of the walls, four white tubular chairs and a polished stainless steel bowl on a rectangular white plinth. A child lay in the bowl whom I recognised as being myself. Or at least I assumed it was me because my three parents

Zsoall Robi

were sitting opposite Obstetrician-Father Sicnarf. He hadn't changed in the six months since my birth. My birth-day is more important to me than my code. I know the code off by heart of course. It's the very first thing a child is taught when learning to speak, even before they're taught their own name.

There was no one else there. Although the meeting was concerned with the legalities of the rest of my life, and a legally binding contract was to be signed by my parents, no legal representation for the child or the parents was acceptable - not considered necessary. The contract was a standard one; the same conditions, penalties and sometimes caveats as always. These only come into play if the genome analysis of the child showed some ambiguity about the child's potential.

"Do you have your copy of the progeny's code certification, death-date certificate and birth date certificate?" I heard the ugly man ask. Why couldn't he use my name. I had a name. TC-S had no prohibitions on parents choosing a name for their child. It wouldn't affect the uniqueness of its code. The ugly man's words came out sounding dead, colourless. The walls seemed to swallow up the sound. But there was no mistaking the tone, that same officious, uncaring tone of the moronic 'idiot' who whacked me when I first arrived. As my BMother searches for the documents in her bag I have time to look at the ugly idiot. The child is also looking at the ugly idiot. We share a common thought as we gaze upon the figure clad in crimson red. We don't like the man.

How can you like a man when the first sight of him is so repulsive? He's a product of the world we now live in. He represents the kind of mind that drives the machinery of TC-S, revealed in his squinting basset hound eyes. They harbour secrets and pain and a desperate desire to balance the account ledger of that pain.

The ugly-idiot continues. "You realise of course," he takes a moment to glance with unfocused eyes at PFather from the contract in front of him, "this is all a formality. There is nothing here you need to be concerned about."

PFather asks a highly irregular question, and some would consider a dangerous one. "May I read the contract?"

                                                    Zsoall Robi

My two mothers turn alarmed looks towards him. Nevertheless, PFather holds out his hand as he finishes the sentence, fully expecting the contract to be handed to him. The daft-idiot lowers the heavy eyelids on his basset hound eyes and sighs. *'Not another one of those,'* he thinks to himself. *'It's the second one this month.'* He doesn't have to allow the parents to read the contract but he thinks of himself as a considerate man. He sighs again and turns the contract towards PFather giving it the slightest little nudge in his direction, saying, "Perhaps you would like to go to page thirty-six and peruse Conditions, Penalties and Caveats. You don't have much time before the contract *must* be signed." He put the slightest ever emphasis on 'must', thereby making it quite clear that 'choice' wasn't part of the equation. Then he suddenly stood up and walked out of the room, clearly indicative there is nothing in the contract open for discussion.

I have no way of telling how much of my Trip time has elapsed, but it cannot have been much. I lie in the stainless steel bowl and listen.

"Conditions:" PFather reads to my mothers …

"One: No part of this contract is to be divulged to any person or persons who are not duly appointed representatives of TC-S. Two: The living entity, code 2359599942APR252105ZALLO-LIOAN-CALI, is the property of TC-S."

I didn't need to hear my parents' reactions to express my own abhorrence at Condition Two. Baby-I burst out screaming, no doubt expressing my BMother's dismay. I couldn't hear the other conditions. She managed to console me sufficiently to become aware of PFather reading from the Caveats section.

"Genetic pre-dispositions give no clear indication of the entity's best area of contribution to the welfare of society. TC-S will therefore decide the entity's role in due course."

My parents looked at each other in disbelief, unable to find the words to express their emerging angst. Just as PFather was about to say something, ugly-idiot walked back into the room. PFather turned to him, still holding the contract in his hands.

The loathsome man raised his palm towards PFather advising, "No discussion is required regarding the contract. Do you wish Counselling before signing the document?" The three sets of dazed eyes obviously gave him the answer.

"I will send in the Counsellor," he said as he floated out of the room again. Anyone watching would think the ugly-idiot actually enjoyed this part of his job. "You have fifteen minutes," he threw back into the room.

The Counsellor clone must have been waiting on the other side of the door because it entered immediately, replacing the dirty aura of the slothful-idiot with its own. It looked almost exactly the same as the deranged-idiot, except for the eyes. I still remember the eyes. Since that Trip I have never liked snakes again. The pupils were in the centre of the eyeball, within the confines of a very thin bordering iris. It didn't blink. Its thin mouth split open to reveal bad, misshapen teeth. The split continued splitting in an attempt at replicating a smile, though the anatomy appeared unwilling. Sounds came from it,

"You wish counselling?" It hissed.

"What does it mean our son is the property of TC-S?" PFather asked, trying to remain calm as he aimed the question at the split faced clone.

I've been told it isn't possible to predict exactly when a Trip will terminate, but the Tripper will get a sense of confusion when it's imminent. That must have been what I felt when I heard the response to PFather's question.

"Do you own property? Yes of course you do. You have several vehicles, furniture etc, etc, don't you? It's your right to use those belongings as you see fit, Yes? So what is it you don't understand!"

"But," BMother began and was immediately cut off.

"You have the pleasure, the life-long pleasure I might add, of enjoying your son." It pauses as It looks from one parent to the other, "and you have certain responsibilities associated with that. I'm sure you will have no difficulty in maintaining the property of TC-S in good order until ..."

I awoke from my coma with a pounding in my head. It was morning. I was at home in my bed. I didn't want to be at home in my bed! I wanted to hear the rest of the counselling session. I lay there stunned, remembering every little detail. I could even feel the cold of the stainless steel bowl. The images of the ugly-idiot and of the split-faced clone will

Zsoall Robi

never leave my mind. What can I do to change the world? Nothing. But I have to try. There is nothing I can do to prevent the billions of individual souls from wanting a physical life. Perhaps they too will have no choices, under such conditions. But maybe I can do something else.

"Miaow … MIAOW … mew … MIAOWrrrr!"

I know that sound. As much as I loved ruminating over global issues, my Kitty has decided I'd had enough cerebral pleasure for one morning, and had begun her wake-up concerto.

"I can hear you Kitty. I'm coming!"

Struggle out of bed, still weighed down by heavy thoughts. Slippers. Shuffle to the front door. Open door. Kitty darts inside … throws herself on the floor, lying partly on my slippers. I bend down. Even before my hand reaches her proffered tummy her motor starts up. It seems extra loud this morning. She must be very hungry. I don't remember letting her out earlier this morning. Oh yes, I was … then the images slam into my consciousness again.

Tober's heard the commotion and comes charging down the corridor with tail gyrating uncontrollably. I have no choice. Full attention to puppy dog while Valisy flees his morning exuberance. Go back to bedroom. Forgot Kitty's bowl and Bird's bowl with the apples. Fill up water bowl, the large one; large enough for Bird to have a bath. He didn't bathe yesterday but dropped a lot of seed husks into the water.

What shall I have for breakfast? "Ulie! Are you awake? Ready for breakfast?"

Take three slices of rye bread, cut to toast thickness, not sandwich thickness … take the butter from the butter tray … place the butter on the kitchen bench, put the three slices of toast in the toaster … take special knife from the drawer and prepare several slices of butter ready for the toast.

I remember how to do these things. At least my body has been sufficiently programmed over the years to be able to do them by itself. Even as I consciously begin the ritual, my brain can still slide into no-mind while the breakfast makes itself. Before removing the tea cups, fill the kettle with water for two cups of tea … place the kettle under the tap and count down …

                                        Zsoall Robi

One - two - three - four - five - six - seven - eight - nine - ten.

That's the 'Ten seconds of water'. Counting helps to settle a chaotic mind. Sometimes I count the number of steps it takes to go from the house to the studio. It's a nice surprise when the count isn't the same as always.

I will take my medication today - it's only fish oil capsules. Take out 'green' tea bag from the pantry, not forgetting the honey and cinnamon. The water is boiling and calling out to Bird with its shrill whistle. Without the whistling kettle, Bird wouldn't know the toast is almost ready. With breakfast prepared, retire to family room lounge. Share toast with Bird.

The sun is out again this morning. We contemplate the activities for the day, silent except for the occasional chortle from Ikik. He's had enough toast and is indulging in the pleasures of 'two cup temperature" green tea. Perfect for sipping without burning the beak, both for Bird and his human.

I sit on the other curve of the couch, half facing Ulie. We start talking about my Trip as the last of the toast is consumed. I don't know if I'm breaking the law if I divulge anything from the Trip. Anyway, she will keep it confidential. Besides, TC-S can say it was all an hallucination during a bad Trip and deny everything. It has the power to create our reality. Just as I'm about to begin she says,
    "You look worried. Did something go wrong last night?"
It is then I realise the impossibility of the situation. Anything she hears, says or sees will be recorded. I can't even write down my concerns to her. It would be bad for us, very bad if we had a visit from the Peace Corps. So I shake my head.
    "No, not really. Just a little confused about a couple of things."
    "Do you want to talk about it?" I shake my head again.
    "Can you talk about it?"
    "No, not really. It's nothing serious. I'll sort it out in my own mind."

If only there was some sort of shielding device to block the transmissions. Surely they must exist. But how does one get one, or even go about searching for one without being detected. I lapse back into my own thoughts this morning. All other considerations fall into the

    Zsoall Robi

background. I stare out into the garden, focused on the slowly rising sun through the palm fronds but not seeing its splendour this morning.

Are we all simply chattels to be maintained and used and then discarded when no longer useful? Do we have a 'used by date? Is that why we have a death-date-code? Why was I cut off at the critical moment just when the subject of my death-date-code came up? BMother … I will speak to BMum, and PDad about it - if they will discuss it.

"Zallo. Zallo! What is the matter with you? I've been talking to you for minutes! Are you sure you're all right?"

"Just lost in my own thoughts … thinking about the day's schedule. Sorry."

I count my steps on the way to the studio. It comes out all wrong. The wrong tally with half a step at the end instead of a full one. That has never happened before – just half a step short at the end. It might not seem like a big deal, but it disrupts what little normality we have left. I should just get on with what has to be done. If I drop dead by lunchtime, so be it … but I think I'm still useful.

The triptych glass mural has to be packed, the shower partitions screened and airbrushed, sandstone bases to be cast and the billboard design for The Sleep Disorder Doctor started. As I begin to plan out the order of activity my mind relaxes and I become the tools I'm about to use. She called me Mr. Millimetre, my painter friend. Well, I like to be accurate. First, the box for the triptych … I'm the tape measure, one of those old style jobs, with character. I wouldn't want to be a laser measure that gives no opportunity to make mistakes and to come up with creative solutions to resultant problems. "Measure thrice" my grandfather said, once for the job, once for yourself and once for me. Whenever I'm the tape measure I remember my grandfather. He used to design and build bridges.

I hook myself to the end to the syn-plank, wood is still available but becoming less readily procurable, and measure out six hundred and thirty millimetres. I measure and mark off again, then I measure from the other end. That's my 'Grandfather measure'. I have a white beard like my grandfather, but not as tidy. For a moment I think, *I hope they are recording all this, but be dammed if I'll tell them what the third measurement is about.*

　　　　　　　　　　　　　　　Zsoall Robi

Measure, measure, measure, mark off, cut. Check length. I love being the saw. I'm sharp and fast. I make a super clean cut. A fly would break a leg on my cut, it's so smooth. Twelve measures and four cuts later I'm ready to be the drill bit. I have great power when I'm the drill bit. I can go through plastic, glass, ceramics, granite and even steel. The heat travels up my spine as my tooth bites into the syn-plank. It's soft and pliable and gives itself over to my intentions. Once, twice, sixteen times it gives in to me. It shall be rewarded with the companionship of its fellows as I become the tool to join each syn-plank to the next. What greater pleasure can a hammer have than to feel the power as its impact thrusts the nail deep into the heart of a syn-plank. One after another each nail is driven home to seal the box to safeguard its precious contents.

I come back into myself and look at the box. An hour ago it didn't exist. I gave it life. I endowed it with the right to occupy space in four dimensional reality. I gave it the opportunity to achieve and then to die with satisfaction when its work has been done. It has no use-by-date.

There are a great many extraordinary weather events on our planet nowadays. Ocean currents are confused. Too much cold water from melted ice caps, too much hot sun through the ozone depleted atmosphere. But there is no chaos as overpowering as the turbulence that emanates from the end of the airbrush nozzle. I prepare myself to receive the cyclonic winds as they make their way from the bowls of the compressor to my minute opening. With the slightest pressure adjustment I eject blood red pigment onto the glass surface. It strikes and spreads and screams in silence at the sudden impact against the transparent resistance. The pigment has no choice. It must do what it was destined to do. It must bend to my will.

The cyclone doesn't abate until all the pigment is spent, prostrate in exhaustion, having created the sensuous contours that will become the design on the shower partition. To make manifest in reality is an act of divinity. *How can such a creator, any creator, deserve a pre-determined end-by-date? Stop that! There is more to be done.*

The billboard for the Sleep Disorder Doctor (SDD). Of necessity there are close affiliations between the SDD and TC-S. Consequently, the content and design of the billboard has been defined to intricate detail by TC-S. Every word, every colour, the nuances of spacing and punctuation, all have their significant influences on the human psyche. There is no room for creativity here. If I'm owned by TC-S then it is just and fitting I should be a good and faithful tool. I am still useful.

The work begins. It progresses uninterrupted. The com-link would have sounded by now if the work wasn't satisfactory. All, absolutely all sensory input is recorded and monitored. They hear what I hear and see what I see. They watch as I work. They approve in silence and disapprove with penalties. Today there is silence.

Lunchtime has come and gone. It was the same as yesterday and as the day before, and the day before that. It will be the same tomorrow and the day after that, and the day after that – if I'm not terminated. It was a good lunch, the type the body and the mind can both enjoy over and over again. Fruit. Grown locally. Placed with attention on a white plate because it is a painting of the essence of life that needs my full awareness. A defrocked banana, a peeled mandarin, a not too large carrot and a cored apple. Lastly a short stick of celery and a glass of clean, cool fresh water. I'm already looking forward to tomorrow's lunch.

I count the number of steps on the way back to the studio. That was better. Only one full step out. Thirty-six steps from the studio to the house, and thirty-five steps from the house to the studio by taking exactly the same route. Sometimes I think my legs are getting shorter, otherwise there can be no reasonable explanation for that kind of anomaly. I will count again when I return to the house for dinner.

The SDD - I continue working on the billboard, but get interrupted. It's Kitty. She desires a cuddle, her motor already idling as I reach down to pick her up. There is always time to give Kitty a cuddle; like there is always time to have a cup of tea with a visiting friend, even if it's in the middle of a working day. It is a precious pleasure. A true freedom that must be cherished, exercised and honoured. My friend didn't come today. Perhaps tomorrow. So now I give Kitty a big cuddle. She purrs double time when I rub her fur backwards and make it all stand on end. She licks her one paw furiously in ecstasy, then suddenly jumps off the table. I'm still useful it seems. Sleep Disorder Doctor. Why do I keep thinking about that name? No, it's not just because I'm working on their

　　　　　　　　　　　　　　　　　　　　Zsoall Robi

billboard. I couldn't care less about their billboard. Damn the billboard. For that matter, Damn TC-S. I have a sudden moment of panic … then relief … no, they can't record thoughts … yet.

The time of day has arrived when the sun bleached heavens go to sleep. Sometimes I put the tools away. Tonight, no.

I want to know how many steps to the house. I try to take absolutely normal steps. It's hard not to think about what is a normal step. What if I have to avoid stepping on a green tree frog? We still have them here. There is grass and there are trees. Each tree is registered and each is protected, and inspected at regular intervals. We still have tree frogs. Step, one, two … sixteen, seventeen … I can see the front door now and try to estimate how many more steps it will take. Twenty-four, twenty-five … it will be thirty-five. No … thirty-three, thirty-four, thirty-five, thirty-five and a half. Not good. It should have been thirty-five.

My parents didn't come to visit today.

                                                                Zsoall Robi

Dream

House
2172 – Pir, April 27th – 6:30pm

It is Kitty catching time. The heavens go to sleep and Kitty cat awakens from her daytime slumbers ready for the evening hunt. She has freedom, the kind of freedom most of us can only dream about. Kitty will not come when called, unless she actually wants to. She will fearlessly defy authority. There are no penalties or reprisals. I can call or shout, cajole or plead. I can threaten or entice, pray or froth at the mouth. She will not come until she decides it is time to end my anxiety. I don't really think she even cares. She is free.

"Come on puss-puss, time for din-dins. Here kitty! Where are you puss-cat?"

I step back into the house. It's still too early for her. After she was bitten by brown snake one night two years ago, which almost killed her, I became anxious every night that she would not come home when called. But she taught me to let go of my fears. She taught me that whether I fear for her safety or not, what will be, will be. I have learnt not to fear for her life. But I still can't go to sleep at night until she's in the house. I hope, with time, to become better at that. Now, since my last Trip, I have begun to have other fears. Perhaps that's too strong a word for it. I'll call it 'uncertainties'. I'll talk to my parents. I hope they will speak with me about those difficult matters.

Stepping back into the house I realise the temperature is dropping steadily. I enjoy winters. It's a time to be warm in a cosy, non-stifling non-humid kind of way. The ancient heater still occupying its favourite place in the corner of the sitting room, is almost beckoning to me. It must know how much I enjoy setting the fire. Solar space heating is much too impersonal, too utilitarian. Our old wood burner has soul. The dead trees I cut with my friend Nethenk in late summer, are stacked and ready to release their warmth. They have already warmed me once, then again during transportation and stacking. Now they will dance with flames and warm me again. It is possible to get permits to

                                   Zsoall Robi

gather dead wood. Kitty will wait till the fire's going. I'm upset with her yet again. Patience - that's the only way to live with a cat.

Newspapers are still printed. The news is as predictable as the editorials. I don't know why people even bother to buy them anymore. But they do have one good use, to prepare the fire bed (also practical as a soak layer under the kitty litter). Living beside the rusting old heater is a new cane basket, at least it's a new companion for the heater. We have resurrected its life. We didn't have to train it, for it used to be a cane picnic basket until it retired. A perfect shape and size for its new profession as a guardian of kindling. I heard a whisper from a dusty corner in the antique shop whilst visiting it one day - '*Kindling*' - and turned towards it. I must have heard it because when I pointed it out to Ulie she immediately said "kindling." She must have heard it as well. It became our 'rescue' picnic basket which carriers exactly the right amount of kindling to set a week's worth of fires. So I open the rich, aged honey colour of the top and take out several handfuls to layer them cross-thatched on the paper. Tober is beside me watching intently. He knows what I'm doing and just watches. He doesn't try and distract me with his favourite ball, which is beside him - just in case.

A single match is all it takes to bring life to the arrangement behind the glass door. I sit on the ground beside Tober and watch as the baby flames become unruly adolescents, then an adult all-consuming fire breathing hungry dragon. The dragon must be fed, so with care I open the front and give it several large pieces of wood. For a few minutes the fire struggles under the heavy burden. Patience. Again all it takes is a little patience, and a little daydreaming to give the dragon a chance to find the full expression of its power. Within minutes I have to adjust the damper. For the next half hour the fire will not need attention. Time to try and find Kitty again.

"Valisy … Valisy!" There was no need for me to stand outside in the dark and shout into the evening stillness. She was there beside the flower planter, nonchalantly coming out of hiding. In the mornings she will often sit on the top, wide edge while calling to me to wake and administer to her needs. The evenings are for hunting and hiding – and of course for frustrating her human.

"Kit-cat, where have you been puss?" Obviously a silly question for she doesn't deign to dignify it with an answer. Instead, I'm invited to stroke her exposed tummy as she executes a deft manoeuvre, turning a

 Zsoall Robi

barrel roll while simultaneously stretching her full length and coming to rest directly on my right shoe. She begins to recite her dinner order even before I have her in my arms. Dinner is a special event and has certain procedural requirements, which, if not met to the letter then the dinner is considered a failure and will not be eaten.

The mix of sea foods with crab meat and shrimp has to be served on a small rectangular glass dish which is decorated with light blue mosaics, the same colour as her eyes. It must be placed on the floor in the en-suite next to her water bowl. It must also be garnished with a sprinkling of small biscuits, some on the floor beside the plate and some directly in the plate. It is indeed a wondrous thing to see Kitty inspect the arrangement before giving final approval by sampling the biscuits first. On numerous occasions the seafood has been left uneaten, simply because the garnish was missing.

The rest of the evening is mostly an anti-climax, apart from the enjoyment of a crackling fire for the next couple of hours. Tober likes to annoy Kitty. She'll put up with the young pup for just so long before all three of her legs propel her at him with a sudden explosion of energy. A puppy is no match for a three legged fearless lioness in full attack mode! Eventually the fire begins to die down and my thoughts turn towards sleep. Some nights it is hard to fall asleep. Some nights it is hard to stay asleep. I will read and try to take my mind off the events of the last Trip. Flashes of it have been coming back during the day. I fervently hope the unpleasant experience doesn't entwine itself around a dream. It has been known to happen. Some people have even been known to go into a coma, into a strange sleep loop that doesn't allow them to awaken. The contents of a Trip can so entangle the original reality of an event that the resultant confusion confounds the mind. Electoconvulsive Therapy is the only known treatment. Even that isn't always effective, though it be applied several times a week. I have not had the night terrors yet after just two Trips. The next one, I promised myself, would be to an event of a purely pleasant nature.

There is no escaping the demands of a feline female.
    "Miaow … MIAOW … mew … MIAOWrrrr!"
    Let me translate for you.
    "Human! It is bed time! It is past our bed time! When do you intend to come to bed, human?"

Accompanying the yowling is a flurry of galloping to the bedroom and back into the lounge, several times. I let her do it just to enjoy the pleasure of her indignation. The purr motor kicks in almost as soon as I start making my way in her preferred direction. Kitty runs ahead, does a sharp ninety degree turn at the bedroom door, dislodging the rug at the same time. She almost hits the door jamb. A moments pause to check her human is following, then up onto the bed. Tail goes from horizontal to vertical, a semaphore indicating her readiness for a stroking.

I kneel on the floor beside the bed and begin the ritual. Valisy arches her back, ramps up the decibels and slowly turns her head towards me. Up until that moment I had a close up view of her pencil sharpener. Presenting that spectacle is the feline equivalent of saying, *"it is time for you to pay particular attention to my wishes."* Still with back in a graceful arch, Kitty half closes her eyes and at the same time executes a semi-jump turning towards my face to plant a forceful head butt on my forehead. I reciprocate. She returns the acknowledgement. We continue for several more mutually satisfying head butts. There is nothing else in my mind. She and I are one. Of the one mind, absorbed in a perfect union of understanding. Humans are incapable of such a total emersion in one another. But I don't think about that whilst in the moment of soft ecstasy.

While I go through my evening ablutions Kitty consumes her dinner, prepared beforehand as ordered. It isn't long before I'm in bed, book ready but Kitty not. One cannot expect a complex female like Valisy to 'simply' come to bed. No. First there is the mad cavorting around the bedroom from one corner to the next, onto the bed, off the bed, under the bed, onto the couch and behind the couch, yowling intermittently. Obviously the dinner was found to be satisfactory. I pat the bed beside me making a small nesting hollow. We are almost ready to settle, but not quite. Suddenly she flies right up to my left exposed arm and bites into it! Ears back, eyes threatening a storm she bites again - not hard, but hard enough. I believe she's just reminding me who's in charge of the bedroom. I don't think it's meant as a blood-letting exercise, though it does achieve a small measure of that as well.

"Ah! No! Don't bite me!" Is my usual response … her's is to curl up in the newly prepared hollow and begin her sleep-purrs. We're both ready. I take a moment to consider our relationship. The bite does hurt,

                                                   Zsoall Robi

but would I have it any other way? I think not. Sometimes true affection can hurt. I'm already looking forward to it tomorrow night.

I haven't thought about dreaming during the entire going-to-bed ritual and now the book claims my full attention. As I read I gradually become the protagonist. The hours jump ahead when not being watched. It is late and a drowsiness comes upon me.

Half awake, I get up and put Kitty to bed in the en-suite forgetting to close the door. A cool night tonight, doona right up under the chin … it's been a long day … will have to finish the, the … those colours were not quite right … get up early … tomorrow is … is …

… Why is she running so fast? I can't keep up. Those buildings shouldn't be there. They're protruding out the side of a hill. She runs inside one of the tall ones without windows. It's too far away. I'll have to fly to catch up. So I run, extend my arms and try a little jump into the air. There's a man chasing me. I try running faster and raise my head and lift into the air. I can fly! The man is still running on the ground, following. He has strange eyes. I don't like those eyes. Where is she? The building is gone. She's standing on a white box. I'm so high that the box almost disappears, so I dive and loose control.

The man is sitting on a white chair. Another man is standing beside him. They are laughing through thin lips; hissing laughing. The woman is up against a white wall. Looking around I see we are inside a white cube. I can no longer fly and look back at the woman. She's upside down. No, I'm upside down. Trying to focus I realise I can no longer see. That noise, a crying … it's coming from me. The man is standing holding me in two hands pulling me out of something soft and warm and dark. I don't want to come out! The man keeps pulling on my head. He holds me upside down and I cry out in pain. "He's due to be terminated on …" he says and I scream. I don't want to know. My eyes open and I can see myself running towards some buildings protruding from a hill. Why are they protruding like that? I don't need to do anything to stay in the air, just concentrate. I'm flying low, followed by an ugly man running on the ground. "I don't want to know the date!" I think I'm shouting, then I hear a soft voice. It's calling to me from far away … "meow … meow … Meow."

                                      Zsoall Robi

𝕾uddenly my eyes are open to the morning - Kitty is standing on my chest. I feel sweaty and I'm thinking about something I should be remembering, but I can't. As I lie there my thoughts go into a loop. Something to do with dates. Kitty keeps yowling. Now Bird has started up. Pushing Valisy off the bed I let Bird out of the cage.

𝕶itty thumps herself around the bedroom on three legs, trying to escape pursuing Bird. Kitty is hungry. First under the bed, then on top, flashing past dog at the door. Out into the corridor, then back to the bedroom.

Why aren't you following?

'MIAOWrrrr! Come on, get the mince out of the fridge and let's go!'

𝕴'm not ready to get up yet. It's only five thirty. So I go back to bed and pull the covers right up to my chin. Date … Dates. I have to remember some dates. Ulie's birthday, our wedding anniversary. I'm not good at remembering dates. In fact, I don't want to remember … I hear an ugly man saying "You can apply to have the …" He says something about a date. I don't want to know the date!

"MIAOWrrrr!"

𝕬nother hour has just fled as I look at the clock. My palms are sweating and the bedding is clinging to my damp skin. I must be getting a fever.

"I'm coming Kitty!"

𝕿oday is … Pir … no, it's Tyr the 27th … no, the 28th. Date. Date. I can't remember the date. Getting up I have the feeling I should be remembering something important about a date. Ah, yes. Tomorrow, the 29th. I have to visit my parents. The three of them are always so busy. It's hard to get them all to the one place at the one time. Must not forget!

𝕴'm relieved to have remembered about the date. But I still have a vague feeling about something from a dream, something to do with a special date. Can't be important. Tomorrow is important. I begin to look forward to the pleasure of breakfast with Ulie and Kitty and Ikik as I get dressed.

"How did you sleep?" Ulie asks.

𝖂e ask each other that every morning. Neither of us sleeps well. It would be good to be able to share a good night's sleep, especially when I don't have to get up several times during the night.

Zsoall Robi

"I slept right through," I say.

"That's good. It's about time. You've not been sleeping well lately."

"Yes, well it wasn't all that good. I woke in a sweat. Even now I have the feeling I should be remembering something … about a date. It's probably nothing important."

Zsoall Robi

Parents

Parents domicile.
2172 – Woden, April 29th – 9:00 am

hat happened to yesterday? I can only remember the breakfast. Another bad dream last night. I don't remember much of it. There was a huge basset hound. I was looking into its eyes and it was grinning at me. I think he was in a white room, full of people. They were all talking. I was cold. The basset hound started sneering. Then there was this very odd thing about me flying, not in a plane but under my own power - not exactly flapping the arms, just flying; and the very strange sensation of not having control of myself in the air.

I have to keep reassuring myself that today is Thor. It's almost nine o'clock. They don't like me to be late. I arrived on the antique motorcycle. It used to run on fossil fuel. It's been converted to hydrogen. Clean, quiet. Lets me think while I'm riding. At last ... a long ride. I tried not to think about the questions I was going to ask them. The morning sun was too nice to waste on sombre thoughts.

My parents are in their nineties but still very active. Some people are given a distant use-by-date. PDad is an official in the local branch of the Australian Church-State offices. He never talks about his job. He said once when I was young and inquisitive that it was best if I didn't ask him questions about what he did. I think he was in some kind of law enforcement, perhaps even the Peace Corps. But I don't really know. Anyway, he never comes out to meet me.

BMum always comes out when I arrive, even if it's raining. PMum stays inside continuing to do whatever she's doing. But she's the one who looks after me when I visit. BMum is all cuddles and coos, whereas PMum is the practical one. Our family unit worked well, except for my brother. I have not mentioned him yet. Greeog was a rebel. We lost track of him after he disappeared from the Adjustment Institute (AI). PDad could do nothing to get him to conform ... to anything. The Peace Corps kept annoying us for years looking for him. But I think he must have had one of those forbidden surgeries and had his artificial

                                            Zsoall Robi

neural net somehow de-activated. Otherwise he could not have become a Ghost. Maybe he's dead. We just don't know – it's all just guesses.

"So what is so important that it couldn't wait?" PDad asked, seemingly a little annoyed. "Your mother and I have to be at the office in an hour, so you had better make it quick."

"Give him a bit of peace," BMum gently admonishes him.

PDad frowns, PMum gives me a hug. Greeog was always his favourite in spite of his rebellious nature; perhaps because of it. We sit in the family room of the ground floor apartment that has been our home ever since I can remember. Nothing's changed. Everything's still where it was when I was a boy. It's even the same long couch in the same place opposite the window. Society had to start using more durable materials. Rubbish dumps were taking up too much valuable real estate. BMum sat with me while PMum prepared a hot drink and something to eat. It was a long trip into the city and it was cold when I left home.

"Well, what is it boy?" He called me 'boy' in spite of my age.

"Can't this wait until Siila brings in the tea? What have you been creating dear?" BMum asked.

"Just the usual boring things. There isn't much opportunity for creativity these days. TC-S defines everything. There's the occasional private commission. I'm doing a billboard for the Sleep Disorder Doctor. Do you know of them?"

I glanced at Dad just in time to see an unexpected flicker of his eyelids. *What is that all about?* I know my Dad very well. He never, never reacts to anything. At the same time PMum came into the room with the tray, and almost dropped it. She's ninety-six but could still thread a needle without glasses. Steady as a rock. I didn't think twice about why she almost dropped the tray. She has the sharpest brain of all of us. She works in Codes, in the same building complex as PDad. That's what makes me think they will be able to explain things for me. I had too many questions and wanted to blurt them all out at once. But I took a moment to sip the tea while looking at PDad. He was silently, intently watching me.

"I've been having some dreams," I started rather lamely, "and I've been on a couple of Trips." Perhaps I should have said it the other way around.

"There you are dear, that's your problem. Those History String Trips might seem very exciting but they are really quite dangerous," BMum said immediately.

"Is that why you came today, boy?"

"Well, yes and no. My first Trip was back to my birthing day." I noticed they all looked at one another. "Then the second Trip was to the Post Natal Counselling." PDad and PMum again looked at each other, for longer this time, then Dad turned to me.

"Why?" He was always so direct and brief. It made discussions with him difficult, but at least it opened the door to my first question.

"Why did I get my Death Certificate on the day I was born?"

"Contrary to what you may have heard in rumours," he began, "TC-S cannot afford to leave anything to chance, son."

It wasn't often he called me 'son' and generally only when about to embark on an extremely serious subject. "It is because of population pressures, the need to keep it all in balance, you understand." Was that a question or an assumption? Everyone knew the planet could not support anymore people. No one cared to know how the balance was achieved, or at least nobody talked about it openly.

"Does that mean our life spans are ..." Before I could complete the question PDad responded. He must have known all along what I was going to ask.

"Yes, only in so far as Fate would have chosen for each of us. Without going into detail, which I don't know anyway, a 'random' selection process is applied at birth and the date recorded. That's all I can tell you. It is for the common good of all."

I didn't know what to say. The suspicion was lurking in my mind ever since the first Trip, but I wasn't prepared to face the reality of it. Now I had to ask myself whether I wanted to know what my 'expiry' date was. What difference would it make to my life? Would it help me to live it better, or more fully - or more carelessly? What if there was an event that made my death premature? I could not conceive of such a thing. Yet accidents did happen. TC-S could not possibly control everything. These thoughts buzzed around my head without finding a safe place to land. Dad was silent, watching me. Perhaps he went through the same trauma when he was young. History String Tripping has been around for a long time. Finally, I gathered my thoughts enough to ask the next question.

     Zsoall Robi

"Do you know …?" This time it was BMum who cut me short.

"No dear. We don't. Not yours or ours. It's easier to live with uncertainty." She said this with such conviction and such an air of authority that I didn't think to question her statement. Strangely, it put my mind at ease, at least temporarily. "I hope this hasn't caused you any trouble sleeping," she added quite naturally. That hit a nerve. Perhaps I should tell them about my dreams. Putting the thought aside for the moment I had another question.

"So I take it the cause, that is the circumstances of … of …" PDad came to the rescue. I don't know why I had so much trouble talking about death. It wasn't as if I was far from it at age sixty-seven. Perhaps it was because it had become a tangible reality, my own personal reality.

"Some people choose to know these things. Your mothers and I have a different philosophy. We are, what you might call, Naturalists. We understand things are as they are because of overpopulation. We accept that. We accept a balance has to be maintained. But we also believe we can have more fulfilling lives by living it with a certain amount of ignorance."

Dad was speaking in such generalities it made me think he wasn't telling all he knew. It was just a feeling. When I add that to the uneasy glances between my parents earlier in the conversation … well, there are things here that I shall have to think about later. Besides which, I can't recall him ever having dedicated so much of his time before to talking to me about anything. Was there a reason to hide anything I wondered? We all forget the implants are always working, always recording everything about us. Occasionally, though very rarely we suddenly pull ourselves up short … oops, better not say this or that. I was beginning to feel it was almost like that for my parents now, as we touched on these difficult subjects.

Our drinks were getting cold and PDad was getting restless. Whether he really had to go back to his office or not … I don't know. I've never doubted him before.

"Yes, I have been having some uncomfortable dreams since the two Trips. But I had to go. Something was nagging at my memories, very old memories." BMum put her hands on my knee as we all took a sip of tea. It could have been any kind of chemical concoction, but BMum once said it tasted like Green Tea. I don't know what that is, but

                                        Zsoall Robi

I got into the habit of having it in the mornings with breakfast. It was nice to share that little pleasure with them once again.

"Dad, at the Post Natal Counselling you asked a question, which I gather you were not supposed to do." He nodded in confirmation of the fact. "You asked about property. Why? I don't have children, so I don't exactly know what happens when the children are born." Dad nodded again, and kept nodding his head whilst obviously deep in thought.

"There is great wisdom in our system of government. It is a combination of centuries of experience gathered by our leaders, and the dictates of our Gods as made known to us through the Saints' interpretations. That wisdom is accepted by all of us belonging to the one body of Faith. We all belong to one another. We all belong to The Church-State."

He stopped abruptly, as if he had finished reciting some political mantra. Was I supposed to understand all that?

"Yes, but what does that mean?"

"It means, dear, that our mother is The Church and our father is The State. We belong, each of us, to our parents."

These were the first words uttered by PMum. Again it was like listening to a catechism recitation. It didn't answer my question, and I had the feeling that further probing wouldn't be any more fruitful. But it all sounded terribly like we were being treated as property by our rulers, who could dispose of us at will when our expiration dates matured, or before, if that happened to be expedient. There was no other way possible for me to think about it. PDad could see I was turning something over in my mind. He stood and came over to the couch, and put a hand on my shoulder.

"Son, it looks to me like you're having a lot of trouble sleeping because of confusions in your mind. Why don't you go and see someone at the Sleep Disorder Doctor clinic? It's said they are very good at helping in these kinds of situations." Having imparted the advice, he left, PMum following close behind.

"Yes, dear, that's a very good idea. Let us know how you get on," she said. I was left sitting there with BMum.

"I remember from my dream that you were also there. You all seemed extremely concerned at one point when Dad read out something to do with a caveat. Do you remember that mother? He

                                         Zsoall Robi

read, as far as I can remember, something along these lines … Genetic pre-dispositions give no clear indication of the entity's best area of contribution to the welfare of society. TC-S will therefore decide the entity's role in due course."

"I think I know what you want to ask me but I'm not very good at these kinds of questions. What I can tell you though is that both your education and your conditioning have been tailored to bring out the best of your potential."

Obviously it was no use trying to get more specific answers. Like for instance; I wanted to ask who determined my potential, and what method was used to do that. Mulling over how evasive everyone had been today led me to think back over one very peculiar thing PDad said. The advice he gave me came across like a normal everyday suggestion from one adult to another. Nothing strange about that. The strange thing was the way the suggestion was communicated. Dad never suggested or requested anything. They were invariably orders when he wanted anything from me in the past. Sometimes the order was expressed convivially, sometimes more 'officiously', but he never 'requested' or 'suggested'. Why now? What was so special about today's circumstances? Nothing has happened that I can recall that would have made the slightest difference to his way of speaking. He also called me 'son'. All very unusual.

As much as I would have liked to have asked him about that, it was quite impossible. These days I think, most people live with many an unexpressed and unanswered question. It was simply safer to keep most things to oneself. What was it I said just before he made his 'suggestion'? Oh yes, my bad dreams following on from the two Trips. Many people are having sleeping disorders, consequently there has arisen a major industry dealing with them. And there are numerous types of sleep clinics in every community. So why should PDad suggest that particular one. It seemed a bit of a coincidence that I'm working on a job for them as well.

On the way home I thought more about my visit, and the more I thought about it the stranger it became. I almost started to feel apprehensive there might be a visitation from the Peace Corps soon. But there was nothing subversive or dangerous in our conversation. Unless of course I'd stepped out of line with delving too deeply into things that perhaps should not concern me. Well, I won't dwell on it. Today is a working day and so is tomorrow.

Best just to get the head down and make some progress on that special job, for now I was starting to think there was something out of the ordinary about the SDD billboard.

As much I as enjoyed riding my machine and looked forward to every opportunity to do so, too many thoughts interfered with my enjoyment today. Perhaps having to ride most of the way through densely populated areas didn't help. Everywhere there were delays. Traffic control systems were not adequate to handle large volumes of people wanting to be somewhere other than where they were a little while earlier. Perhaps I should explain why I found all the traffic strange.

Although I live in a rural environment, nevertheless I have to make reasonably frequent forays into civilization to procure the wherewithal to carry out my studio activities. Within thirty kilometres of our home there is a rural city centre that has just about everything I need. On some rare occasions I even enjoy getting in amongst the noise and commotion. I have to reluctantly admit to that. A frequently flooding river meanders its way between a score of buildings there, each building about five hundred stories high. Picturesque bridges connect the buildings at different levels. There are myriad ground level paths between the buildings which are all surrounded by lush vegetation, most representing food of some kind. Even here some people of one building want to be in another building, although each is almost self sufficient in supplying its nesting population. I can understand a certain amount of migration. Not every building has the capacity to cater for all the requirements of all its dwellers.

However, in a large centre where the buildings are so tall and have such a large footprint, and each having such a complex array of services, enough to cater for a small city, the people still insist on travelling. Much of the to and fro is by small vehicles that create the traffic congestion. The thing making it worse is that the buildings are separated by large plots of land all dedicated to growing food.

The mega-monolith structures, domiciles-come-business-come-employment buildings, are so comprehensive in their infrastructure that a person could be born, live and die in the same building without ever

                                                    Zsoall Robi

having to go to another. With each building having an average height of one point eight kilometres and a footprint of about one hundred and thirty thousand square meters, a person could spend a lifetime exploring just one building and never get to know it all. It has me mystified why there is so much inter-building traffic.

Watching all those people coming and going, the outstanding thing is that so few of them actually smile. Surely some pleasure could be found in the simple act of being amongst one's fellow adventuring human beings, if one absolutely had to be out there.

I had taken a different route to get out of the shadow of the monoliths, but it made no difference to the congestion. There was one thing though which stood out. I was almost out of the city when I saw the advertising screen. There it was plain as day, in my rear vision mirror. I had to stop. "Are You Having Nightmares?" It asked boldly while an image of a child thrashed about on a bed. The other lettering wasn't large. It was nevertheless large enough to be read even from a distance ... "The Sleep Disorder Doctor."

Extraordinary. It seems whichever way I turn lately SDD keeps cropping up. It took another hour and a half to get home. Eventually, most of the unpleasant thoughts were blown away by the wind. It rained. Unusually, not heavily. Our climate had undergone some dramatic changes. Extreme weather events were the order of the day. In-between those, there was sufficient time to recover if one had not prepared beforehand. There were still people living in remote areas who have not been able to come to terms with the idea that the Earth has had enough. It has finally rebelled against us for abusing it over so many centuries. It will survive and it is going about the business of repairing itself. Humanity still has a choice, but not for long. It isn't enough just to keep the population numbers stable.

I was enjoying the rain and aromas of the countryside around me. Intensive agriculture and farming have claimed all arable land. The smells of productive earth could still be discerned in spite of the rich mixture of unidentifiable synthetic fertilisers.

It had taken a good part of the morning to get to my parents' tower and even longer to get home. So it was nearing darkness by the time I opened the gate. No matter where we go there is one thing we can always look forward to. Tober was already at the gate even before I started opening it. He gets most excited when expecting Ulie, but I'm just as good an excuse to wag the tail furiously. What a joy to get that welcoming greeting every time. People should learn to wag their tails. It would make the world a better place.

As I ride up to the studio Tober follows barking all the way. He's only distracted from announcing my arrival when he sees Valisy. As much as Tober is attached to his human mother, Kitty has the same infatuation with me. Hail or shine she's there somewhere near the studio, waiting. Cats being what they are, hold their enthusiasm in reserve. It's a matter of polite decorum. Dogs will never learn to control their emotions, like some humans. Unfortunately, many more humans are like Kitty, unable or unwilling to express their feelings after so many years of restraint. It just goes with living in a world governed by the joined forces of The State and The Church. Kitty however only holds back a little. As soon as I'm off the bike she's beside me, vociferously explaining what a dull boring day it has been for her. To emphasize the point, she yawns an all teeth exposure yawn, before throwing herself on the ground exposing her tummy for me to rub.

Tober will have none of that. With an explosion of barking he lunges at Kitty. There is no intent to do harm, just to do some mischief.

"No! Tober, Stop It!"

He takes very little notice. His blood is up and Kitty is running. A dog must do what a dog must do. The chase is on all the way to the front door. By the time I arrive Kitty is safely seated on top of the planter looking down her nose at the silly dog creature. Meanwhile the silly dog creature continues barking, thinking it will make Kitty want to run again. Kitty must be thinking to herself *'Good kitty-Gods, when are these stupid dog creatures ever going to learn!'*

I let them eyeball each other for another half a minute before scooping Kitty up with my free hand. I nuzzle my nose into the white fur on the back of her neck. She responds without words, winding up her purr motor in record time. Ulie is at the door, Tober runs inside.

"Where have you been. I've been worried. I was expecting you much earlier," annoyed in her own peculiar loving way.

"Sorry, I was distracted by The Sleep Disorder Doctor. I'll explain later," unperturbed by the admonishment.

                                                    Zsoall Robi

Weekend Ride

On the road
2172 – Sabt, May 2nd – 12:00 noon

I awoke with a number doing continuous loops in my head. Sixty zero forty-two seven one six eight forty-one. It just kept endlessly repeating itself. It had crept into a dream where I was dreaming about another dream with numbers in it. Complicated. It was all getting very confusing inside my head. For some reason the number was wrong. I didn't know what the number signified but it was wrong. Not all wrong, only the last three digits. It had to mean something. Why did it have to wake me? Sixty thousand million odd … it was a big number. It first appeared when I was trying to get back to a house. There were all these small houses, all looking like small cubes one on top of another. Some were spaced out along the hills and along the cliff edge. Most were white. Many were coloured; primary and secondary colours. Every time I reached the crest of a hill, another hill folded up in front of me so that I could not see the house I was trying to get back to.

Then I saw this number. I started saying this number to myself and the houses all disappeared. At first I couldn't remember all of the number and had to say it over and over again just to get the rhythm of it. It was a number I had known before, but had forgotten the end of it. So I kept repeating it until the repetition of it eventually woke me in the middle of the night.

Now I'm fully awake and the number continues looping in my brain. I can't stop it. Why should the last three digits be wrong? No, it's only the last two digits. I try to think about something else. Kitty is on the bed, between my legs which have become stiff and sore. So I get up and put Kitty in the bathroom. Back in bed the number returns to my thoughts. I say it quickly. It sounds correct so I say again. Good, that must be it. I repeat it, repeat it, repeat it then I wake up. It's six thirty-seven. Kitty is calling me.

I prepare for the day's activity after the breakfast routine unwinds to its final crescendo with a kookaburra laugh as it snatches the mince from

Zsoall Robi

Magpie. I've not yet told Ulie about the conversation with my parents, or about my strange dream. She likes to interpret dreams. I find that hard to listen to because I don't think dreams have meaning. They definitely have a connection to reality, but in a highly unstructured way. Often the brain gets bits of one reality mixed up with bits of another reality. That is exactly the kind of problem that can result from Tripping, especially if it becomes addictive. Virtual reality is safer in many respects than actual reality. We have more control over virtual reality.

Good Gods, imagine what could happen if one person's virtuals mix with another's, and then that mix up became part of dreams. But TC-S tells us that can never happen. So it must be true … probably true … perhaps, given the state of mind I'm in.

It's back to the billboard today. There is a certain pleasure in repetitive tasks. They allow the mind to go blank, with muscle memory taking over the bulk of the work. The emptiness in the mind lets data to flow unhindered, backwards if one is being creative. Daydreaming is the next best thing to night dreaming. At least one can keep a thread attached to actual reality. It often happens that I start work, in my mind, on another piece whilst my hands complete an unchallenging aspect of something else in hand at the time. Daydreaming and creativity are closely linked. A well defined aesthetic problem can become the magnet to attract useful stored information.

It isn't only TC-S that stores input. So does the mind of a creative. To activate the reverse flow of information one needs a focus, like a design issue needing resolution. The artist's filter recalls and sorts data, then sends it down the same neural pathways that transmitted it into the brain in the first instance.

So a colour comes out of its pigeon hole and finds its way to the 'mind's eye'. Thus I see that colour in the context of the defined problem. More and more data are released until an image is created that meets the criteria of the required design. This particular type of search and re-routing process is peculiar to creatives in that incoming data is flagged differently to normal people. Many more connections are pre-set to each datum before it is stored. From an algorithmic aspect these connections contain no logic systems and are consequently impossible for a computer program to replicate.

Zsoall Robi

TC-S data interrogation algorithms are not capable of that kind of recall and filter functions. Nor can they relate unrelated bits of datum to one another even after they have been located. That incapacity gives people a certain degree of freedom from interference by TC-S.

If they had that ability then they would have taken the first steps towards knowing our thoughts, and I would now be in serious trouble.

Today I have only one task, to finish the billboard. I can do that while engaging in the pleasures of subversive thinking. It is a great pity I cannot share my thoughts with others, not even Ulie. I can think these things but I had better not say them. Even writing them down for another person to see would be to betray myself. Perhaps Ghosts are free to do such things. I wonder if Greeog is a Ghost.

Which reminds me of some of my thoughts during the conversation with my parents. I speculate about those rumours of an operation that can de-activate our NNETs. I would like to meet a Ghost one day. Perhaps I already have and just don't know it.

It has been such a busy day, not just with the billboard but also with my own thoughts, that I had not taken the usual pleasure in the lunch event, nor the evening meal. Even the memory of having lunch escapes me. Actual reality finally asserts itself fully as I lie in bed ready for my nightly read. Pain has a tendency to bring one back to empirical reality. It is Kitty biting me on the arm again. She has no confusions about the hierarchy of important things in her life. Unusually she's making a big fuss instead of coming to lie beside me within stroking reach. It amazes me how thick I can be sometimes. Valisy has not only stood on my chest and vocally expressed her considerable displeasure with me, as well as the attempt to take a chunk out of my arm, but she has proceeded to scoot around the bedroom while continuing her litany.

I just stared at her, not even being able to open the book in peace let alone start reading.

"Kitty puss-cat, what is the matter with you?"

She acknowledges this by running into the bathroom with tail fully erect. Ah! At last I get it. Her dinner. I'd completely forgotten her dinner! It happens sometimes. I might forget, but she never does. A special treat is in order to make up for my inhuman neglect of her wellbeing. Even though I don't do such terrible things on purpose, it

Zsoall Robi

does give me the opportunity to enjoy our special little conversations. The pleasure doesn't end there. As I walk back into the bedroom with her little tray of prawns and crab meat she's waiting in hiding.

Not only do I have the obligation to provide the sustenance, I also have to follow correct protocol. Place the tray on the floor … take a handful of tiny kitty biscuits out of the package, making much noise in the process. Kitty knows what will soon follow, and she prepares herself by sneaking up to the door jamb pretending she's truly invisible. Next I have to throw one small morsel past her nose out onto the bedroom carpet. She catapults herself into the air in the general direction of the escaping tit-bit, making a big show of pouncing exactly on the spot where it came to rest. No time is wasted in consuming the rogue delicacy.

The sneak – throw – pounce – eat routine has to be repeated at least twenty times. Obviously a girl needs to convince herself of her hunting prowess before giving in to the curl up – purr – sleep routine. I know Kitty has forgiven me when she hobbles offhandedly into the bathroom to inspect the rest of my humble peace offering, the consumption of which barely gives me enough time to get back into bed.

I'm not allowed to do quite as I please just yet. If I don't cajole in a suitably inviting manner she will go and lie at the end of the bed, on my foot. That will not do … for me that is. She needs to be beside me, on the left hand side and within easy reach of my hand. Neither of us could go to sleep if I can't stroke her while reading, and she could not immerse herself in sleep inducing purrs.

Although nothing out of the ordinary happened today I'm still slightly apprehensive about tonight, mostly because of yesterday's conversation with PDad. It's what they didn't tell me that's unsettling. Which is peculiar. How can something you don't know, have that effect? I think it is my suspicions of the implications of what they didn't say that's the worry.

There were only a few pages left of my book to read, so I find myself sitting up in bed, stroking Kitty and thinking. My mind wanders back to numbers. I've worked out what the eleven-digit number, starting with sixty, was. Still is, in fact. It is a code that defines what I do.

60 042 716 832, then add it to my personal code …

Zsoall Robi

2359599942APR252105ZALLO-LIOAN-CALI, not to forget my communications code ... 011 61 02 665 78316 ... supplemented with the licence to use a vehicle code ... 30 31 841 274, then a current status code ...

What point is there in having a name, or even a personality for that matter. If it can't be reduced to a code, then it obviously has no significance in the greater scheme of things. The idea of a soul, such an undefinable entity, has long ago been relegated to the status of an historical curiosity. I wonder if our current Gods think of us in terms of numbers and codes. Perhaps one God does and the others don't.
There used to be a time when there were many Gods. Most of them creations of fertile imaginations: Or creations of the ruling powers at the time as a device to control the lives and aspirations and hopes of the people they ruled over. It isn't so different now.

The current Gods of the Churches serve the State well. Allah, God of Jesus, Yahweh, Elohim and Jehovah seemed to have formed a Committee, with President-Saint Sutsugua as the chairman. One could not expect the Gods to debase themselves by coming into our presence, so it is their representatives on Earth, the Saints, that attend the committee meetings. They have an exclusive channel of communication to their respective bosses. What they tell us isn't in fact an interpretation of the Gods' collective wishes, rather a translation into a language we can understand of the desires of the Saints. They don't represent the people: They represent the Gods. They are not accountable to us, as one would expect politicians to be in a democratic government. They are accountable to the Gods. Convenient. The Angels are no better. They carry out the bidding of the Saints, so the Saints don't have to soil their minds by being too involved in the daily lives of the people. The Angels are accountable to the Saints. Again quite convenient, and efficient. To be an Angel, Politician and/or a Priest is a great responsibility. We are comforted in the knowledge that our paths through life are not random but guided by the Saints through the administrations of the Angels, and that we are not without constant support.

It is getting harder and harder to have meaningful thoughts these days. You can only truly know what your thoughts are if you are able to express them vocally and so hear with your own ears what your mind is

                                    Zsoall Robi

unfolding. Six six six, the number of The Beast. Perhaps The Beast is the Secretary of the Committee. I realize, with eyelids beginning to droop that my mind is having a wonderfully fanciful time meandering on untrodden paths.

…

There are simply too many numbers in our lives. Just look at the lady over there, next to the large white building. She has all her numbers tattooed on her back. They cover almost the entire surface. She turns around, grinning … at me. I have this sudden great urge to flee, but hold my ground. She comes closer, still grinning a toothless grin. There is another tattoo on her forehead. It extends from beside her ear on the left hand side of her face, across her forehead all the way to the other ear. I recognise four numbers in the middle. They look like the numbers representing the current year. On the end of the code the numbers become letters, like the letters in my own code, except they are different letters.

I try to focus on the rest of the code, but it's hard. She has the smell of death about her. As she leans against the door of the white building her eyeballs roll up into her head to reveal their white orbs. I try to get closer to her, but before I can take two steps the code on her forehead begins to fade and she collapses. The door she's leaning against suddenly opens revealing a completely white room. There are two people in the room and a child.

The closer I get to the collapsed figure the more her features become less distinct, but I recognise the dress she's wearing. It is just like my BMother's. I jerk my head away from the corpse to stare at the people in the room. The ugly man behind a desk is grinning at me through a slit in his face. Backing away I trip over the dress covered bones of the skeleton.

Suddenly everything is black. I can feel my heart beating fast and the bedclothes are sticking to my sweating body. Reaching up to my eyes I test to see if they are open. Yes. I'm awake. There is no light in the room at all. It must still be night. The clock confirms. Where is the moon, the white light of the moon? The white walls of the room - I begin to remember the dream through my gasping shallow breaths. It was wearing BMum's dress. I panic … pick up the comms …

"Is that you Dad? Is BMum alright?" I tremble into the comms.

63

Zsoall Robi

"Son? What's the matter with you? Do you realise what time it is?"

"Is BMum alright?" I persist.

"Yes she is, but awake now. What's the matter? … You've had another one of those dreams haven't you. Walk up and down in your room ten times, then go back to bed. Go and see the SDD."

"Don't let BMum wear the blue dress with the red spots!"

"What are you talking about son? Get a hold of yourself!"

"But I saw the code, the code on her forehead! That's where they put it isn't it. It was fading and she died."

A slight pause, "There is nothing wrong with your mother. She's not going to die. Now go back to bed."

"Is there something you're not telling me Dad … about mother … I mean about her … her … her death date?"

"I'm telling you son, There Is Nothing To Worry About! Go back to bed."

To this day I still don't know if either of my parents knew their death-date-codes decoded. Probably not. I wouldn't want to know mine.

After the conversation I eventually went back to bed, forcing myself to think about the motorbike ride later in the day. Must check the tyre pressures … fill up the tank … maybe give it a wash before we go … a round trip, two to three hundred kilometres … up the coast … PDad would like that …

"Dad! Is that you? Is mother alright?! The dress, with the red code in the front, don't let her wear it! … Why should I go to the SDD…"?

"MIAOWrrrr!"

Suddenly I'm awake staring at the ceiling. I look at the clock then the comms. It's on. Why is my comms still on? Dad! I remember … the dream, no the call … he said walk up and down the room. Why would he say that? It must have been a dream.

Gods, I'm feeling worn out.

"MIAOW-Orrrrr!"

"Ok Kitty, OK! Come on let's have breakfast." Ulie's in the kitchen.

"Have you decided where you want to go?" I ask her.

"Not far," she says, "I've got things to do at home."

"Well, what about going down the coast, to that favourite café of ours?"

"No, I don't want to go that far. How about Ripples, just on the other side of Kyogle?

That settled it. Feeling a bit tired but it's a perfect day for a ride. About twenty degrees with a light breeze and a warm sun - the best. About an hour and a half to Ripples. Pity Tober can't come. We should have taught him to ride in the top box when he was younger. Although we are both looking forward to the day, me especially, there's things scratching away at the back of my mind trying to get out. I push them back. I don't want to know, at least not today.

Kitty is fed, Tober is fed, Bird is replete with his honey toastie and green tea breakfast. Magpies and Butcher birds all happy with their mince. A perfect start to the day.

Ulie is trying to ward off Tober jumping on her while she's putting on her bike boots. Tober knows she's going somewhere. He looks at her, barks, sits, jumps and barks. Her cupboard is open revealing the basket that has hidden in the bottom of it his collar and lead. Tober sniffs in the basket. Nudges the contents around and retrieves the lead.

"Sorry Tober, you can't come with us today."

Puppy goes back to the basket and finds the car keys, dumping them on the floor beside the lead. We both think he's a Mensa dog. Just to prove it, he goes to the other side of the cupboard where Ulie keeps her walking shoes.

"Really sorry puppy!" She exclaims, looking at the walking shoe Tober has just retrieved from the cupboard.

Out in the bike garage I get the full story of his discontent transmitted by copious puppy wailing. First the crying then the barking. He has to stay inside the house. Tober has no road sense and although the property is fully fenced he might get out. He has his own little courtyard and a doggy flap to get out of the house. He's a young puppy and he has to learn. Life is not all about him. It is a lesson many people are

Zsoall Robi

struggling with, even after thousands of years of evolution. They should have learnt by now. Life is about the Gods and TC-S. Individuals and their aspirations have no intrinsic value.

Always these thoughts intrude themselves even onto the simplest pleasures that Ulie and I enjoy from time to time. Before donning all the riding gear, I check the tyre pressure … it's down, and there's not enough hydrogen … enough to get to the energy station. Boots, coat, helmet, gloves. Always the same order. Security in repetition, safety above all. Who knows when one's time is up. No need to hasten the inevitable. Ulie is ready and I roll the trike out of its nest into dappled shade. We let the bike warm up and listen out for Tober. He's stopped barking, but I can see his eyes peering over the window sill. Ulie walks off to open the gate. I load music into the sound system.

It is only nine in the morning, ten minutes to our village then we are out in open countryside. Should be back by lunchtime. Yes, one of the back tyres was down; I see to it at the energy station.

"Nice bike," a voice behind me exclaims. "How long have you had it?" Ulie starts up a conversation with a stranger. The stranger has a sports car. Nice. Her husband, perhaps, fills its tank.

"We both have bikes," she said. "Where are you going today?"

"Kyogle," Ulie responds, casting a glance in my direction, *Hurry up, lets get out of here*, her eyes flash. She doesn't like the woman. Dislike, distrust? Who knows. The Peace Corps has many agents.

"See you on the road sometime." We're under way. Down the road a bit, six other riders are getting ready for their own adventure. A perfect day for a ride. They are waiting outside the local Church-State offices for the other members of their group. The building looks like one of the old churches we used to have, built of 'catholic bricks'. You can see pictures of them in the history books. My friend Nethenk calls them catholic bricks because all the Catholic churches in the olden days used to build out of red clay bricks. They all looked the same. But this Church is now only used as the data re-routing centre for our locality. There is a more up-to-date worship and data-administration facility in the Tower. One gets so used to seeing it that it becomes invisible after a time. Occasionally there's a Signarama display at its entrance. It heralds that elections are imminent for the selection of Living Saints to important national positions to represent our sector at world conferences. That's how President-Saint Sutsugua was elected several decades ago. They tend to stay in office a long time.

Remarkable how a fine day brings the riders out. It is one of the few simple public pleasures left to us to enjoy. We have saluted at least forty riders since leaving home.

When travelling on a bike we become part of the countryside we ride in. We smell the aroma of the cows in the fields, the damp grass of the morning, even the honey from bee hives close to the road. We live in an area that has the best remaining environment for healthy cattle, clean water for cropping and space undisturbed by hoards of humanity falling over each other in their daily pursuit of survival and profit.

Although it is Dominica many people are already back at work. It is forbidden to work on a Sabt. Heavy penalties apply for law breakers. So the work piles up and much needs to be done at the start of the week. Not only motorcycles but myriad other vehicles infest some of the major roads. So we make the effort to go further inland. Kyogle is a small country village by today's standards with merely sixty thousand souls. Some of the small buildings are ancient structures housing insignificant small businesses. Still, there is enough through traffic to keep the proprietors chained to the tedium of making ends meet. Otherwise they would no doubt have given up by now, and the quaint buildings would have been demolished long ago.

We ride slowly past one such. It used to be a Bank, when money was still a physical entity people could handle and use as a medium of exchange. The sign on it reads "Est. 1867." Gods ... I can't even imagine there was ever such a time in living memory. It's now a shop peddling artefacts once used to work the land. What the museums haven't snapped up wealthy people collected as decoration and to laugh at the memory of those who had to work so hard to make the land productive. We see another building. It's been refurbished into a café.

"There, Ulie ... lunch later?"

"Perhaps." It takes her a moment to reply. She's completely absorbed in the experience. We have ridden together many times over the years, on different bikes, but the pleasure never diminishes. Cool air, warm sun on the back, the sound of the road rushing under the wheel. It is almost like standing still and the world moving underneath you. A bit like flying a glider.

                                                    Zsoall Robi

Well past Kyogle we head towards a place with a very strange name "Whyamiangry". Picturesque; it has a small park, a little lake and one shop. A few riders are perched on their stationary machines sipping drinks. Several dogs lazing on the side of the road. Not much action. I read about this place in a history book. A great deal of fighting between the aboriginals and the whites who took the land from them. This was so long ago, even before the Bank was built in Kyogle. Many deaths, a great deal of illness. The whites almost didn't survive. Perhaps the place is aptly named.

Eventually we come to The Road of Lions. Strange name for it. There is a legend it was named after a philanthropic organisation that built it. Strange, calling it after an extinct animal. It's a particularly narrow road winding itself into a mountain range. Up and down hills and gullies, across ancient narrow, wooden bridges – a mostly forgotten part of the country. People here still live in the arms of nature.

Leaning into bends on a two wheeled machine creates a mesmeric rhythm of left, right … right, left then the opposite in unending combinations. Giving oneself over to the sensation is the only way. At just the right speed and at just the right lean one is transported into a world of perpetual motion of repetitive pleasure that even challenges the rhythm of the human heart beat. We used to know this.

No such pleasure exists on a trike. Muscle, pure and simple. It takes muscle to force three hundred and sixty kilograms of machine into and out of every corner and every curve. Not so with the modern bikes, only the antique ones with which we attempt to pleasure ourselves on days such as today. Traffic is virtually non-existent here. Nobody comes here except the farmers and us riders. It is as much our country as theirs. Ulie and I wave to the farmer. He's about to raise the axe to prepare firewood for the night. It gets cold in this part of the country amongst the hills. He waves back and smiles. We understand one another. We understand the little freedoms we can still enjoy and the pleasure of living in the bosom of nature.

Four rickety bridges later we come to the café entrance but find the establishment closed. Perhaps there is a reason. We speculate. Was it the consistently poor service? Maybe the below standard food? One would expect better quality food in this locality. Real food from local produce.

                                    Zsoall Robi

Not plastic food with everything artificial one finds in the city. Or maybe the recent floods had something to do with it. Every bridge for kilometres around was closed recently because of the heavy floods. Our climate brings inundations more often than not, cutting off access to remote areas like this. Businesses could not survive long without regular custom. But the building is still there. We'll try again some other time.

Resting for a few minutes and after stretching the leg muscles with a short meander we head back to Kyogle. Pity. The odour of life here is strong; the animals, ripening crops, wet soils. It fortifies the soul against the stench of modernity, the miasma of TC-S.

Almost time for lunch. We're not on a schedule but habit is hard to break. Everything seems to be so completely regimented by time constraints. Slowing down at Whyamiangry we consider stopping at the little shop. No. The ambiance isn't right. We seem to be drawn away towards our original lunch destination.

I call Kyogle the 'Ratty' town. It refers more to the name I gave one of the cafes. We stopped there a few years ago. It was the only place open then on a Dominica. It was quite busy with only one small table left free in the back corner. Reasonably clean but not excessively. The glass counter had a few smudges, the floor not recently swept. A smell of food pervaded the space. Not the wholesome, inviting smell of fresh cooking. No - slightly stale, yesterday's aroma or perhaps the day before.

We order and sit at the table in the corner. There's a refrigerator humming directly behind my chair. Ulie looks around at the other patrons. I follow her gaze. Mostly old folk, like really old folk, pushing a hundred plus. I notice two old women walk in, one of them quite unsteady on her feet, supported by her friend. She's looking at the ground.

"There!" She exclaims to her friend, "did you see that!"

Ulie and I both follow the direction of her pointing crooked finger.

"Did you see it?" She repeats. We both saw it - a rat. Not a big rat, but a rat nevertheless. It ran along the wall, stopped for a moment under a table by the wall, now unoccupied. Looking around it must have decided it was unsafe to be out in the open, so it ran under our table and behind the refrigerator.

"Did you see it," Ulie asks me, incredulous.

Zsoall Robi

"Yes, but don't tell anyone. The people would panic!"

Our order arrived. Coffee and toasted sandwiches. We didn't feel like a big meal. Just as well. I don't think we could have stayed there for very long. The two old women started towards the empty table.

"Yes I did." Eventually the friend said. With that having been firmly established, the two ancients turned and left the premises instead of sitting down. We haven't been back there either since then. That's our Ratty Café. We haven't told anyone. The rat is probably dead by now. Maybe it had lots of little ones. It's become a rarity to see rats. They are no longer in plague proportions – unlike people. Perhaps because they had no Gods and Saints and Angels to protect them.

The memories faded as we ate our sandwiches in silence on this occasion. While listening to the inconsequential babble of the patrons I looked around the establishment. Pretty run down and unkempt. No wonder it had undesirable patrons. There are probably other rats nesting in warm, safe nooks in the kitchen even today. As my eye meandered over towards the entrance I happened to glance across the road.

Impossible!

It beggars belief. Easier to believe in five Gods than what I saw above the entrance to another old shop. Faded, probably because inferior quality paint was used, the sign read: 'The Sleep Disorder Doctor.' Fortunately, I wasn't sipping my coffee as I would have ended up choking on it. At that moment I made up my mind. Emersed in my own thoughts I didn't immediately hear Ulie asking me,

"Shall we go home another way?"

"Yes, why not." I wasn't really listening. Already things began bubbling into my consciousness about my Trips with Playback Inc.; the dreams and mostly about those things my parents didn't tell me.

I ask Ulie, "Have your parents been open with you about things, you know – like about when you were born and your certificates."

"Where did that come from? What's on your mind?"

"Never mind. Let's go. We'll talk on the way home."

I was in a quandary. How could I talk to her openly about the things worrying me. Lately I've been getting rather sensitive about personal privacy. There was nothing we could really discuss in any depth … like

Zsoall Robi

our fears, or our misgivings about the nature of our society and the surveillance we all lived under. What could she possible say that would be of any help.

"No, never mind," I repeated. On the way back to the bike I confided in her that I was going to go and see the Sleep Disorder Doctor.

"I think that's a very good idea. You haven't said anything, but I could see something was troubling you, and you haven't been sleeping well. Did you tell your parents the other day?"

"Yes. PDad suggested the SDD."

Happy Time Trip

Playback Inc. Centre
2172 – Faith, May 8th – 7:00 pm

arly Pir morning, prior to starting work, I made the appointment before I could get cold feet. May 25th, 7:00pm. I gave myself time to prepare. But on Faith I was going on another Trip. The courier from Playback Inc. arrived on time as usual, at 4:38pm, to pick up my body. It is an odd time for it, but apparently the data cloud storage services for our region are only available within a limited time band-width. History Strings for people living in our rural area are not stored at the local facility, so access is strictly apportioned.

This time I wanted to get away from traumatic events, go to sometime – pleasant. I had settled on an outing arranged by my father many years ago. It wasn't difficult to pinpoint the exact position on the History String, as we only had the experience on one occasion. The only way I could enjoy it again was in virtual space.

It was a fabulous day from what I can remember. Flying was one of his passions before he embarked on his political career with TC-S. He didn't quite make it to the high rank of an Angel, but close.

On the way home on Dominica from the bike ride, after the Ratty Café meal, my thoughts naturally turned to my father because of the sign. I found it amazing he should place so much emphasis on my visiting the SDD, and then to see the two signs within days of each other. Strange that I'm working on a job for them at the present. Dwelling on PDad led to other thoughts, and I ended up daydreaming for the rest of the ride home. After over a million kilometres of road under the belt, a little daydreaming on a motorcycle wasn't a cause for alarm. The perverse thought also flashed through my mind that if my death-date-code had not matured, and the manner of my pre-determined demise didn't include a motorcycle, then I could get away with almost anything. That was fallacious thinking of course, as natural 'disasters' could still follow their own timetable independent of TC-S decisions.

 Zsoall Robi

I scanned my memories, or rather gave myself over to memories emerging of different things we did together as father and son. By that time Greeog had left the family unit. It was actually about the same time he'd refused to go back to the Adjustment Institute. He'd disappeared from one day to next. To this day I don't know what's happened to him. PDad and I went flying together, just the two of us. My mothers could not cope with the possibilities of us falling out of the sky. They didn't understand that glider flying was the only true way of flying, and the safest.

Part of the pleasure was the long trip to the airport at Benalla. It took three days of driving to get there. We used to talk about many things on those rare occasions we were together. Well, Dad did most of the talking. I loved to listen to him reminiscing over his youth when the passion for flying first took hold of him. It became the one and only truly great renewable pleasure of his life. But now, like myself with my own modest pleasures, he can only re-experience his by Tripping. I don't know if he's ever actually done that.

He told me about his first flight in a glider he built himself.

"My own PFather - let's just say he admonished me rather severely. In retrospect, he probably had good reason. I was so proud of myself – I designed and constructed the glider myself - from readily available re-cycled materials, mind you – not the prescribed 'official' stuff. That was part of the challenge. I used strong light weight timbers for the skeleton, and I managed to get hold of some carbon fibre tubes to construct the wings. Don't ask where I got the graphene from – but it was enough to cover the entire framework of the plane."

I didn't quiz him about it. Just as well. Even in those days it was easy enough to forget the global surveillance network keeping an eye on all of us. He must have been very devious.

Despite all his aeronautical and engineering genius, the first flight ended in disaster. Perhaps if he'd given more thought to the obstacles further down the hill from where he launched, he might not have broken a leg and a collar bone.

"The accident was just bad luck – good luck if you considered that it forced me to refine my designs and flying skills. I don't think I

                                        Zsoall Robi

would have taken out the National long distance gliding champion otherwise."

By the time I was a fully accredited adult, PDad spent very little time in the air.

Only half an hour was allocated for my Trip. I specified that the whole experience should be provided, from the moment of our arrival at the airport, to the moment when we rolled the glider back into the hangar; spanning several hours. Playback Inc. managed such requests by fast forwarding at the least disruptive moments of the experience. The result was unsettling, especially for me, as I had not been through that process before. It was explained to me when I first booked the Trip that the sensation would be almost like having a dream. Things might seem to happen out of sequence and appear as unrelated episodes. I was assured there was no neurological danger as long as I was aware of what was happening.

That's all well and good. But once you're in the experience it's so totally real as to be virtually real. Although at the beginning there's an underlying awareness of the process and a sense of disassociation, once emersed in it the brain cannot distinguish the playback from reality. It is only the mind that's able to retain some degree of independence from the renewed experience. The rewards are as great as the dangers, some people say.

I've seen a sensory depravation tank, at an orientation session before my first Trip. It's the only time people get to see one, because for all their Trips they arrive already comatose. The chamber ensures there are no external stimuli to interfere with the playback data. Amongst other effects, those could be detrimental to the Tripper and could corrupt the already stored data, which was considered to be a far more serious eventuality and to be assiduously guarded against.

"Are you ready, boy? Have you studied up on gaining and maintaining altitude? Don't forget what I taught you about staying away from the clouds." He was already lecturing as we got out of the car. I've heard it all before, so I was only listening with half an ear. The aroma of freshly cut grass in the morning sun assailed my senses. PDad droned on about the pre-flight as we walked into the hangar. More elegant than an albatross in flight, the white birds in the hangar lay with one wing

                                    Zsoall Robi

dipped as if greeting their pilots. We move through them with infinite care towards ours … *fast forward* … "Instruments zeroed, Controls full and free movement, set trim for take-off" … I was sitting in front and PDad was finishing the pre-flight before the cable was connected for the aerotow. No sound. Even the wind coming through the vents I'd just opened made almost no noise at all. I watch the cable being connected and heard the marshal yell "Take up the slack!" … I get a jolt as suddenly the wind rushes in through the vent and the horizon tilts hard to the right … *fast forward* … I'm still aware this isn't reality. The wind is coming in so hard I have to adjust the vent on both sides.

"Do you want to take over?"

A couple of eagles escort us, whistling threateningly. I watch their wing tip feathers vibrating and realise our own wings are in slow oscillation. One eagle is just below us, and the other slightly behind our left wing. They fly like us, we fly like them, rising on the thermals …

"Do you want to take over? I've trimmed." This time I hear him. "Stay away from that cloud - here you go."

I'm not ready, but I take the stick. Tension locks up my arm and I can't feel our white bird responding as I pull back. So I pull back a bit more …

"Don't chase it Boy! Relax. It will fly by itself if you let it … that's it … gently … bring the nose down a bit … don't worry about hitting the eagles … follow them into the thermal."

I take a deep breath and close my eyes for a moment and I can feel our bird bump and jolt as it hits warm pockets … *fast forward* … The horizon is tilting around to the left … airstrip ahead … I begin to panic but realize PDad has the stick. How many minutes has it been? Too short. We're speeding onto the landing strip, which is strange compared to the seeming motionlessness whilst in the air; nothing moved then, except the horizon, not even the clouds. Serenity was waiting for me up there but PDad didn't give me long enough. Yet I feel refreshed, alive, energised … *fast forward* …

"Let's put it to rest today. That was a long flight. You did well to stay with the eagles for a little while."

I don't know what he was talking about. The flight was too short. I wanted to stay up there much longer. "I don't remember," I say.

Zsoall Robi

"Sure. That's how it is sometimes - like an out-of-body experience, timeless, weightless. You must have really enjoyed it."

I couldn't tell him and disappoint him. It was just a few minutes, a quarter of an hour at the most. We each take a wing tip and begin to walk our bird towards the hangar, when suddenly my foot slips and I almost hit my head against the roof edge of the car.

"Watch it Boy. I don't know what the matter is with you today. Better snap out of it. You're driving first."

… *fast forward* … After that, things become a little confusing. I'm watching the eagles effortlessly soaring beside us and I think how good it would be to stroke their wings and feel the power of flight in those giant feathers. So I open the canopy and begin to step out of the cockpit. Next second I hear a loud thump and someone shouting my name.

"Zallo, Zallo! What in Gods' name are you doing!"

Ulie is on the ground beside me pulling my hands off her shoulders.

"You've fallen out of bed! They brought you back over an hour ago. Have you been dreaming?"

"Yes, no, I don't know." She helped me get back into bed and even before she covered me up I was already asleep again.

The brilliant white of the body and the elegant wings were overwhelmingly stunning. I stood there looking at the first glider in the hangar, overcome by the exquisite sleek beauty of the flying machine.

"Come on Boy, we haven't got all day. In the air, that's where we want to be."

It took a lot of maneuvering to get our plane out from amongst the others. Pre-flight and launch all went smoothly; text book. The sense of weightlessness and motionlessness dominate the experience during a good flight. To some extent those two sensations make flying a little difficult at first because there is no sensual reference point other than the horizon. That isn't enough. So I experiment with little adjustments of the stick. PDad says nothing. I have control.

For an hour I follow one of the eagles. The other has veered off in search of prey. I forget the controls and just fly. The two of us, together in brotherhood with the air and the wind and the thermals. He leads and I follow. I have him in my sights for a long time before he suddenly drops and I lose him. It's then I feel the stick moving and it's not me doing it. PDad's resumed control. I want to protest, but he starts to say something - I can't understand …

"Meooooww!"

My eyes snap open and I see a whiskered face centimetres from my nose. Later that morning I decide work can wait.

"Nethenk, Nethenk? It's Zallo. Are you busy today? Do you want to go flying, gliding?" He says nothing. "Come on, let's do it!" I urge my friend before he has a chance to object.

"Kia Ora mate. Yis, we kin go, but not gliding bro. I'll be there in teen meenuts."

I had this incredible urge to be up in the sky again. Somehow there was this feeling of incompleteness without it. The Trip last night was better than the previous two, much better. Such a pleasure to be with PDad again on those days when we had time to spent together. It wasn't just about the days of travelling to get there and all his stories. It was also about being in the air. It must be something I inherited from him, but never had the opportunity to explore flying as a career option. Perhaps that wasn't written into my birth contract. People have said Tripping can become addictive. I can see how that could happen. But I wanted to expand on the experience, not just re-live a previous one, especially the sensations before I woke up. That was the best part.

Ulie tried to talk to me this morning. Something about my falling out of bed. I don't remember anything about that. I only remember Valisy waking me up in her usual way. Anyway, Nethenk will be here soon. The project for SDD can wait a day.

"Teke off is optional, lending is mendetery, end don't forgit it," Nethenk says to cheer me up as soon as he arrives at the studio.

"Weether's not bed, could be a bit rough."

"Come on then, let's go," I say. I hear none of what he's saying. My mind is already in the air.

"Whet's the big hurry?"

"No hurry. I just need to be up there."

"Ulie said you've been teking Trips. Is it enything to do with thet?" I'm not looking at him. There's a wedge tail eagle soaring over the hill on our left. It seems to be keeping pace with the car.

                                        Zsoall Robi

"Don't get hooked on thet stuff," I hear him say, "It seems hermless enough. But I've known guys lose all sense of reality. Teke it easy, ay."

"See the eagle? How high is it you reckon?" I know what he's trying to tell me. It's all under control. I'll be seeing the SDD soon enough.

Arriving mid-afternoon at the local airstrip of the Aero Club there's already plenty of activity. The wind has settled and the sky is blue. I can feel my excitement building. Nethenk has taken me up a few times before. He's a good pilot. It was always interesting to go up with him, but today is different. I want to be with PDad again. Nethenk doesn't fly gliders. His bird is an old, very old, Jabiru J230, kept in immaculate condition. That's how Nethenk is, thorough and cautious. Someone had already pulled it out of the hangar. White, glistening in the afternoon glow. The best colour for a bird, pristine white, almost something spiritual about it.

As soon as we're in the club house Nethenk gets side tracked. Pilots' jabber jabber …

"Derf came a cropper just the other day."

"Yee, I'm not surprised. He's always teken chences with thet flying kitchen chair of his. Whet did he do?"

"Climbed too steep, stalled it. Gods know how he's still alive!"

"Write off?"

"Yep, him too almost."

"Did you heer about Retep's new …"

I listened for a while drinking in the atmosphere. Some of those guys have thousands of hours under their wings; one of them, one hundred and ten years old and still flying. Not only flying, he's also an instructor. After a little while the chatter became just background noise as my eyes kept lurking towards the white bird out on the tarmac. Nethenk could see my attention wander so he filled out the paperwork and dropped a few credits, while I disappeared outside.

Definitely not as elegant as PDad's glider. In fact, a bit industrial in comparison with the short wings and big belly. Even the prop seemed to be out of place, like flies on your nose. Still, a nice machine, and quick. Not too loud and good manoeuvrability. I like the high wing, gives good vision to the ground. I stroke it softly with the palm of my hand as I walk

                                        Zsoall Robi

around the bird. Someone must have cleaned the top. It was so smooth and shiny a fly could not have landed on it without breaking a leg. Nethenk caught up with me as I was admiring the Jabiru's symmetry from the tail end.

"She's a mad plane, bro!" I think he's had a long love affair with flying. You could see it in the way he intimately touched and checked all the protrusions under and around the wings.

"Needs juice." No need for a lot of words. When you're in the experience why talk about it. Just be there. He took the front and I the back to wheel the bird over to the avgas pumps.

"Earth it." I follow instructions. Nethenk's worked out how much we need in the header and the wing tanks. He watches till I'm ready. It's all taking too long, but I guess we don't want to come down unexpectedly.

Shadows were starting to get longer. Still a few hours left.

"All set?" It took effort to get into the small, though comfortable seat. Much more room than in the glider; spacious in fact. He's letting the motor warm for a while before we taxi out. Nethenk clears take off with air control.

"Lismore Traffic, Jabiru, 7296, Entering end becktrecking runwey fifteen."

Remarkable how quickly we're in the air. The crackle of the radio disturbs the peace until we are well clear of the airfield and heading into the sun.

"Can we do a couple of circuits?"

"Yea bro." We don't talk. Nethenk's busy with the radio and the instruments.

"Lismore traffic, 7296, zero nautical miles, west at five thousand descending to two thousand, estimating the field at seventeen."

He flies differently. He's flying in the cabin, I'm out there, in the air. It doesn't take long for all sound to disappear. At first my eyes concentrate on the ever diminishing buildings and people and animals. The roads have become tidy silken grey ribbons on the landscape. There is a rhythm to their meanderings, a rhythm that soon loses focus of destinations. I try to follow one as far as my eyes can see. It disappears into the textured folds of the hills created by the trees in the distance.

Zsoall Robi

I catch a movement out of the corner of my eye. For a second I think it is an eagle. No. Disappointed. A shadow from another plane higher than we are. Nethenk brings my attention back into the cabin with a steep bank to port. We hit a pocket that jolts the little craft. I glance at Nethenk. He's been watching me.

"Now thet I hev your ettention, lets get beck to the lesson."

At first I don't understand what he means. Then I realise his hand is off the stick and the Jabiru is beginning a long slide. Nethenk indicates with a jerk of his head in the direction of the control in front of me.

"Oh!" I take the stick, check horizon and bring the bird back to level.

"Nose up a bit." I pull up on the stick.

"No point being up here if you are not flying," he says.

But I have been flying. From the moment we left the ground I've been flying.

"Come on, pull beck on the stick a but, bro. Don't lose too much eltitude or you'll heve to look for a place to lend."

I didn't like the sound of that.

"Watch you ettitude. Look out the window bro… thet's it … nice … just keep it there."

It wasn't a warm day, but by then I was decidedly heating up. I prefer my kind of flying. Yet it was exhilarating to have control of the little bird.

"Keep en eye out for other aircreft! Now … benk slow to port … we'll meke our way beck. Do you want to lend it mate, yea?" He sees the panic stricken look in my eye, "Na, only jokin' bro."

"On final – Lismore traffic, Jabiru 7296, on final for runway 15, full stop lending, Lismore."

I knew he was only joking but on the spur of the moment it struck fear into my heart. Even some birds have trouble landing. We're in sight of the airfield and Nethenk's got the controls again. I can relax.

It's late afternoon and the amber glow of the sun bathes the landscape in mango coloured ice cream. My spirit is still in the air in spite of Nethenk's little tricks. It's always interesting to go up with him.

"Lismore Traffic, Jabiru 7296, becktrecking runwey fifteen, Lismore."

                                              Zsoall Robi

I almost couldn't feel the moment of touching the ground. He's such a good pilot. Yet last year he was nearly ready to ground himself after a little incident. A bad cross-wind caught him while he had a passenger. Nethenk stayed glued to the ground for months before the lure became too much and he had to go up again. So now he's upgrading his licence and heavily involved in lessons and tests for Instrument Flight Rules (IFR) endorsement.

"Lismore Traffic, Jabiru 7296, clear of runwey fifteen."

"Thank you, Nethenk. And you're right about the Trips."

That's all I said on the way home, and he didn't press the issue.

"We'll see you tomorrow night, about seven."

Trivial Pursuit

The Pub
2172 – Sabt, May 9th – 7:00 pm

 nce a month Nethenk and I recycle our store of useless trivial knowledge at the local watering hole. It's a small country Pub, with nice uncomplicated country folk. We don't make a habit of frequenting the establishment except to take the girls out to dinner occasionally, and then to join them at the monthly game of Trivial Pursuit. It is indeed a remarkable thing that such a trivial pastime should survive the ravages of time. But it's a simple pleasure, and one that can be renewed with little effort. It's one of those inherently relaxing activities partly because of the friendly, easygoing company and because it's an occasion when one can completely forget about the stress of surveillance. There is nothing dangerous or subversive to TC-S going on during a night of Trivial Pursuit.

The evening started like most evenings. It was their turn to pick us up. With the most innocent expectation of a pleasant evening we turned out onto the main road in their limousine (an ordinary vehicle by many standards, but a real luxury for us, with it's heating and music and comfortable seats and plenty of leg room), little knowing that 'Avarice' was going to rear its ugly head.

From habit we were all alert for the kangaroos. It was already dark by six in the evening. They're not normally around this late except for the dead ones on the side of the road. Arriving incident free, Nethenk found a parking spot directly in front of the pub; a good omen. We hadn't realised how cold it had become so quickly made our way inside. "How very pleasant," I remark at seeing an open fireplace in the lounge with logs burning away contentedly. The aroma of burning timber is as much a pleasure as the warmth and the sight of the flames. Winter is really the best season. It creates many opportunities for convivial get-togethers with friends in pleasant surroundings.

Others are starting to arrive so we all enter the dining area and Ulie goes with Eneri to order supper. The cook uses only local produce,

                    Zsoall Robi

which is a luxury denied to city folk and here it is available for reasonable credits. Even the simplest fare has the outstanding quality of freshness and taste; the kind of taste that doesn't leave a bad aftertaste from preservatives and other additives. It isn't all about taste either. Nourishment. I doubt if people in the city towers even understand the concept. Sure they grow a lot of their own food on the terraces well above the pollution altitude. But for how long can one use the same soil over and over again before it dies, just simply dies. And the quality of what it produces is anybody's guess.

We have become a little complacent about the simple pleasure of good, country food and I don't even think about it as Nethenk and I go to get the refreshments. On the way I pass a guy standing by the fireplace with beer in hand, gazing into the flames. It makes me smile … not the beer … the flame gazing. He's still there as we return to our table. We reminisce about the olden days when we tried to fight against coal seam gas mining, and lost. Inevitable, now that we look back at it. Just another example of the illusion of freedom. My eye wanders around the interior of the old establishment as we talk, waiting for the girls to return. I notice the old wooded carved entrance that must be at least four hundred years old. It separates the dinning area from the lounge with the open fireplace. From the look of it, it must be the original one with the heavy timber lintel. The guy with the beer in hand is still standing there. He's not looking at the fire anymore but at something in front of it. I don't take much notice as we are deep in conversation. But gradually I realize what he's staring at. He's just standing there as if in a stupor, focused on something on the hearth.

The drongo is so sloshed he doesn't realize what he's seeing. A burning log had fallen off the fire grate. It's smouldering and producing copious amounts of smoke. At about the same time that the scene penetrates my consciousness, the drunk realizes he has to do something about it. So off he goes, presumably to fetch someone. Without thinking about it I jump up in mid sentence and walk swiftly to the fireplace. Nethenk follows. He's saying something but I don't take any notice as I move the fireguard out of the way.

"There's no fire tongs." I ignore that. There's only a short length of metal pipe … useless. My mind makes the decision even before I realise what my hands are doing. I spit into the palm of each hand and

Zsoall Robi

rub them together, then pick up the smouldering log and toss it back onto the fire grate.

Problem solved, but not before a great deal of smoke had filled the room. By then the barman had arrived with the drunk in tow, still clutching his (by now warm) beer. I look at my hands. They're black - there is no sensation of burning. More to wash my hands than to check for any burn injury I hurry to the bathroom and use cold water. Completely uninjured.

Methenk can't believe it and says so several times as he elucidates on the details of the event to Ulie and Eneri. Half way through his tale several fire alarms begin to complain, one chirping, the other clanging and the third whining. All the smoke detectors had been set off, but nobody moved; not in the dining-room, not in the bar and no one came running down from the residential section. Maybe there's never been a fire in this part of the world and no one knows what it is. Or perhaps they are just too relaxed to bother to do anything about it. 'She'll be right' could be the local motto of the village. Everyone just continued sitting and talking and eating and drinking. One especially bright lad, he must have belonged to the local Mensa Club, worked out it might be a good idea to open a few windows, so he proceeded to do just that to let the smoke out.

Immediately there were complaints about it being too cold for open windows, Ulie being among the complainants. One patron got up and closed the windows with a huff, which the Mensa lad would not tolerate, so he opened them again. Joy, the sheer unadulterated joy of seeing country folk in action in their habitat!

One would think a word of thanks might be in order for the brave soul who was prepared to sacrifice his hands for the common good. No. Not even the Publican who arrived in leisurely due course had anything to say. Perhaps we should forgive her the oversight as she may have been distracted by other noises over and above the din of the fire alarms.

Two fire trucks arrived simultaneously, sirens blaring, late of course, and stopped directly outside the open dinning room windows. It seems the good lady Publican neither knew how to turn the alarms off, nor was she able to call off the Fire Brigade in time. We all felt so much safer with the arrival of the trucks and their flashing sirens adding to the

                                    Zsoall Robi

already deafening internal cacophony. Still the customers continued eating and chatting and drinking. No one even bothered to look out the window. Well, that's not strictly true. The Mensa lad's sidekick closed a window nearest their table. Which was fine until the smoke started to build up in their corner, so he opened the window again after a few minutes.

Our meals arrived. The meat wasn't charred, thank goodness, nor did it smell of smoke. So we began our repast unperturbed by the flurry of activity subsequent to the arrival of the local fire volunteers in their magnificent outfits. We only interrupted the enjoyment of our meal with the free entertainment, to comment on the professionalism of the fire truck's crew. With exaggerated slow motion alacrity two officers ascertained the origins of the incendiary malfunction, determining that the danger had passed. It was good to see these brave men and women retain so much composure in the face of an emergency; that they had the presence of mind to warm themselves by the same fire that had very recently threatened the lives of countless souls in the Pub. After all, it was a particularly cold evening and a fire was mandatory.

Eventually the smoke cleared, the tables were cleared, the fire fighters cleared out and we all made our way into the lounge room in preparation for Trivial Pursuit. Though I must say I was thinking it would surely be an anticlimax to the evening after the excitement of the free dinner entertainment. A fresh log was put on the fire.

First round; Outstanding Polipriests - guess the year of their birth. It would have been impossible to guess their code. So to make the game a bit easier a number of Years were provided, randomly matched to faces. Even that was difficult because the advances of current genetic breakthroughs were widely used by the wealthy to maintain their youthful appearance. Our team of four laboured for ten minutes over all the possible combinations, some dates of the birth years were very close together. All our hopes for a perfect score were dashed with a single word. One of the other contestants declared that one of the years provided didn't match any of the faces. True. First round … Null. Disappointment mixed with laughter greeted the faux pas, no doubt because some of the other teams have also been unable to make much headway.

85

Zsoall Robi

Second round: Multiple choice; 'What is considered to be the root of all evil?' Great question considering that 'evil' as such no longer existed in our enlightened society, as we all lived under the watchful eyes of numerous deities. We are continually told by TC-S that all crime, the manifestation of evil, had been eradicated by the advent of the neural transmitters. But dare I say it? Evil doing per se may have been greatly curtailed, however one could not fail but see the evil intent in the crafty manipulations of some of our illustrious leaders. Data could be collected, categorised and analysed till the Gods got tired of sacrifices.

But 'intent' as such wasn't data and was an elusive little worm in the minds of many of the fourteen billion trying to rise to the top. But I digress. The official answer given was 'Credits'.

"Not true," I cried!

Our hostess turned towards me bestowing an incredulous, glazed-over eye blankness upon my person. Nevertheless, I continued, without waiting for permission to do so. "Avarice is the root of all evil." She continued to stare at me. "I know this for a fact because the Romans even had a proverb I could quote to you!" I said in a loud enough voice so all could hear. Still the incredulous woman remained silent, glaring. What could I do in the face of such complete ignorance but persist. "Greed. Greed is the root of all evil, not Credits!" I'm sure my team was one hundred percent behind me, yet my pearls fell on deaf ears.

Our hostess turned back to the rest of the gathering and announced, "If you had 'Credits' for the answer you were right," without so much acknowledging anything enlightening had interrupted the flow of her game.

"I read money was the root of all evil." Finally, Nethenk came to my rescue.

"Exactly! Greed is synonymous with what used to be called money. But to be accurate, it's all types of greed!" I proffered with great enthusiasm.

Ulie had started off by being surprised at my courage in contradicting the hostess. Then she began sniggering under her nose as I continued to beat my head against the immovable wall of non-comprehension. My latest offering almost sent her into paroxysms of laughter, had it not been for the forceful shushing of Eneri. Round three had already started and we were missing it.

 Zsoall Robi

Third round: "What are the elements of carbohydrates?"
Did she ask the question accurately? Such as 'What are the chemical elements of carbohydrates'. No she didn't. Had she asked correctly I would have had the answer. I said as much to our team, while ringing my hands in frustration. What had promised to be a pleasant evening meal with post degustation entertainment, was turning into a frustrating farce of ignorant ravings.

"Why should I bother coming again if this is what I can look forward to."

"But it's just for a bit of fun," Eneri tried to smooth things over. At the same time Ulie teetered on the brink of another hilarity outbreak.

Rounds four and five at last had a semblance of intelligence. We all contributed eagerly and achieved some good scores. '*At last,*' I thought to myself, '*we're getting somewhere.*' The Gods must have been especially bored that night, for it seemed all their combined mischief was concentrated on our insignificant little gathering. The lights, without any warning, were suddenly dimmed. "What now!" A more or less silent protest managed to fight its way out between my clenched teeth.

"Happy Birthday to you … Happy Birthday to you … blah, blah, blah … heralded a procession with a lighted birthday cake in the lead. It meandered between the chaotic scattering of tables and chairs, to arrive ceremoniously at our neighbour's table. Most of us didn't know the birthday octogenarian's name, so we mumbled something nonsensical. I waited patiently, still wringing my hands in impatience, for the slices of cake to be distributed at their table.

At last, round seven. Ulie noticed my manual antics,

"You're not going to want to come again, are you?"

"It's just for a bit of fun," I replied with a Cheshire cat grin, not wanting to offend the other members of our team. Then, just as we were about to listen to the round seven question, our very considerate neighbours came over with an offering of their left-over morsels of gooey, over sugared cake bits.

"What was the question again please," I could not prevent my mouth from asking.

"It wasn't a question, but the next clue to the mystery item." Came the curt reply, then silence.

                    Zsoall Robi

"Could you repeat the clue, please." Obviously the hostess had taken displeasure at my previous audacity regarding 'the root of all evil', and was going to make me suffer for it.

"It comes in many odours." But rather than saying it my direction, she turned so my radar had to decipher her sound waves through her body's generous amplitude. Fortunately for us Nethenk heard the clue the first time and ventured …

"It is either toilet paper, toothpaste or … or …" Someone shouted "Deodorant!"

"If you had 'toilet paper' you are wrong. If you had 'toothpaste' you are wrong. 'Deodorant' is the right answer!" She triumphantly announced, I'm sure with special emphasis on the 'wrongness' of *our* most excellent guesses.

Because our responses to round five produced a perfect score, and we had chosen it to be our 'bonus' round, our hostess was obliged to present us with a ten credit voucher, redeemable that night. Nethenk, being particularly keen on some refreshments whizzed off to acquire same, and upon his return we were also rewarded with the announcement our team had come in second place overall. Whoopee!

Well, that was that – and - believe it or not, as a parting surprise, yet another birthday and another cake. I suppose with so many people on the planet it is inevitable one would come across the odd birthday celebration here and there.

It was just one of many forgettable, though repeatable evenings of nonsense Ulie and I enjoyed with our friends. One little lasting memory wormed its way into our heads, the birth of which occurred on the way home in the limo. We were immersed in our own thoughts for a while until the injustice through ignorance rose again to prominence in my mind.

"Radix malorum est cupiditas!" I suddenly announced. "If you want to be accurate about it. The Latin proverb clearly, unequivocally states; 'Greed is the root of all evil' Nowhere is there any mention of money."

A moan escapes the lips of the other passengers, before Ulie begins to stifle a giggle again. "You're not still on about that!"

"It's true! I know this for a fact because I wrote that very same proverb on a kite I made back in my art school days."

Zsoall Robi

That was enough to tip Ulie over the edge and she burst into a fit of screeching, breathless laughter … and it was totally infectious. Even I couldn't help myself as we all burst into tears over it; not the proverb, Ulie's unique rendition of laughter. I was trying to be serious and to educate, and all I got in return was screaming laughter.

"I flew that kite with great pride. Many people asked me what was written on it." The tears continued to flow. 'Cupiditas' actually means 'greed'. You could say covetousness or envy or any number of lusts, but not that actual subject of the unwholesome desire - credits!" I almost had to shout to get heard above the laughter. That only made them more frenetic. Then Nethenk managed to get control himself and asked Ulie, in as serious a tone as he could muster under the circumstances,

"What would an Aussie put on his kite?"

"What?" Julie squeezed out between breaths.

"Show us your tits!"

Uncontrolled fitting burst out of all of us. Ulie was bouncing up and down in the back seat, and Eneri was having trouble breathing. Nethenk had to pull over to the side of the road for fear of crashing into something. Ulie clutched my left arm and dug her fingernails in deep as she was beginning to hyper-ventilate.

Yes, that was a good night out. Might do it again.

Zsoall Robi

The Sleep Disorder Doctor

2172 – Pir, May 25th

t seemed like a long time before we were able to continue our journey home. Nethenk was the calmest, so he drove the rest of the way. Not only is he a good pilot, but a man with an overdeveloped funny bone. Sometimes I think that's the major prerequisite for surviving with an intact mind in our current society. There are just too many ways TC-S has curtailed our freedom and tainted almost every aspect of our lives with fear. And it's all due to one single device, the neural network transmitter and it's web across the sensory cortex. Well I hope the bastards at the data centre enjoyed themselves as much as we did the other night!

The SDD billboard was finally completed near the end of the month and my client was keen to get it installed. TC-S had approved it, so there was no reason to delay it. Of course they approved. What a stupid formality. They'd been keeping check on progress anyway; watching through my own eyes, ever since I started. Besides, under no circumstances could I deviate from the brief. There really was no point.

The SDD local offices, situated in one of the still standing 'historical' buildings of our village, boasted a large frontage above which the billboard was destined to scream its silent message at all the poor insomniacs. Though I would not have classified myself as such that subject somehow came up in my conversation with the manager of the facility, Dr.Peels. I had no excuse with which to reject his offer of a free consultation with one of their sleep technicians. Dr.Peels treated my affliction with as much concern as a shop assistant in a shoe store flogging a bit of outdated footwear. It made me feel so much better. His receptionist was the epitome of efficiency.

"Your code." No good morning, no smile.

"2359599942APR252105ZALLO-LIOAN-CALI. Would you like my name?"

"Don't need it. Sit and wait."

There was one other person ahead of me. Obese, blotchy skinned, bloated face and red eyed. I wasn't like that at all. The more I thought

Zsoall Robi

about it, the less I felt I should be there. We didn't talk. What for? Obviously we had nothing in common. *Maybe he's got trouble sleeping - Ha!* I thought to myself. Time trickled by in the silent waiting room. The receptionist never looked up from her screen, not even when I arrived. *It's only been a few nights troubled sleep.* I said to myself. *It's happened before.* Gradually I started to talk myself out of the whole thing. I wasn't anything like that overweight, worn out individual sitting opposite me.

"Zallo?" I was just on the verge of getting up to leave when I heard my name. It was almost a shock. Hardly anybody used first names anymore. It was always some abbreviated form of the personal code. Taken off guard by the friendly tone I automatically rose to follow the man into a consulting room. *GODS … it is all so white!* One shock after another. I had an immediate flashback to my dream about the white room, and my first Trip back to the hospital-cathedral's birthing facility.

I must have blanched because the man enquired about my wellbeing.

"Are you not feeling well, Zallo? May I call you Zallo?"
"Yes, that is … I'm alright."
"Have you been Tripping lately?"

Without any preamble he came directly to the point. Perhaps he could already see my problem wasn't due to ordinary bad habits causing the sleep depravation. Before I could answer he volunteered I should call him 'Werd'. Most unusually friendly. For a moment I thought perhaps he knew from my records that I was the son of an officer in the Peace Corps.

"Yes - Werd - three of them, only recently."
"Ah."

That sounded like an expression of understanding. I was beginning to like Werd. I wondered if I should tell him the details of those dreams, not the intimate stuff just the essence. He was still looking at me, not taking any notes. To my mind that was a sign of a person thinking. Professional health workers who took notes even without looking at you, didn't care what they were doing. It was all about statistics and TC-S imposed standard procedures. You were not an individual to them, just a code, a chattel.

"I take it your sleep pattern has only changed since the Tripping." Again I nodded.

"Yes, yes … and did any of those Trips have anything to do with finding more information about specific past experiences?" I nodded. *This guy is right on the ball. I should tell … oops … I just remembered we are being monitored.*

"There's your problem right there. During Tripping our historical events data and our memory often conflict and cause confusion. That manifests itself most prominently in our dreams. Dreams themselves are highly complex and irrational events, which further exacerbate the problem. Have you had an ordinary, that is to say a pleasant experience Trip? No problematic dreams afterwards I take it?"

"Perhaps I should just tell you that I went back to my birthing, and then to the post natal counselling."

"Ah … don't tell me … your death-date-code, right?" I nodded. *He's good!* "You don't know the date, do you?" I shook my head. He seems to know the whole story. Maybe my problem isn't unique. "Do you want to know?"

Oops, Ouch. "Sometimes yes and sometimes no. It seems to have something to do with my sense of freedom, not so …"

"Quite. You don't need to explain. I think I understand." Strange he cut me off like that, just when we were getting to the core of the issue. But again I had forgotten about the monitoring. Perhaps it's just as well.

"We can help you. But only if you are prepared to work at it. Follow these instructions and come back to see me in a month."

The procedures were not at all complicated, other than having to (temporarily) give up my quest to decipher my death-date-code. 'Carry on with your normal daily routines, especially those before going to bed.'

Valisy will be happy with that - So will I. It's one of those simple pleasures I look forward to at the end of each day anyway.

'Don't read anything even remotely connected with any past Trips or future Trips if they have any connection with death-date-codes. Limit future Trips to only pleasant, enjoyable events.'

That seemed self-evident. I'd already made up my mind to get more into the 'flying' thing, partly with my PDad and partly with Nethenk.

Zsoall Robi

The last instruction I found a bit odd, almost something I could have rebelled against.

"Don't talk to anyone about any of your Trips." That seemed like a bit of an overkill, especially as we were considering only pleasurable events. I determined to do my best. Werd seemed like a genuine sort of person, and certainly appeared to be very experienced and knowledgeable, more than just a professional in fact. Odd.

On the way out I was confronted with the sight of 'obesity' still waiting his turn. Not a pleasant image to take away from a health centre. The I-don't-want-to-know-you receptionist didn't even acknowledge my departure. It couldn't possibly have been just an act. Her disinterestedness seemed too genuine.

On the way home various thoughts kept revolving in my head. It was too easy to get an appointment. Although SDD was a big organisation with many regional offices, there were still far too many people suffering sleep disorders needing treatment. One could reasonable expect to wait a couple of months for an appointment. The job I did on the billboard was pretty good, if I say so myself, but it was by no means brilliant. Certainly not something that could warrant getting special treatment.

What about that woman receptionist! Perhaps it was only the remarkable contrast between herself and Werd that made her manner seem to stand out. But maybe I'm being over sensitive. Most people are treated with a goodly degree of disdain in these quasi government facilities. We've come to expect it, and even enjoy the vicarious anonymity it seems to give.

The biggest surprise was Werd himself. I can't imagine how he could have been so savvy about my situation. Surely not that many people agonise over knowing the exact moment of their deaths. Living in ignorance seems to make most people happier, than not. He seemed to be right on my wavelength. I really took a liking to him. So now I not only have a nice clear set of guidelines to follow, but most extraordinarily, another appointment. I haven't heard of such a thing. Generally, it's a one-time visit … a quick diagnosis … a standard remedy … and good bye - A 'Don't bother us again policy'. Yet I do have another appointment. He knew things I didn't think he'd know. Perhaps I should ask PDad about Werd. He might know the man, or at least something about him. The strangest thing was how he cut me off in

Zsoall Robi

mid sentence as I was about to tell him how I felt about my sense of freedom, which I believed to be severely curtailed in a deliberate attempt to keep me ignorant. Being stopped like that was most unsettling.

My next Trip was already booked, even before I went to the SDD. As it happens, it falls within my new guidelines for happy sleeping.

Trip 4 ⸱ Back in the air

2172 - Tyr, 9th June, 4:38pm

"Is it worth the risk?" Dr.Peels asked his colleagues as though he was quite certain of a negative answer. It was a strange hour of the day to be having a serious discussion at three in the morning. The three employees of the SDD clinic had remained behind at the end of the day and went to sleep in their emergency bunks, which they used from time to time. When Dr.Peels' wife entered the building late in the evening, which she did regularly to catch up on administrative matters, she flicked several switches. Only one of them turned on a variety of lights. The others activated three NITS. One each for Dr.Peels, Werd the sleep technician and Sisi the receptionist. She wasn't just the receptionist it seems.

It was her idea to coin the term NITS for the Neural Interference System that had been activated by the switches. The three people having the discussion had been implanted with the NITS, which specifically acted as a neural activity transmitting blocker, effectively neutralising the output of their neural network transmitters implanted prior to birth. Because the technology of the day wasn't able to distinguish internal sensory data produced during sleep episodes, and externally received sensory input, the NITS was a way to continue sending sleep theta brainwaves while blocking the beta waves of an individual when fully awake.

"You know the guy's father and you also know he's a sympathiser." Werd was quick to add, "I think he could be an asset to us. Wait until I have another look at him at the next session. Sisi, could you let him know we'll have to run a 'sleep' test with him at the next session."

Sisi had been doing some clandestine background checking and found out Zallo's first two Trips were concerned with exactly the kind of enquiry one could expect of a person seeking 'freedom'. "I think, yes, it's worth the risk to do a test implant. But we'll go with your assessment, Werd. He's also a creative. That's most important." Sisi wasn't just a receptionist, but also one of the high ranking leaders of the freedom fighters for whom the SDD was just a front. "And don't forget his brother Greeog is one of our best Ghosts," she added before the discussion had to be terminated. It was best to limit those sessions to short durations. By then Dr.Peels' wife had finished her work and turned the lights off on her way out, turning the NITS off as soon as the three were asleep again.

*

Nothing really happened at the SDD clinic, they hadn't done anything to me and yet I actually felt a lot better for the visit. PDad was right. Just to be able to discuss the situation with someone who actually understood. I didn't get the impression that it was all an act. Quite the opposite. It's only the receptionist woman I can't work out, attractive but so … so … officious. Oh well, a couple of weeks of hard slog in the studio and then the next Trip.

My next big job, not a really big one but important, was to make a very strange item for a boardroom table. This boardroom hosted meetings of Saints and Angels. Why the Polipriests needed a fancy table for meetings with their high ranking administrative staff and personal assistants is anybody's guess. I was only asked to make the lighting for the table, not the table itself. At a cost that would make my annual income credits seem paltry in comparison, the table was to be made from solid timber, the top being 100mm thick. I got to see it because the lighting design had to match its grandeur.

Our ruling Saints were always considered to be inscrutable. I guess it went with their incredible power and the unfathomable reasons behind many of their decisions with which they ruled our world. How does one reconcile that kind of perception with an appreciation of antiquity? The table itself was going to be four meters long, and the ultra contemporary light feature had to be 25 mm thick glass and 1800 mm long. The absolute pleasure for me was to create a design that would accommodate on that slab of glass, fifteen small antique objects to be used to support beeswax candles. One could be forgiven for thinking perhaps some kind of unholy ceremonies were being planned to take place in the boardroom – why else would candles be needed?

The thick slab of crystal clear glass, curved into a long s-shape and melted over roughly tumbled river rocks created many reflective facets for the dancing, perhaps apprehensive, flames of the candles. The objects of antiquity were provided by one of the Angles. I'll describe

 Zsoall Robi

several of them as they are a joy to behold. For me the great pleasure was in imagining the lives of the people in ages past, who would have perhaps taken these objects to be nothing out of the ordinary; simply objects that witnessed great joys and great tragedies suffered by people who had the freedom to live, to express themselves freely and associate with whomever they chose, without fear. Could that actually have ever happened? I hold these treasures in my hand and let my thoughts explore and imagine.

Standing on four solid silver lion's claw feet protruding from a rotund silver belly, the miniature mustard pot proclaims its right to three dimensional existence by virtue of its functionality. No more than fifty millimetres diameter and only thirty-five millimetres tall it is proud to offer the finest mustard from its cobalt blue glass liner. In an age when craftsmanship was still valued, this modest little pot may only have given pleasure to its creator, for it is a design of simple elegance and well balanced proportions. As I gaze at its polished belly it seems to be telling me the tale of its many incarnations, each bestowing upon the new owners the pleasure if its elegant form. Even today it serves humanity well and is no longer an unnoticed object on an over-ornate baroque-set table. In our minimalist and highly utilitarian design ethic, this little gem sits proudly and prominently on the most lavishly prepared dinner table settings.

By contrast the modest glass inkwell, I think that's what they used to call those little containers set into school desks when handwriting was taught almost as an art form, evokes only images of happy childhood. Warm summer days when the ink would run without any concern for decorum or the guidance of the students' hands. On those days the ink was happiest when it could stain the fingers of the urchins who cared more about the day's-end escapades than the flowing lines of a well scripted capital 'S'. Pedagogue heaven was attained only on the day when every child in the classroom could show clean fingers after a challenging handwriting lesson. If I look deeply into the dark green cast glass of the inkwell, I can almost imagine seeing the wicked pleasures of existence for the little canister of mischief.

In a country once know as Portugal, it wasn't until sometime around the 18th century, after growing grapes for four thousand years that Portuguese wines began to be mapped and regulated. But I don't see

                    Zsoall Robi

that history in the miniature silver wine goblet. As I hold it between two fingers and a thumb, slowly bringing it to my mouth I can sense that it is a vessel of pleasure. One does to grasp such a delicate creature with a slender long neck as one would a beer tankard for swilling ale. It is made to savour the subtleties of the fortified wines of the Duoro Valley. This goblet is a rare creature but not as rare as the wines it once brought to the lips of wine connoisseurs, giving their palates the pleasures of life from the Elysian Fields.

Day followed day, each with its routine of beginnings and endings. Each bringing me closer to the next Trip. I'm starting to think it's not a healthy thing to be expecting an escape from reality with such relish. Friends have warned me about this, but I have a plan … I think. It is the only way available to me to investigate certain critical periods of my past. Perhaps I could even get a clue as to what happened to my brother. Surely he's still alive. TC-S would not allow me to overtly investigate my past, any past for that matter. So covertly I try to go directly to the very source they are trying to prevent me from accessing. Tomorrow is my fourth Trip. I will be in the air once more with Nethenk, but this time he's on an advanced training flight with an instructor. I'll be an observer/passenger and free to fly my own way without interruption.

Those 4:38 pm pick-ups throw the day's routine right out the window. It doesn't give me a chance to enjoy the Valisy going-to-bed routine, nor the pleasure of falling asleep to a good book. I'm even beginning to wonder if the Trips are worth it if they cause so much of a problem with my sleeping patterns. Perhaps SDD and the sleep technician Werd can help with that side of things.

Death isn't immediate when you fall out of an aeroplane. There is time to think about things before hitting the ground. From three thousand meters there is about sixty seconds to contemplate one's mortality. But what would be the point of being maudlin about it? Why not enjoy those seconds of eternity? You have nothing more to lose. With a little forward planning you might be lucky to be flying under your own steam above a magnificent landscape of mountains and valleys, rivers and lakes. I would counsel you to take great pleasure in the spectacle, as it

                                    Zsoall Robi

will stay with you for the rest of your life. An unprecedented opportunity has been given to you to immerse yourself in a comprehensive experience, the memory of which will be enduring, though for a short time.

Strange as it may seem such thoughts crept into my consciousness as Nethenk and his instructor deviate from their pre-planned flight path, all part of Nethenk's training for learning the IFR, towards the ranges west of the aerodrome. Strapped in securely in the back seat, with two qualified pilots up front, there is no need for me to scan the skies for other aircraft. I can just relax and re-live the experience. My conscious memory of the original event seems to be a little different to this replay. I don't recall thinking about falling before. Perhaps I should sit inactive at home for a full sixty seconds and see just how long sixty single seconds can be when they are joined end to end.

A wedge tailed eagle appeared from above and behind us, seemingly pulling out of a dive, to take up a position no more than twenty meters from our port wingtip. Within seconds I felt myself transported out of the little craft to take up my place beside him. It must have been his eyes that pulled me out of one reality into another. He turned his piercing gaze away from me as soon as I joined him, towards a speck between us and the ground.

In unison we banked to port, veering away from the plane before realigning ourselves with the speck. I can see it clearly. It isn't a speck but a small bird that hasn't yet seen us. Maintaining altitude, I manoeuvre myself to fly a little behind him in his blind spot. Thermals create the turbulence I don't need at that moment, but it only takes a minute effort to keep my position. With a split second decision I pull my wings tight against my body and brace my head to resume the dive. At two hundred kilometres an hour every feather is working hard to keep me true to my target. My eyes are fixed on the small bird - I see nothing else. Existence has shrunk to a bubble with only myself and my prey encased in it. It takes less time to close the gap than to free fall to earth. The turbo boost kicks in at the last one hundred meters. Suddenly thrusting both wings backwards I'm almost blinded by the immediate burst of speed.

      "What was thet?" Nethenk calls out, jolting me back into the seat. While Nethenk was recalculating his course the instructor had to take evasive action to avoid colliding with another eagle. He'd pushed fully forward with the joy-stick causing a temporary cessation of all heartbeats in the small aircraft.

"Sorry, Zallo. There was no time to warn you."

I didn't care about that. My only though was, *"I can fly!"* Although I do recall having spotted the first eagle during the original event, most of what followed afterwards during the Tripping was all new. I can definitely see how an addiction can develop for Tripping. The pleasure wasn't only cerebral, not just in the mind like reviewing photos of a holiday. I felt the wind, the racing heartbeat, the thrill of expectation at the last two hundred meters of the dive. *"I can fly!"* Sixty seconds of eternity are no longer relevant. I know death will not claim me through an impact of my body with the planet.

That's a comforting thought. Perhaps by a process of elimination … No … I don't want to know. What I do want is to live in the knowledge that my demise has not been pre-planned, pre-engineered to suit the political aspirations of an elite few. That would be true freedom for me; knowing that no one knows when or how I will die, including myself. Is this a completely unrealistic dream? Is it so totally outside the realms of possibility that it could not be attained? Dare I even hope that whatever has been pre-ordained for me by mere mortals could be changed? If there is nothing else left in life other than pleasure, then they cannot take away from me my joy in being able to fly.

The night after the last Trip seemed not to happen at all. I cannot recall any dreams as I lie in bed in the morning, with Ikik roosting under the doona around my chin and Valisy curled up at the foot of the bed. Kitty is purring. That sound of contentment cannot be ignored. It fills the bedroom with peace and tranquillity. So why am I having thoughts of dying?

I try to refocus, to remember the Trip and find myself smiling at the memory of my flight. The wind. The dance of the air molecules against my feathers is an indelible memory, a sensual memory. Then the sudden jolt back into the pilot's seat of the aircraft. What price to pay to escape reality?

　　　　　　　　　　　　　　　Zsoall Robi

Back into the pilot's seat! That's not right. Where did that come from. No. It can't be! I'm getting mixed up. Did the instructor apologise to me or to Nethenk? I wasn't flying the plane in the primary event!

Some months ago, when Nethenk had the first hour of IFR instruction I was there with him. I learnt about the different instruments, their functions and their locations on the dashboard. Particularly strong in my mind is the sequence in which those instruments had to be scrutinized during a flight. But I wasn't the one taking instruction. There is no possible way I could have been in the pilot's chair during a training flight.

"Miaow … miaow … miaow!"

Definitely time for breakfast. Kitty first then Ikik then Zen toast … but first a call … "PDad, are you home this Faith?"

"Yes son, I've been expecting your call. Come anytime."

Now, there's something to think about. More often than not I get put off to an indeterminate date. He definitely hasn't called me 'son' so often in the past. And this business of 'come anytime', that's almost ominous. Today is Woden, so that gives me a couple of days to get my thoughts together. He likes to get straight to the point and the point is - I'm a bit lost. There are things happening that are most peculiar, not least PDad's strange change of attitude towards me. I want to talk to him about the SDD visit more than anything else.

It is already Thor and I don't feel like there's been much progress with the work. Strange how it always seems to feel like that when the kilns are not cooking the glass. Most of the sculptures were painted yesterday, which means I'm still on schedule. Thor is loading and firing day. This morning I loaded the moulds, and made several unique ones that could only be used once. Then I thought about trying to put my questions for PDad on paper. It wouldn't work. What I see with my eyes, TC-S sees and records. Best to keep it all in the mind. Even during lunch, I was turning things over and over without making much sense of the latest sequence of events.

Firing stage one: Up to 550 degrees at 350 degrees an hour. Stage two: Up to 770 degrees at 480 degrees an hour. Stage three: Hold at 770 degrees for two minutes. Programming the kiln's computer control can

Zsoall Robi

be laborious. The last five stages take five to six hours to ensure the glass is annealed adequately. One good thing about today's society is that we can no longer afford to make junk. All resources are precious and wastage has to be kept to a minimum. Products have to last. There is no room for rubbish dumps. Even 'recycling' centres are in the minority.

On cold days having the kilns on is a blessing. Today is hot. I forgot what 'seasons' are, the weather is so changeable. Yet I still make the afternoon snack the same every day regardless of the temperature. Zen toast with a difference. Special grainy bread cut into little finger thick slices. Just three of them. Into the toaster set to dark. That gives some of the seeds a chance to roast a little. Instead of waiting I put the kettle on (five second count of water as it's only for one person). There's time to prepare the coffee mug with one spoon of coffee and one spoon of sugar. As soon as the rattle of the sugar bowl lid reaches Ikik's attention in the bedroom his lightning reaction brings him to my shoulder before I could replace the lid.

Beak over foot he makes his way down my sleeve and perches on the rim of the sugar bowl. I have to stay there until he's sated, which only takes three or four dips of his beak. He has a sweet beak but knows how to regulate his desire. (I make a mental note for future reference when combating some of my own addictions). The shrill kettle whistle calls to both of us. Ikik likes to sit on the warm handle. At the same time the toast pops. Left hand turns gas off, right hand takes out the toast. Butter is already on the bench, cut into thin slices.

The ritual isn't complete until the butter is on the crisp toast and melting into the well browned surface. That's the secret you see; to have the butter melt into the bread so each bite is juicy whilst tasting the roasted seeds. I head for the front door with toast and coffee in hand, with a goodly degree of pleasant anticipation. Ikik veers off my shoulder to fly back to his room, while Valisy takes over escorting me to the studio office.

Rituals have an importance we humans should not underestimate. They represent one of the strongest binding mechanisms between us and our animal family. You only have to look at Tober as he takes his human for a walk to realise that. Thinking about it makes me contemplate what it is that binds us, the people, to TC-S, the rulers. It is Fear – it is resentment at their absolute control over us – it is even

Zsoall Robi

hatred for them for not recognising and respecting our humanity. They are not Divine after all. From their actions it is evident they don't, by any stretch of the imagination, represent divinity, even if the Divine does exist.

Office procedures in the afternoon commence with the arrival of afternoon refreshments accompanied by one human and one kitty. Why she should insist on being there is beyond me. She doesn't have coffee and she doesn't like the toast. She likes the lap. My paperwork is in front of me, toast to the left, coffee to the right and Valisy right in the middle in my lap … purring. It seems that her pleasure, even the least little bit of pleasure has to be expressed with purrs. I should learn to purr.

That night the purring continues beside me in bed. I read only for a little while before falling asleep. Tired from the heat, tired from the work and tired from too much thinking about Tripping and flying and PDad and the SDD. Too much. But the subsequent dream was surprisingly uncomplicated. Unsurprisingly I was flying again, back in the small plane, alone. It wasn't a replay of the previous dream, nor a rehash of the Trip from Tyr night. I was in the cockpit flying above some nearly white, broken stratus clouds. Wind speed light and steady. Temperature cool and getting colder. Nothing to worry about … until the eagle appears. A big white-chested sea eagle. He's come level with me to starboard. As I become transfixed by his presence his eyes turn towards me. He looks at me, through me …

… I'm watching the pilot staring at me … an updraft catches the plane but I maintain altitude … loosing interest in the plane and its pilot I begin to descend below cloud level. There are some interesting structures that need exploring. Those exceptionally tall towers … perhaps an opportunity for a good nest … not that one … I keep turning my head and sliding to the left and to the right …

It's cold. I wake up because it is cold. Half my body is hanging out of bed and I'm cold. Six thirty in the morning. Kitty is still asleep … just. As soon as I stir she's awake and Ikik starts up his morning clucking and whistling. Why should I be so interested in the towers? I don't think I've ever been higher than the fiftieth floor in any one of them. PDad lives near one. Then I remember it's Faith today - I'm supposed to visit him.

PDad

2172 – Faith, 12ᵗʰ June

oth BMum and PMum were out when I arrived. He's probably arranged that for our privacy. It's odd I still feel almost like a child when I'm with PDad sometimes, even though I'm well and truly into middle adulthood at sixty-seven. Although I had a lot on my mind and both looking forward to the interview, and not looking forward to it, I took the motorbike. There is absolutely no reason why there should not be something to enjoy each day. I don't know when my last day will be.

"When is your next appointment at the SDD clinic?" No doubt about my dad. Always right to the heart of the matter.

"Not till 9th July. I had a call from Sisi, the receptionist. They want me in the late evening. Something to do with a sleep test."

"Yes, I know." That was like a bombshell. How come he knew? Why did he know? Who told him? He was watching me as these questions raced through my head.

"I spoke with Werd, the Technician," he added before I could ask any of my questions.

We both sat there for a few minutes with neither one of us saying anything. I was still trying to work out why PDad should have become involved. He was watching me absorb the fact that he had. I was on the couch facing the window, with the sun coming in, and he was opposite me. So when I looked up at his face the light was too strong and I could not really make out what his face was doing. Our seating arrangement was probably by design as well. No doubt his position at TC-S had habituated PDad to taking certain 'security' measures. But perhaps I'm being unkind.

"What do you know about the SDD?" I asked eventually.

"Let me ask you first, how do you feel about Werd?"
So I told him what my thoughts were right after the first appointment.

"I was impressed with his professionalism and his knowledge; his ability to get to the heart of the matter. I found him to be rather sympatico."

Then I asked again, "What do you know about the SDD?"

104

He waited as if weighing up some serious problematical issues before stating rather matter-of-factly,

"Greeog, your brother went to see them a couple of times … before …"

"Oh." What could I say?

"What about Sisi? How was she?" This wasn't going the way I had expected. Why was he quizzing me about these people? I thought it best to go along with it for a bit longer.

"Officious. Didn't like her. Do you want to know about Dr.Peels?" PDad looked at me with what I thought to be raised eyebrows. Although the light coming through the window behind him made it difficult to tell. He nodded.

"I'd finished the billboard project for them and delivered it. Somehow my sleeping - irregularities - came up in conversation. He offered me a free consultation. Imagine that!"

"I had a word to him."

"Do you know these people? I'm beginning to feel like a laboratory specimen under observation. What's going on?"

"So what did you think of him?" PDad still wouldn't answer my questions.

Ok. I'll take a different tack. "Impersonal. He couldn't give a damn. Probably would have ignored me if you hadn't spoken to him."

"Yes." Dad said.

"Do you want to know what happened?"

"Yes."

"Werd was uncanny. I didn't have to say much to him at all. It seemed like he'd dealt with this kind of thing all the time. I wasn't aware so many people would have been having sleep problems caused by Tripping."

"Some do." Dad was certainly in a very talkative mood.

"He worked out I'd some concerns about my death certificate … and … er … that I could not make up my mind about wanting to decipher my death-date-code. He gave me some sleeping guidelines and arranged the next session."

"Yes, I spoke to him about it. Now listen to me, son. I understand your fears and your underlying concerns. You can trust these people."

Zsoall Robi

𝔥e just said … underlying concerns … could he possibly be referring to my thoughts about freedom?

"I want you to go and do the sleep test. Listen to what they say. Perhaps we would still have Greeog with us if he'd listened to them."
So that's it! "What about my brother?"

"You know he had problems at the Adjustment Institute. He had a lot of trouble sleeping as a result. So we sent him to the SDD. It looked like he was getting better. But one day he didn't turn up at the Institute. You know the rest. We all miss him."

𝔦 was too young to know much about the whole affair at the time. Except I remember the constant hounding by the Peace Corps. But I did miss him. Still do. Greeog was such a rebel. Not just because he didn't want to do what he was told, by anybody, but because of his ideas. He and I sort of discussed some of those, although always in round-about ways. Even then, when we were still young, the spectre of being watched was very real and frightening. I had graduated from the Adjustment Institute, so that's probably why TC-S left me alone.

"Are you sleeping better now? Have you taken their advice?"

"Yes, and yes. I'll do the sleep test, but honestly, I don't see the point. Perhaps I should stop all this Tripping and just stick to working in the studio."

𝔦 could feel the conversation coming to an end. PDad somehow managed to convey the feeling he was watching over me, that he had some kind of connection with the SDD. Never before had he shown so much concern about my wellbeing. At least I can't recall ever taking notice of it before. It made me fell a lot better. I'm glad I came to see him.

"Do what you feel is the right thing, son."

Zsoall Robi

On the way home I couldn't help thinking about my brother and his connection with the SDD. Then there was PDad's connection with them. I think he was more deeply involved than he would let on. But what was the link? He worked for TC-S, and the SDD was like a subsidiary of TC-S. Perhaps that was it. The thing that really surprised me was what he said about my 'underlying concerns'. A harmless enough statement if taken out of context. But I had a context. I wasn't happy with society in general, with the whole control thing, with the unrelenting attitude towards curtailing our freedoms. I was apprehensive that the next universal restriction would result in us not being able to have privacy in our own thoughts, and that I was thinking about doing something about it.

Zsoall Robi

NITS

2172, Thor, 9th July, 9:30 pm.
The SDD Clinic

 lie wanted to know all about my discussion with PDad. She wasn't being nosey, just normally curious. She knew how few words he had to spare for anyone in the family, and basically held himself aloof from day-to-day matters. So she was interested to know why he was so ready to talk to me all of a sudden.

"I think losing Greeog affected him a lot more than he led us to believe. Perhaps he's worried something might happen to me, although I can't see how. My little problems have only cropped up since those Trips, and only one or two made me lose a bit of sleep. No big deal, really." I tried to explain without going into too much detail.

"You haven't told me what happened on your first interview at the SDD. Are you keeping secrets?"

"No secrets and nothing special happened. I met this technician called Werd. He was surprisingly astute. Without my having to say very much at all he worked out the probable cause for the unsettled sleep. He even gave me some exercises and arranged for a sleep test tonight. So don't expect me home till the morning."

"Alright. So tell me - what's the issue?"

"It's about … about the … er … the certificates you get at birth. It's all so weird. I know everybody gets their birth certificate and their death certificate at the same time. Somehow I don't understand that. It's hard to find out anything about it. Even my parents are elusive. They are probably right about just getting on with life and not worrying about the future. I remember them teaching us History at the Adjustment Institute, and how people's life spans were always so random. So it's all completely normal."

Ulie listened and stared at me as if I was talking heresy. She made no comments at all. Odd really, because she has strong opinions about everything and generally not reticent in expressing them.

Time was slipping by so fast lately. The morning disappeared before I had a chance to even think about tonight. Werd said I should just get on

Zsoall Robi

with my normal daily routine. Get the jobs done that needed attention and not leave any loose ends. Essentially finish the day without carrying any distractions into the night.

The afternoon was uneventful, other than thinking about my last dream. Before the Tripping I could hardly remember my dreams, but now they are more vivid, more real. There is greater clarity and a sense of cohesion about them. That's not a bad thing. It's a pleasure to remember pleasant dreams. Occasionally I can get back to sleep after waking, and wilfully continue a previous dream. Compulsive Trippers must have a real problem with differentiating between dreams, re-lived episodes from their History Strings and actual reality. That's probably why The Sleep Disorder Doctor exists; to help people sort these confusions out.

My last dream was a collage of all sorts of disassociated elements. Perhaps that's why I knew it was a dream while I was having it. Like, people don't usually take their cats flying. Yet there was Valisy sitting up in the co-pilots seat bristling her whiskers at an eagle escorting us. Even more amusing was watching Tober jumping out of the plane when we landed, instead of Kitty. Yeah, that's what dreams are supposed to be like.

There was still plenty of time to have a good evening meal before I had to get on the road, but they said not to eat too much. I hope the test isn't going to be demanding. Tomorrow is still only Faith and I'll be busy with delivering orders. Ulie said I should take her car. Safer than riding the antique motorcycle if I end up exhausted by the morning. I'm authorised to use my vehicle licence code with her car. They'll know who's driving it anyway the moment my thumbprint is registered as the car starts up.

SDD were ready for me when I arrived. Even Sisi was there, which is surprising. I thought she was just a receptionist. My appointment wasn't till 9:30 pm. She said nothing about my arriving fifteen minutes early. Instead, she shoved a forty-five-point questionnaire in front of me to fill out. All the expected types of questions, like "Do your legs want to dance when you're in bed because they feel restless?" As if that could be considered usual. However, there was one very odd one … "Why do you want to go to sleep?" That is strange. So I answered … "To re-live the day's pleasurable experiences."

Zsoall Robi

It took a while to get through them all and Werd arrived before I finished. I was glad of that. Sisi really got on my nerves. By half past ten I was changed and on a 'slab' of metal, though with a comfortable body-moulding surface. It was one of those contraptions with wheels and all kinds of adjustments. Fine. They know what they're doing. I trust this guy Werd. I'm in trouble otherwise because he'd started attaching sensors all over my body, most of them around my head. The room was odd. It looked more like a small operating theatre than a 'sleep' centre - not that I knew what they were like. But this one had some big light fittings and various monitors around the walls. Strange. While I was absorbed in coming to terms with the set up of the room, another arrival added itself to the rather small space. The person I least expected to see was Dr.Peels. Why would he be involved in a simple day-to-day routine? Even more unexpected was his manner; quite friendly this time.

"Zallo, how are you? Comfortable? Has Sisi explained the procedure to you? No? Ok, let me fill you in."

Maybe PDad's been talking to him again.

"Do you listen to music before going to sleep? No. Read? Ok. Did you bring a book? … Good. How about you read a bit when we're out of the room and just let yourself fall asleep."

Up till then Werd had said nothing at all. Disappointing somehow, as I got it into my head we may have had some kind of rapport. But there you have it. You never know with people these days. "I'll be back to check on you soon." That's all he said. Sisi just stood beside the contraption I was lying on and kept her eyes fixed on me, like I was some sort of specimen. She was studying me, for sure. I thought she was like a lizard mesmerizing a fly before pouncing on it. Then she put a hand on my wrist as if taking a pulse, leaving it there for a few heart beats. That wasn't necessary, the sensors were already doing that. Then she smiled and left the room with the other two following her.

She smiled! *Lizards don't smile!* I thought to myself.
Normally I would fall asleep within half an hour after starting to read. This time it was a bit longer I guess. It felt longer. The book was a good one, but it was somewhat unsettling to be all trussed up with sensors and lying on something reminiscent of a sardine can lid. I can sort of remember someone come into the room, but I was too close to dreamland by then.

                                          Zsoall Robi

"Time to wake up! Come on, that's it. Open your eyes."

It was Sisi's voice talking me back to reality … Sisi talking me back to reality … No. I'm still dreaming. Then I felt the warmth of her hand on my wrist and I immediately snapped my eyes open. No dream. At about fifty years old, black hair, athletic body and piercing black eyes Sisi was no lizard and no dream. Her irises were as dark as her pupil and set right in the middle of the eyeball. Definitely no lizard, maybe a 'dream'. Beautiful in fact. Why did I not see that before? I'm thinking all these things while trying to take in her broad smile framed by very full feminine lips.

"That's it, you can do it. That was a big sleep! Do you often sleep so deeply?"

"I … I … er …"

"Never mind. Come on get up. We have good news."

I just kept staring at Sisi not realizing Werd and Dr.Peels were also there. Then Sisi left the room while I got dressed, but my eyes followed her all the way out.

"Amazing what a good night's sleep does." Werd remarked, no doubt seeing my fascination with Sisi. "Sisi is very good at her job; an enormous help to us." We went to the consultation room where I first met Werd. Sisi was already there.

Dr.Peels opened the discussion with what he probably considered encouraging, "There is nothing wrong with you we can't fix." The statement had the desired effect of bringing my mind back to where it should have been in the first place and not on lizards that were not really lizards.

"Fix?"

"All the scans indicate a normal healthy neurological structure," Werd continued, "there are no structural, biochemical or electrical abnormalities in your brain. The NNET is functioning normally and isn't interfering with any of your neurological processes."

Sisi joined in, "It means that with a little fine tuning of the overlapping brainwaves you should have much fewer disturbing dreams. The dreams of course have to continue, you understand." I had trouble focusing on her words, because of her, but I guess they got in because I responded with something sensible. The idea of having people tweaking and prodding things inside my head wasn't entirely appealing. It's one

                    Zsoall Robi

thing when TC-S does things while you are still an uncomprehending foetus, and quite another when you're an adult with apprehensions.

"Fix? How?" I realised I was starting to sound a lot like my PDad; laconic. Maybe they took a lot of words out my psyche.

Werd said, "Come back on Dominica night and we'll make the adjustments during another sleep session when we can monitor your theta and beta waves."

"Couldn't you have fixed me last night?"

"No. We were only monitoring. Whatever we do must be with your consent." Dr.Peels sounded most definite about that.

"Dominica night, same time … Ok?"

Sisi was broadcasting words I understood but my mind was on the warm hand she again placed on my wrist. They let me deal with all that was being said and waited till I was ready to get up and go of my own volition. By the time I was in Ulie's car the sun had lit the day, the fog had lifted from my mind and I felt I was able to concentrate on driving home. Just one thought kept cruising around my brain … *Why did Sisi keep putting her hand on my wrist?* Surely that wasn't standard professional procedure.

"Well, it seemed to go as planned. I don't think he has much to worry about. We'll do the adjustments next session and perhaps the short psychological profiling for TC-S and then he's done."

"Dr.Peels, tonight we'll need to wind up last nights tests and prepare the room for Dominica. There are several more clients tomorrow. So it all has to be done tonight."

"Right. I suggest we all get a bit of sleep first and then get on with it."

The three of them retired to their usual sleeping areas, following the same routine they had followed many hundreds of times. Everything routine, nothing unusual. Just as Dr.Peels' wife arriving later in the evening was also completely routine. When she entered the building to do some admin work, she flicked several switches. One of them turned on a variety of lights. The others activated three NITS. The conversation the three SDD personnel wanted to have could now proceed, waking after only a short sleep.

"Did you feel any adverse reaction to the implant, Sisi?"

"None at all. He's stable. But I think he may have another problem."

"Yes, well we noticed that also. You seem to have that effect on men … and women. It can be useful, as we've experienced in some cases." Sisi didn't blush. She was used to getting passing attention. But Zallo seemed to be more … intense. Maybe it was because he was an artist and trained to observe and absorb.

'Werd, you did the implant. Is the NITS fully functional?" Dr.Peels asked.

"It had better be, or we are all in a lot of trouble. Yes. Everything is perfect. I have already tested it and the beta waves are blocked from the NNET and replaced with his normal theta signals."

"So we'll be able to 'confide' in him on Dominica?" Sisi asked the question Dr.Peels was about to ask.

"Yes." Werd was most positive.

"We'll follow standard procedure. You each know what to say. Sisi, monitor his reactions … as only you know how. If there is the slightest problem, we'll have to terminate. I'll speak with his father. He can pass it onto Greeog if he wants to. Our time is almost up. My wife will be leaving in a few minutes and switching us off."

Many thoughts stumbled over each other in Zallo's mind on the way home. He kept trying to reconcile the considerable change of attitude by the three people at SDD towards him, between the first consultation and the second. Somehow it just didn't seem right that a receptionist should be involved in the actual hands-on technical work carried out by Werd. Then there was all that business of touching and peering by the attractive lizard woman receptionist. Zallo didn't once think about how rested he felt. He was looking forward to getting back into the studio and making the time go as quickly as possible between then and Dominica night. Only Faith and Sabt to go.

Why am I wanting to get back to SDD? Who in their right mind wants to have their brain tinkered with? The realization hit him as he was about to open the front door of his home. Ulie was there at the door, still in her nightie waiting for him.

"Well?"

"I'm feeling good. Yeah. But a bit weird. Just let me come inside and have some breakfast and I'll explain."

Predictably it was Kitty most put out by the monumental change in her routine. How can a girl get proper rest at night if her human is not home? Anything could have happened to him. "MIAOWrrrr!"

"How can you expect me to get a good night's sleep if you're out there somewhere with strange people doing who knows what to you!" Ulie exclaimed even before they got to the kitchen, Kitty with flag erect following close behind. Zallo thought Kitty was more upset than Ulie. Ulie knew where he was. There was no danger to him. TC-S wasn't after him, nor was the Peace Corps.

"It might have been just testing they did and a heap of monitoring, but I slept really well. Surprising if you'd seen the metal slab I was on. What can I say - I feel good."

Ulie watched him closely as he skimmed over his experience. She knew him. He was definitely 'skimming'. "Come on, out with it. What else happened?"
For a fleeting moment the vision of the lizard woman flashed through his mind and how he could not get his eyes off her, or get her out of his head.

"Nothing else happened … but … they want me to go back on Dominica night … to … to fix something."

"Fix something? Fix something! Fix WHAT?"

"Now don't get all anxious on me. You'll make the animals nervous. Nothing. Nothing much. Just a small adjustment to the balance of my brain waves."

"RIGHT! They want to mess with your head! I knew it!"

She was right. It was crazy. Yet he still felt it was something he needed to do. Besides, he really did want to see the lizard woman again and feeling decidedly guilty that he was relieved the fortuitous 'brain waves' diversion worked to satisfy Ulie for the time being.

"Would it make you feel any better if I spoke to PDad about it first? He seems to have some kind of connection with these people at the SDD. Did you realise Greeog had been to see them before he disappeared? As soon as Zallo said it he realized he'd just made the situation worse.

"Are you trying to tell me you have plans to go walkabout, like your brother!"

"No, no, not that. PDad said that after Greeog had several sessions at SDD he felt a lot better. There's no connection between them and his disappearance. You know what he was like, an absolute rebel. It's just as likely the Peace Corps got him."

…

"PDad, can we talk?" I knew the commlink wasn't private, but it didn't matter. This was personal. It had nothing to do with TC-S.

"You don't need to worry, son. Dr.Peels has already rung me and explained everything. Nothing showed up on the tests to indicate there is a problem. The Tripping has caused a temporary imbalance to your theta waves, which can be easily adjusted. Your brain would make the adjustment by itself over time anyway. I suggest you go and get the adjustment done, just to speed things up and get you back to having good night's sleep."

Zallo didn't know whether to be relieved or not. The whole situation seemed to be well and truly out of his hands. Werd obviously knew everything, his PDad knew everything and the lizard woman acted as if she knew him inside out. At least Ulie calmed down after Zallo spoke to his Dad. She had always trusted him.

Zallo's PFather wasn't a Ghost. He didn't have a NITS implant. But he was a sympathiser and worked actively for the cause. He and Dr.Peels became intimate associates over Greeog's case. Ghosts and sympathisers had developed a kind of code language enabling them to communicate about 'delicate', shall we say 'subversive' matters in an innocuous way. At least it would seem that way to the Peace Corps if they happened to be reviewing their respective History Strings. Ical was happy that at last his second son had the opportunity to give real value to his life by helping to restore freedom to the people.

It had begun to worry him that Zallo spent more and more time in the pursuit of pleasure. True, it was just simple renewable pleasures of daily life. But now he'd started Tripping. That was highly addictive and could escalate into life destroying directions and possibly even into other more addictive habits. By their very nature renewable pleasures change over time. Some become unusable. The body and mind become accustomed

Zsoall Robi

to others, needing more intense experiences from them. One spoon of sugar in the coffee will not be enough for ever. Eventually the body will demand two.

Fortunately, they managed to intervene early with Zallo, not like his brother. The Cause could use a good creative mind like Zallo's. He also had courage and the conviction of his beliefs. These attributes were not highly valued by the Saints and Angels of TC-S. It was agreed between himself and Dr.Peels that they should definitely try to recruit Zallo, and as soon as possible.

Early mornings are the best time to split and stack the wood. Faith morning was perfect; cool, breezy and an overcast autumn start to the day. My work schedule in the studio wasn't so crowded after completing the job for SDD and so time would drag in the studio. Splitting and stacking always warmed me up and chewed up hours within minutes. We have enough timber for heating this season and the new lot is destined to warm us next winter. I remember PDad saying the best form of heating was burning timber in a wood fire. It warmed you when you cut the tree, warmed you again when you split it, when you stacked it and when you burnt it. The activity began to release its pleasure potential at the splitting stage. There are of course pneumatic splitters, but why rob yourself of the biological pleasure of giving your body the chance to loosen up and tone up. All it takes is a five kilogram splitting axe to build up a good sweat. There are so many benefits to a good sweat and I can feel my body revelling in it as it expels toxins and the perspiration keeps me from overheating.

As an artist I particularly enjoy stacking the split timber. A good stack isn't only stable but a thing of beauty. It has texture and rhythm. These are more exquisite because of the result of random chaos with overtones of aesthetic order. I only need to concentrate on placing each small log so they fit close together with as small gaps as possible, and on keeping the ends flush with the face of the stack. The finished wall is a tapestry of nature within which it is possible to discover the life of the tree. The wall will reveal the size and the age of the tree … its probably height … its species … slow or fast growing … and … well it is best to experience the pleasure of the discovery yourself.

                                                    Zsoall Robi

Lunchtime has come and gone. No studio work done. It's now three in the afternoon and time to enjoy the happy exhaustion. I feel my body relax into a chair letting the coiled springs of my muscles release their tension. I don't think about that. It just happens as a bonus. A glass of cool water is the focus of my attention. Possibly the last of many I have enjoyed today. So there's a change to our afternoon routine, which means my mind can dwell on matters other than the forthcoming adjustment or work. Tomorrow will take of itself, if only I could get another good night's sleep.

Recruited

2172 – Dominica, 11ᵗʰ July, 9:30 pm
The SDD Clinic

My happy anticipation faded as I stepped into the reception area and saw a stranger sitting and watching. Sisi sat at her console. "Your code." Once again no greeting, no smile. The lizard woman seemed to be colder than last time. "2359599942APR252105ZALLO-LIOAN-CALI."

As soon as I'd finished defining myself the stranger came over to stand beside me - very close. Sisi didn't acknowledge his move and continued working. The stranger took my arm trying to lead me outside. I resisted. He pointed to a small badge that seemed to be cowering on his left lapel. 'PC'. One doesn't resist a Peace Corps agent.

The vehicle I was 'invited' into unceremoniously had a passenger and a driver. The passenger placed a dog's collar like thing on my head, which came down over my forehead. I'd seen this done to many people over the years, although it had never happened to me before. Yet I wasn't particularly worried about it. There was nothing in my past, distant or near, that could possibly be a reason for a random security check; for surely that's all it was. No flashing lights or warning beeps sounded from the instrumentation the passenger was fiddling with. I was getting ready to get out of the vehicle.

"Why are you here?" The agent asked.

That should have been obvious to the agent and I almost said so. "Having sleeping problems after Tripping." The passenger continued to examine his instrument. All quiet.

"Why are you here so late?"

"Part of the procedure. They have to … er … make an adjustment to the … er … theta waves while I'm sleeping. It will help me to …"

"You can go." Which I did without delaying for small talk. They were not the 'small talk' kind of people. It was only ten in the

Zsoall Robi

evening as I stepped back into the reception area. I saw in the glass reflection that the vehicle was still there.

"Sit," the lizard woman commanded.

So I sat and waited.

Her commlink sounded. "It's for you."

"Son, you can relax. It was a necessary check. Just routine. You alright?"

I didn't know what to say on the spur of the moment. The whole thing took me so completely by surprise that thought had fled my mind. I just held the device and stared at it.

"Son?"

"Yes - Dad? … Shall I stay here?"

"Yes. Get the procedure done. Then we can talk some more."

No sooner had he finished than Dr.Peels appeared, and firstly looked out into the street. The vehicle was still there. When he turned back to me his previously friendly demeanour had disappeared.

"Come with me. Everything's ready." That was it. I may as well have been buying stale cod from a deaf-mute at the fish market. I wanted to ask him about the Peace Corps agent but he was totally unreceptive. We went through the exact same procedure as last time, except for an interruption just as I was settling down to read. Dr.Peels and Werd came back into the sleeping room followed by the PC agent. He looked at me, checked my sensors, scrutinised the electronics and left without so much as a nod to anybody. My only thought was that these people must really enjoy their jobs … or absolutely hate it. I don't think there is a middle ground somehow. He behaved almost like my PDad, until only recently. Cold, brief, distant. Then there he was in my space again. PDad knew exactly what had happened. I'm almost convinced he does indeed work for the Peace Corps. How else would he have known?"

The book I brought with me didn't get a chance to have its pages turned as I was already drifting off when Sisi appeared. The lizard woman had softened again. She looked at me, put her hand on my wrist, smiled, waited a few minutes and left. I don't remember anything else after that until being awakened by soft shaking and her eyes peering into mine from very close, so close that I could smell her scent. She didn't smell like a lizard.

Zsoall Robi

"We don't have much time," she said, "you don't have to say anything, just listen." Sisi kept her hand on my wrist. All the sensors had been removed from my scalp and body. If they had not been, the rapid rise in my pulse rate may have alarmed Werd. Then Dr.Peels said the strangest thing I'd ever heard.

'You've been switched on. It will be safe for you to hear everything … in a minute." I waited to see how this would unfold. It felt like a dream, a mystery dream. I liked those.

"You are now a Ghost," Werd said.

The effect of the statement would not have been less explosive if they'd actually detonated a small bomb in my head. Too stunned to say anything I just lay there like a stunned mullet, hearing him add, "if you want to be. Your brother is also a Ghost and will make contact with you … IF you remain a Ghost."

If I want to be! Did I have a choice?

Dr.Peels drew my attention by saying, "Look at me Zallo, I will say this only once. Do you understand me?" I just nodded, only partly comprehending. "Right. We will monitor you from now on. If you tell anyone you are a Ghost, even Ulie, you will be terminated, immediately, without hesitation, permanently. Do you understand?"

I nodded again. All I knew at the time was that it represented freedom! "I want this!" I thought I knew what being a Ghost was all about.

"Good. We have given you a NNET interference device. We call it a NITS. It will make you invisible to TC-S and the Peace Corps. Your family knows, but they're not Ghosts. That will be explained later." While Sisi was telling me this, the pressure of her hand on my wrist increased slightly before she released me. Pity. My heart rate was still up.

"I … er …"

"No questions," Sisi said softly, "another time. You have a little time to decide. If you decide it isn't for you, we will remove the device and reset your Memory String."

"You can do that?"

"I said - No questions. That's all for now. Go back to sleep. We will switch you off as soon as you are asleep. You will remember everything about tonight, including the random security check by the PC. Sisi will contact you for another session with us."

                                        Zsoall Robi

My head was reeling from all that happened in the last few hours. Oh my Gods! Life was getting exciting. Greeog! I was going to see him again. And PDad and PMum, BMum … I never would have guessed. No wonder they were so distant with me.

On reflection it seems my dissatisfaction with TC-S had been brewing for years. With only rumours about an organisation dedicated to regaining our freedom it is impossible to formulate any course of action. And it is impossible to talk to anyone about these things because of the NNET. Gods! This is fantastic. It took me a while to fall asleep.

On waking it seemed like only minutes since the conversation with the SDD team. Sisi was the only one around when I left. I smiled to her and she smiled back. I knew straight away it wasn't a dream, the warmth of her hand on my wrist still vivid – I could almost feel it again.

Lizard woman doesn't smile without a reason. Thinking about her on the way home I realised that the fascination was all to do with the mystery of her. Yes, she was incredibly attractive, in a fatalistic sort of way, but she was a Ghost! How the hell am I going to cope with Ulie? I think PDad is going to have to help out here. Ulie is far too inquisitive for my continued welfare. That morning she was waiting outside the door when I arrived. No surprise there.

"Some guy from the SDD called. He said you'd be home soon. He sounded pleasant enough." *That must have been Werd. At least they had the tact not to get Sisi to call.* "So how do you feel?" Her tone was ambivalent.

"Tired. There was a bit of excitement last night, if you could call it that. But everything is Ok. Dr.Peels has reassured me the procedure was straightforward, no complications. And I should start getting the benefits pretty well immediately."

"Excitement?" Trust Ulie to latch onto that. At least I won't have to go into the 'other' thing. Dr.Peels sounded very convincing about the 'termination' aspect.

"When I arrived at SDD there was a guy there from the Peace Corps. He …"

"The Peace Corps! What could they possibly want with you!"

"Let me finish. It was just a normal, random security check. I'd already spoken to PDad about it. Nothing to worry about."

"Life is never dull with you around. So what's next?"

I knew it was a rhetorical question, so didn't bother to answer. It sounded almost like a trap. No doubt it would be extremely easy to fall into one. Ulie will be a good training ground for me in avoiding them.

Both Kitty and Tober were milling about my feet. So good to come home to that. They don't ask a lot of tricky questions. Breakfast was pleasant and enjoyable as always and I decided to have a little catch-up nap before getting back to work. That, as it turns out, wasn't a brilliant idea.

                                    Zsoall Robi

Daydream

2172 – Pir, 12ᵗʰ July, Early afternoon
Studio

hen the body and mind are feeling lethargic and the opportunity presents itself to just let go, that in itself is enjoyable. Then gradually losing wakefulness whilst being fully aware of the process heightens the pleasure. The sensation of breathing becoming shallow and regular, and one's thoughts beginning to meander through shadows in the memory forest, then slipping into the void is – tranquilizing, to say the least. It can only happen during the day. Falling asleep at night is a different experience altogether. Daydreams are different too. More erratic. Probably because of outside influences. Every sensory input seems to become part of a daydream. They make the daydreams more interesting, though the relaxation not as refreshing.

Just before lunch I woke up after only a couple hours of half sleeping and half waking. I can remember Ikik walking all over my head, trying to get in under the doona, and Valisy crying for attention under my window. Even Tober managed to disturb me by barking at birds that dared to come to their bird feeder for a snack. Still, it was a rest, of sorts.

Fruit for lunch as normal. Ulie has already had hers. Synchronising our rituals is a constant problem. Although today it is understandable. I'm still in a bit of a daze so I don't take much notice. Ikik is on my shoulder wanting some of the apple. Sometimes he munches right there, dropping bits to the ground for Tober to snap up. He likes apples. Strange little man. Mostly Ikik flies to his tree branch set up in the family room; a large branch that reaches our two-and-a-half-meter tall ceiling. He likes to perch right on the top and feed the forest floor from there with his cast-offs.

I'm convinced forests thrive and the ground dwelling creatures living there thrive because the parrots feed them. Have you ever watched a parrot demolish a seed? Only a small percentage actually ends up in their tiny stomachs. Most of it is crunched into tiny pieces and dropped to the forest floor. Mix that with their seemingly constant production of

          Zsoall Robi

parrot poop and you can understand how the ground can become exceptionally fecund.

Valisy leads the way to the studio after lunch, no doubt wanting to get on my back to purr sweet things into my ears. It would be lovely, but I've lost a fair bit of studio time in the last few days that need to be reclaimed. My mind is on many other things besides cutting glass, but I force myself to go through the drudgery of it. Yet there is an element of satisfaction when the process works well. Good, reliable suction cups help me to pick up a two square meter sheet of four millimetre float glass. The table is covered with felt so when the glass sheet lands on its surface a whoosh of air is expelled and the sheet settles without breaking.

Water jet cutting is still used in some industries but I use the traditional hand cutters. A well made cutter can last for years with proper maintenance. Such a simple thing really. An old coffee mug with a triple folded cloth in the bottom, covered with a centimetre of kerosene lubricant. It keeps the tempered metal wheel of the cutter rolling freely and insulated against the corrosive effects of oxygen. Over the years the wooden handle has patinated to a satin gloss honey colour. Also worn a little in two places it now fits my hand as if it was an extension of it. Thousands of times I have picked it up and although not always consciously aware of its pleasing qualities, nevertheless my hand welcomes its rightful place between the forefinger and the thumb.

Several sheets need to be cut exactly the same, into twenty centimetre squares. So each time I run the cutter across the glass I can hear the crisp even tone as the furrow is ploughed into the surface. It's difficult to see the score line and assess the success of the cut, but the evenness of the sound is what I listen for. Sure enough, the first piece comes away smoothly with a 'thwack' as I put pressure on either side of the score. That is most satisfying. So I settle into the repetitive pleasure of the sounds of the plough and split, and my mind begins to drift.

I'm dimly aware of Valisy watching from another table top as I work. She's a constant and comforting companion. It's all routine so the conscious mind doesn't fully engage. Still a bit dopey from the attempt at pre-lunch sleep my mind is primed to wander. After a little while sounds seem to stop having meaning. I'm still conscious of Kitty purring in the background. She's happy. How many pieces have I cut? I don't

                                        Zsoall Robi

know. Best to count them. By the time I get to twenty I'm already thinking about other things. Start again. The commlink sounds but I don't react. What I'm doing isn't quite right, but I'm no longer fully conscious of it.

My eyes are open but focused inwardly. Sometime ago Ulie and I visited a timber furniture factory, out here in the country. Exclusive and extremely expensive. More credits for a table than I could earn in a year. They had some ready made furniture. Exquisite! But the storeroom with stacks and stacks of bark-to-bark slabs seasoning was overwhelmingly aromatic. Some stacks were as high as a person. I tried counting the slabs.

It's confusing. There are too many. I start the count again, backwards from a hundred … three, two one … pre-launch sequence completed. Towrope hookup completed. Wingrunner has given thumbs up to the tow pilot. I wiggle the rudder back and forth to signal the tow pilot. Traffic clear. I hear Nethenk advise the tow pilot "Canopy and air brakes closed and locked." The launch begins and the glider accelerates. There's a sudden noise! I'm running beside the glider at the wing tips trying to control it. The wing snaps out of my hand, and I catch a glimpse of PDad glaring at me from the cockpit.

Valisy has jumped to the ground and upset a bucket with broken glass pieces. My head snaps around to the location of the noise. I've completely lost concentration. Ah! Cut finger! Not too bad. Doesn't happen often. Kitty wanders out of the studio because I haven't been paying her enough attention. Back in actual reality the finger needs attention. Too much blood getting onto the glass. Messy. I don't like messy. A little pain is Ok. There's the sound of a car pulling up in our driveway. I wasn't expecting anyone. Holding onto the bleeding finger I go to check who's arrived. For a split second I think I'm looking at Nethenk getting out of his limousine. But that can't be - He's on a cruise around Australia. Apparently I was still coming out of the daydream. It's a visitor for Ulie.

Wide awake now from the shock of the cut and jolt of the hallucination I'm determined to get on top of the situation. How could I possibly think my friend was out there? Maybe the adjustment has some side effects. I don't normally get this dopey during the day, not even after a short mid-day snooze. After bandaging the finger of the left hand I tried to get back to work.

                                        Zsoall Robi

It all went well until I put some music on. Should I talk to PDad or Dr.Peels about the daydreaming? The sounds of Albinoni's Adagio in G Minor help to make the transition from reality back to another daydream. Unintended of course. Dr.Peels probably knows a lot more. Perhaps it's a side effect of the NITS implant. I hope it's temporary. Another session probably. Late at night again. Which book should I take? I hope Sisi is there. She's not really a lizard woman … once you get to know her a little better … once you feel the warmth of her hand. I'd like to get to know her a little better. Sisi is dancing a slow motion ballet to the Adagio. Her long black hair is moving in the opposite direction to her leap across the stage.

"Crack!"

Damn! I've broken another piece. The rain and wind outside have brought a tree branch down onto the tin roof of the studio, jolting me out of the daydream. This is no good. Some days are like that. The first thing that happens sets the mood for the day. I should have stopped earlier. I decide to make the call.

"Sisi, Hi. Zallo here. Look, I'm having a little problem staying in touch with reality."

"Who is that?"

"2359599942APR252105ZALLO-LIOAN-CALI."

"You had an adjustment last night, right? There should be no problems."

"But I'm having daydreams, and hallucinations."

"Hold on." Sisi was acting like the lizard woman again.

"Werd here. What's the problem?"

I explained about the daydream and seeing my friend when he could not possibly have been there. I left out the bit about Sisi dancing; though I did mention the injury as a result of loosing concentration on what I was doing.

"You should have gone to bed and stayed there for the rest of the day. It's just the effects of the events of the evening. Go to bed."

And he hung up. These people at SDD can be so changeable. Then it hit me. They are operating under cover. It's their 'front'. That's why Sisi is so On and Off. Maybe I should take their lead. On the way to the house Valisy found my leg, gave it a head-but and decided to accompany it. They always seem to know what is going on.

     Zsoall Robi

That night the SDD team met again under cover of the NITS screen to discuss Zallo's problems. There were no real concerns, but best to review the situation. Too much at stake.

"We've done nothing to interfere with his History String," Werd stated categorically. "It was a straight forward theta wave adjustment. It was minor. Didn't even need to be done, but we had the inspection so it was best to have the event on record."

"What about the NITS implant?" Sisi queried.

"Functioning one hundred percent. I did several tests."

"Well then Werd, it can only be one thing," Dr.Peels speculated, "It's his Tripping. I've come across this once before. The individual had several consecutive Trips about very similar past experiences, and they were rather intense in nature. For a short while, reliving the past like that, caused some bleeding into present reality. But it was only temporary. I'll see what Cali knows. He's been making an effort to get closer to his son. At this stage there is no need to do an analysis of Zallo's recent data acquisitions on his History String."

Although TC-S has gone to a great deal of effort to reassure the population their NNET system was perfectly safe, there was still a small element of risk. That only existed because they still didn't have the technology to capture and store thoughts and daydreams. They also believed the data filters were sufficiently well developed to completely prevent data migration from one History String to another. Theoretically it wasn't possible. But the human neural network was still essentially a mystery.

To ensure the integrity of the existing data stored for each individual it was essential all History Strings were closed loops. That isolated each History from the billions of others. A bit like the DNA double helix. But unfortunately, as with a DNA strand, a kind of 'mutation' was still possible.

Zallo went to bed and slept for the rest of the day. He didn't have dinner and slept for the rest of the night. The next day was uneventful except for a call from Sisi.

"Come see us in three months. The effect of the adjustment is temporary and there is *no other contributory factor* to the side-effects you're experiencing other than your most recent Trippings associated with flying."

Zsoall Robi

Zallo thought about it for a while, replaying the conversation in his head. Sometimes he could be quite slow in his thinking. Did he imagine it, or did Sisi put a minute extra emphasis on the words *no other contributory factor*? He came to the conclusion she had, and that it was all part of the clandestine vocabulary of Ghosts getting messages across to one another undetected.

So that must mean the NITS implant had nothing to do with my daydreaming. I was new to the game, but I was beginning to understand. History Strings! That's where the whole issue of our loss of freedom hinges. They lied to us, hoodwinked us into believing that collecting all the data was for our protection; Protection from crime, protection against illness and all the other little lies. The innovation was nothing more than a more sophisticated way of controlling the masses other than through religion, through economic restrictions, even through brainwashing techniques transmitted through the social media networks.

How am I going to get through the next three months? There isn't enough work to keep me busy every day of the week. Ulie's been bringing up the subject of a deck for the house lately. Perhaps I'll work on that. We have a friend who's keen to work in a garden, as she lives with her family of two young girls in an apartment tower on the one hundred and second floor, in a larger coastal city. I could also do some research into the development and workings of History Strings in my spare time, as much as they will let me anyway.

"Hello granddad!" Loytar and Idda shouted together as they jumped out of the vehicle almost before it stopped in the driveway next to the house. Loytar being a bit shy allowed me to give the top of her head a kiss, while she turned her face away.

Idda isn't like that at all. At age three and a half she's already a consummate social being, giving the biggest hugs a granddad could possibly cope with. She gives me her hugs with all the trimmings. First an enormous smile contracting to puckered lips to give an acoustic kiss full on the lips, followed by a hug so tight she must have stolen it from one of those enormous bears one only sees only in zoological gardens nowadays. The prelude to hugging is a long distance run and leap into open arms, tiny spindly legs clamping to my sides, and arms extended to

                                    Zsoall Robi

hold my face in both hands. They are not really our biological grandkids, which makes it all the more a pleasure.

How is it possible to be a granddad without having children of you own? It's a process unknown to TC-S and therefore without sanction or prohibition. The resultant relationship has no legal or religious ramifications and is therefore pure. The idea came into Loytar's head one day, several years ago during one of their visits. Ulie and the girls' mother, May, are the best of friends. May's parents are no longer part of their family, so the girls had no grandparents from her side. When they came on their regular visits it was generally for a few days to a week at a time. The girls never wanted to go back to their apartment in the sky. The day before going home from one of those extended visits Loytar asked me of they could call me Granddad.

Such a simple thing for an innocent to ask. However, one doesn't become 'granddad' in name only, as any adult would know. The title isn't just honorary. It carries responsibilities. Being thus promoted well beyond my capabilities, presented a good variety of 'discomfort' issues for me. As if it wasn't enough of a challenge learning to be an adult around children, there was the added task of learning to be an adult exemplar.

Three years after my promotion, my position in the family structure is cemented into multiple layers and I have to keep that in mind as I embark on my 'Ghostly' adventures; wife to Ulie and granddad to Loytar and Idda. To ensure I don't forget, particularly my grandfatherly status, there is a beer mug in the pantry with "Granddad" and a motorcycle helmet etched into the surface. Keeping the mug company on the shelf is my personalised coffee mug, similarly endorsed.

My education is almost complete. Summertime around the swimming pool presents many opportunities to bond with grandchildren; playing in the water with 'put your life jacket on' reminders, 'walk don't run around the edge' reminders; and smothering them in dry towels when their tiny bodies are shaking from cold and happy exhaustion. Reinforcing good manners around the table with 'eat what your mother tells you' support to their mother ensured I wasn't just a play-in-the-pool granddad.

                                            Zsoall Robi

It's only recently I graduated from granddad training to gain my Diploma after passing the 'growl' test. Growling! My final test was the ability to growl menacingly and with great theatrical conviction when the little ones didn't want to settle in bed at the end of an exhausting day (for me, Ulie and May – not them). If one growls rarely and with impeccable timing, then the warning never needs to escalate to the actual devouring of the child by the growling granddad bear. So now I'm a fully qualified granddad with a Doctorate in Growling.

Zsoall Robi

The Deck
And
History Strings

2172 – August – September,
At home
Tyr

n entire week of screeching! Between two young girls, one six years old (going on eighteen) and the other three (going on ten), and two women whose words allocation for each day has no limitations, it is almost impossible for a human being of the male variety to remain sane … except … if he has some tools in his hands with which he can make sufficient noise to drown out the noises of humans of the female variety.

One would think that days spent constructing a deck, and evenings dedicated to research would provide the perfect recipe for sanity. One could be forgiven for thinking that. Exhaustion at the end of the day certainly ensured good sleeping and inconsequential dreaming. A great boon under the circumstances. Tripping lost its allure during those months, especially when the girls were visiting and helping with the decking … All of them. A mere man doesn't have sufficient instinctual knowledge to carry out major constructions, like a deck, without their expert assistance.

The greatest pleasure is during the birth of the concept, the design, scale, proportions, the creative vision of the completed structure. From there the hard work begins, with periods of satisfaction experienced at the end of each day's progress. In a sense I dread the completion because it's invariably such an anti-climax. Of course it's a joy to walk on it and make comments about its stability and solidity; to sit on it and marvel at how we could possibly have lived without having it before; watch with big smiles as the girls play with their scooters on it. And yet there is always a sense of loss - of a "what shall we do now" feeling.

                                         Zsoall Robi

Take lots of images during the construction process and squeeze every ounce of value out of the work each day. That's the only lasting solution, apart from Tripping of course along the long loop of our personal History Strings.

Helicopter children. They know something is about to happen, but not what. So they hover around us as May and I discuss the complex engineering considerations of building on a site with ground sloping away from the house in three different directions. We walk to the left of the house and they follow us on their bicycles: Then to the right of the house, again accompanied by Grasshopper and Pumpkin. They are the names I have given the urchins because one is so excruciatingly cute, and the other has stores of energy sufficient to move the moon out of its orbit as and when required.

Two hours of measuring, calculating then re-measuring and re-calculating brings us to the understanding of exactly the range and quantity of materials we will need. 'Exactly' being a relative term to describe a plus or minus twenty percent accuracy. Grasshopper and Pumpkin are girls, so they should not be interested in 'boys' stuff. They don't know that yet, so they do get very excited. The joy of an adventure with mum and granddad going into a small country village for supplies even overcomes the allure of spending an afternoon accompanied by Nana and Tober playing around the pool.

As could be expected there is scant supply of construction grade timber. We have to resign ourselves to a composite of recycled hydrocarbons and reclaimed timber simulations. Grasshopper and Pumpkin managed to elude our attention to wander around the 'timber' yard, for it is still called a timber yard, to discover ancient cast iron equipment. The machinery no longer worked but they looked magical with great steel extremities reaching into the air and flat topped tables barely able to hide enormous circular discs with steel teeth protruding at menacing angles.

I caught up with the two urchins and together we explored into the darker recesses of several half dilapidated sheds. Every one of them housed treasures of mystical machinery. Some had round wheel legs that rolled on double steel rails set into the ground. Others stood two meters tall with banded blades showing off thousands of sharp bone

Zsoall Robi

crunching teeth. It was like walking through an Industrial Revolution wonderland at the museum. All three of us found it hard to leave it all behind. May waited impatiently for the 'three children' to return to reality. Having placed our order, we left.

"Time to go home," I announced most convincingly.

At the first intersection instead of turning right, as we should have done, we turned left. Loytar sparked up immediately, "This isn't the way home granddad!"

"No Pumpkin, it isn't. Where do you think we're going?"

She was still engaged in loudly exploring the likely options with Idda when we arrived at our destination. What would be the sense of going on an adventure without adequate provisions, in the form of ice cream of course?

"Yeah!" They both shouted in unison as they saw the ice cream vending place. In such a small village there were still many businesses not only managed by human beings, but staffed by them as well. This establishment was particularly liked by the girls because the nice lady always gave them an extra little treat. Building a deck has many fringe benefits as we came to realize over the next few weeks.

By the time we arrived home the sun was feeling weary and had begun to droop very close towards the horizon.

"That's it for today girls," I said, somewhat disappointed our little adventure had come to an end.

"What are we doing tomorrow, granddad?" asked Loytar, always the one with questions. She seemed to emphasize 'we'. Perhaps it was just my imagination. Nevertheless, I made a mental note to let the works supervisor be aware he had to schedule activities in such a way as to involve two lively urchins.

Woden

Breakfast rituals need to be sufficiently flexible to allow for instant modification as the need arose, which had had to be implemented with the arrival of Grasshopper and Pumpkin. By six o'clock in the morning the household was awakened to the sounds of reveille in the form of tiny drumming feet charging around the house, with the owners of those feet giving not the least consideration to anyone who might still be in bed. Their exuberance sounded the call to greet the rising sun. Well, not

                                              Zsoall Robi

quite. The sun was still asleep, until the reveille sounded and woke it as well. Grudgingly it winked into the family room with one eye, then another, until the entire room was flooded in morning gold. I didn't want to get up yet and kept my eyes tightly closed. A furtive opening of eyelids revealed two faces peering into my bedroom through the window. No, I didn't want to get up yet, as strong as the temptation was to bear-hug a Grasshopper and a Pumpkin. Last night's research revealed a few things about the background to History Strings that needed further thinking about.

It came as no surprise really that much of our current surveillance technology had already existed for well over a hundred years. At first the harvesting of general data seemed harmless enough. The annual Census was just one example. It was readily understood by the populations of nations that governments needed information on which to plan the future welfare of their citizens. Initially, private particulars of individuals appeared not to be a target of the data gathering exercise. As technology evolved and population numbers increased exponentially it became expedient to collect and store more data. More data meant more analysis and more information. Any thinking person could have foreseen the consequences. But they would have been trumped by the visionary planning of governments and multinational businesses. The danger signs were already emerging.

"Granddad! Get up Granddad! Honey toasties please Granddad!"

Reluctantly I opened my eyes. Four female smiling faces squashed up against the window pane this time is not the kind of enticement a mere male can resist. Let us put the pressure being exerted by the spectacle into perspective. There's myself lying in my single bed; doona revealing only my eyes; Four faces at the window begging for food; one three legged kitty yowling to be let out of the bathroom and to top it all off, a squawking sun conure parrot threatening unbelievable bloodshed by the instrument of its ferociously sharp beak if it isn't immediately let out of its cage. Tober was barking into the bargain, infected by the urchin's excitement.

The inevitable inevitably happened. Faces retreated back into the house towards the kitchen, Valisy was released from the bathroom into

                                                            Zsoall Robi

the wilds of the garden, and Bird given the freedom of the large bedroom. Oh yes - and I got up.

In my role as Majordomo and Chief Butler of the household on occasions of grandchildren invasions, I took over management of the kitchen and buttled my way to satisfying the needs of the entire family.

"Granddad, could I please have a dolphin sunshine toast?" Pleaded Loytar.

"GRRRAHH!" Dinosaur please, ordered Idda.

"Water for four in the kettle," Ulie suggested diplomatically, and May wasn't ready.

What is sunshine toast? It's the one thing that makes a sunny Dominica morning worth living, apart from the faces of the urchins at the window. The recipe is quite simple. Toasted bread blanketed with butter, sprinkled lightly with the ground bark of a tree (cinnamon, still available but scarce), toped with local honey and the ingredients mixed into a paste on the surface of the toast. The critical element is what the butler-come-artist does next. Create the dolphin from a single slice of toast!

All it takes is a small sharp knife to skilfully cut the silhouette of the dolphin from the toast, taking care not to damage the excess pieces for they are important. The bottom section becomes the ocean waves for the dolphin to leap out from. The top segment is cut into small 'fish' the dolphin is going to have for breakfast. As a detail, that only the imaginative mind of an urchin can appreciate, the artist must slice open the dolphin's mouth. "Why?" You ask. Isn't it obvious silly … he's chasing the fish to have his own breakfast!

With infinite care the artist/butler next creates the GRRRAHH for Idda, paying particular attention to making the dinosaur prey as tiny as possible. And what do you thing Idda will eat first? The dinosaur's head of course! Grasshoppers are ferocious creatures and will devour anything in their path.

Loytar also ate the head first as we sat around the round table on the small patio, soon to be enlarged. Ulie sipped her green tea and munched on the cereal she shared with Grasshopper. I managed to take a small bite of my own sunshine toast (in the shape of a square slice of bread) in-between discussing with May the best way to begin the project. Pumpkin

                    Zsoall Robi

listened patiently for a short while and then the need-to-know became too urgent.

"What can *We* do Granddad?" The emphasis being on 'We'.

"You can come with me to get some base-plates and Grasshopper can help mummy measure out the locations of the stumps."

"Yeah! What are base-plates granddad?"

"They will hold up the stumps for supporting the deck, Pumpkin." Then I was hit with the universally inexplicable.

"Why?" At which point I immediately decided this wasn't going to be a 'why' day. One 'why' is never enough for an urchin. Whys will multiply exponentially out of control given the slightest encouragement.

"Because!" And that was the end of that, or so I thought. Was it a mistake to take Pumpkin to the garden centre? In retrospect … no.
In the short term yes, as far as our project was concerned because it meant a substantial deviation from our plan A and from our budget.

"Granddad!" I heard her shout from the back corner of the garden centre. I knew that tone of voice. It meant trouble. There was a request lurking in there somewhere.

"Can we get some sand and make a sandpit?" She was already in the huge pile of concreting sand, happily making sand castles, not even bothering to look in my direction when broadcasting her requirements. The proprietor looked at me with understanding in his eyes, knowing full well what he had to do.

"I'll put a couple of meters in the back of the truck and some edging, as well as the base plates." I didn't have to ask him. He knew. "I'll deliver this afternoon."

"Idda! Idda! We're getting a sand pit!"

"May, we have another little job to do. Might as well get the area ready for it." This was going to be fun. Idda didn't pay us much attention as she was busy with Nana Ulie drawing dinosaurs. Good. She won't get in the way. May already had the tools and the wheelbarrow organised by the time I decided on the ideal location … somewhere close to the house within direct line of sight. "Why? Sand isn't dangerous like a swimming pool. Have you never heard an urchin shout "Mum, watch me!" – That's why.

"What about the stumps?" I queried.

"All marked out and the ground levelled for them."

                                         Zsoall Robi

May is a human dynamo. Both Pumpkin and Grasshopper had inherited her energy DNA. The rest of the day we devoted to making and playing in the sandpit. Tober didn't ask for the sandpit, but even before it was completed he was competing with the urchins for a place in the 'sand' Olympics.

The edging went up easily enough, and the weed mat on the bottom, which Tober had to rearrange several times and which Idda had to rearrange several more times before we were allowed to fill the enclosure with the sand.

Now, there is a law that says << If there is a wheelbarrow with sand in it, and two urchins are in the garden, then urchins must ride on top of the sand in that wheelbarrow >>. It is an universal law of quantum physics. We are all law abiding citizens (as TC-S well knows … and I hope whoever is going to review the event will enjoy it is much as we did … although I doubt the soulless reprobates still have the capacity to 'enjoy'). For each of the twenty trips of moving sand from pile to pit, two small passengers pressed their little bum prints into the load of sand in the wheelbarrow. How heavy is a wheelbarrow full of sand? Well that depends on how many wriggling, giggling, screeching passengers you have to carry.

Three adults at the table and two, no sorry, three diggers in the pit. We had the good sense not to save on space and gave the sandpit ample proportions. Who was having more fun? Adults or children? Tober, the poodle digging machine, was determined to dig his way to China. He had not learnt about China in puppy school, but not knowing something wasn't an impediment to achieving it. It looked like the urchins had been to the same puppy school not to learn about China. Tober had his back legs on level sand, his head no longer visible; partly because it was below sand level and partly because the spray of sand was coming out of the hole he was digging so fast it almost completely obscured the girls as well.

Grasshopper, as we should have expected, squatted beside the first love of her life, Tober, digging as fast as he was. Her cascading blond hair was indistinguishable from the sand she was flinging between her legs, with cute bottom raised to create a natural arch between them. Just as Tober had created both a deep hole down to the depth of the weed mat,

Zsoall Robi

and a mound of sand behind him, he decided to change position. So did Grasshopper. At the edge of the pit, out of the way of the two major sandmining companies, the third company, a construction conglomerate in the personhood of Loytar, busied herself with creating sandcastles on top of sandcastles, on top of sandcastles. Unfortunately, the operations of the two mining companies conflicted with that of the construction company because of their change of strategy. Under normal circumstances it is highly commendable to fill the hole you have dug and so rehabilitate the landscape. However, by so doing most of the sand was landing directly on the mining company's Chief Executive Officer. So began the era of the 'sand' wars.

The day ended with no progress achieved on the deck, a moonscaped sandpit, a sandstone coloured poodle, two crying urchins and an unhappy mother. Sand in the eyes of Grasshopper and Pumpkin wasn't a good preparation for having a peaceful evening meal. Granddad was happy enough. Having built the distraction device and seeing it thoroughly tested and approved of by its future users, he felt reassured of experiencing minimum disruption for the rest of the deck building project - And so it came to pass, except for the nails.

Even during the last stages of dinner, which included encouraging noises by granddad to get the urchins to finish their meals on pain of not getting desert, granddad was already thinking about his evening researches.

In the back of my mind there was the constant worry TC-S would be watching and eventually wanting to know why this particular individual was so interested in History Strings. True, most citizens wanted to know more than what was told them 'officially', and would seek information through the global information network system. Although it had limited credibility as it was a system controlled by T-CS. There was once a community computer information interchange they called the Internet. But it was prone to considerable misuse by the very people using it. One can still get onto it, and extract some old records. The skill to finding out what was the essence of History Strings became a matter of joining the dots; the ones that didn't seem to have a relationship to one another.

So far my research didn't extend beyond just a few hours and I didn't actually download any information. I will not do that unnecessarily, for obvious personal security reasons. The thing I'm particularly interested

                                          Zsoall Robi

and so wasn't fully conscious of the eagle appearing overhead. He circled a couple of times sending the resident smaller birds into a panic, before suddenly diving down to head height and flying above the patio and the scale plan. He was so close the wind from his passing made the corner of the plan flutter and turn the whole thing upside down.

The last thing I remember from the dream was that it was good to get his approval. It must have been approval because he didn't come back to complain.

"Miaow … MIAOW … mew … MIAOWrrrr."

"MIAOW-Orrrrrr!"

"Ok Kitty, OK. You must be very hungry. Did you have an unsuccessful hunt last night in your dreams Kitty-puss. Come on let's have breakfast."

Thor

Most of the decking material arrives today.

"Granddad, could I please have an aeroplane toast?" Loytar asked, with such good manners.

"I want a train!"

"What did you say, Idda?"

"Sorry granddad. Could I have a train - please?"

"That's better. I'll make it a very special train."

There are some things in life much more important than many other things. As adults we are not too good at keeping a balanced perspective. So, first things first … aeroplane and train 'sunshine toasties.' The aeroplane is quite special. It carries many, many passengers and they have lots of luggage. The design needs two slices of toast this time. The first becomes the fuselage, with lots of luggage scattered around the plane. The second slice becomes the wings and the tail, with a big tail fin sticking up into the air. Loytar is sitting up very pretty at the table and the sunshine toasties pilot flies the plate over to the table in a circuitous route that covers half the family room, hovering over the heads of all the breakfasters before landing gently in front of Pumpkin.

"Thank you granddad."

Back to work … I have a train to construct. The toast pops as I get to the kitchen bench. Again two slices of toast. I know only one will be eaten, but it's not about the food. A steam train has a big boiler in front as we all know from seeing them in the museum. Several layers are needed to make up the bulk of the boiler and a small piece for the chimney. Carriages and passengers are made from the second slice. I wonder what Grasshopper will eat first? The carriages are set up to wind around the edge of the plate, and I put a lit birthday candle on the chimney stack of the boiler. To get the best effect I blow out the candle just as the train arrives at Grasshopper Station. Steam train smoke trails into the air above her head, and a broad enchanted smile spreads from ear to ear of a very happy grasshopper.

"Yeah! Thank you granddad!" And before I could turn around to make my own toasties, several of the passengers had become victims of a ferociously hungry Grasshopper Engineer.

Neither May nor Ulie say anything. They just enjoy the performance. Sad to report however that by the end of the breakfast ritual the fuselage was still on the plate, and several train carriages survived the carnage. Perhaps it was the discussion May and I were having about drawing up the plan, or not, for the whole job. I think the girls had forgotten all about the sandpit and wanted to help us.

Ulie takes care of the washing up and we all charge out the family room door. As I suspected, within seconds of spying the sandpit both urchins had run towards it, then ran back to get all their playing-in-the-sand toys. We would have no interruptions from them today.

May had done such a grand job of laying out the sites for all the stumps that within an hour we had the base-plates in location and the brick pillar stumps started. By eleven o'clock the truck had arrived with the decking materials, and by lunchtime the stumps were half completed. I had originally thought this would be the difficult stage of the work. But that was yet to come. Lunch. Clean off the sand, clean up Tober, for he worked in the sand with the urchins. May to make the lunch, Ulie to make the drinks and all I had to do was … enjoy.

Time is a highly fluid substance and I had long suspected it could change its viscosity at will. Wet weather seems to make it stick to you for much longer than when the sun is shinning and you are having so much fun. Completing the stumps and getting their levels right seemed to take only an hour or so. The chronometer was most pleased to inform us it had robbed our lives of precisely four hours, thirty-seven minutes and fifty-two seconds as at the moment when we consulted it. Good to know. Exactitude like that may come in handy one day.

It was time to sit on the edge of the patio and soak in the progress. May's hands must have ached as much as my back from handling so many bricks in such a short time. Yet the result was there, right in front of our eyes. Even the sun seemed to take an extra moment to cast an approving look at our work before it went to bed for the day. It was dark by the time we retired inside, and Ulie almost had dinner ready. The really odd thing is that though we were so depleted of energy, the urchins seemed to have recharged their batteries during the day. They played harder than we worked, they have smaller energy generators under their ribs than we have and yet they still had energy to spare.

However, I had to summon enough of my reserves to produce a growl. Rarely do I need to growl but that night was one of those occasions. Post bathing and pre-bed cuddles, drinks of water, staying up for just another five minutes began the evening ritual. It seemed from the very beginning the day would end in a bear growl. The urchins still had too much kinetic energy. Big cuddles, big-big cuddles seemed barely a sufficient reward for a well lived day, and going to bed just didn't make sense.

"Time for bed Grasshopper. Come on Pumpkin, let's go." That was granddad, being nice.

"BED! – NOW!" That was mum being mum. Whimpering and a little pleading and googly eyes made no difference. "BED. I WON'T SAY IT AGAIN!"

Ten minutes later we heard a scratching at the bedroom door. Just a quiet little scratching at first, which quickly escalated, eliciting an immediate response from mum.

"BED! DON'T MAKE ME COME IN THERE!" Silence. Then more whimpering. "Granddad, can you help me out here." May was losing patience.

A big sigh, a big decision. Was it going to be a big growl or little growl? I decided on the little growl, giving myself room to escalate. It turns out to have been the right decision. As soon as they heard my footsteps, which I made sound like an elephant was stomping in the corridor, they must have crawled back into bed. I found both of them tucked in and owl-eyed in the semi dark. After a few minutes of carrot and stick I left them to sort it out. They either wanted a ride on the motorcycle

     Zsoall Robi

tomorrow or not. A simple choice. They must have chosen to ride, because that was the last we heard from them. Half an hour later May put the question to me. "What is it you do to them?

"Magic with honey … and a threat," I said. I wasn't going to give away all my granddad secrets – it was hard work getting that PhD.

Feeling refreshed after a rest and a shower I decided to continue my research. At that stage it was still all in my head. Nothing recorded, downloaded or written down. All TC-S could see was what I saw. They could not read my thoughts. There was a period in our illustrious history when the sense of helpless frustration drove the Islamic faith radicals to drastic action. It was the only method they felt could balance the inequalities created by the rest of a world that had been exploiting them for centuries. The radicals called their opposition a Jihad against unbelievers. The rest of the world called it terrorism. Extremism on both sides resulted in inhuman atrocities. It wasn't surprising to read that the attempt to eradicate Terrorism was the guise under which the world government had decided to collect even more data. This time it wasn't for the purpose of knowing what the people spent credits on, but to know what they were doing. Mobile communication units became individualised tracking devices. Social media scanning gave information about the content of people's conversations. Public and Domestic Surveillance Networks could identify suspicious patterns of behaviour and provide the basis for proactive security measures.

Cumbersome, time consuming and resources intensive as these measures were they had paved the way for the next development. Predictably, the nation once known as America came up with a lovely system. As I became engrossed in the details I was sure sleep would elude me that night. In this enterprise, groups of people were no longer the primary target. Statistical analysis of mass trends was no longer adequate. The nation wanted data on individuals. The PRISM Program had started as clandestine surveillance under which data was collected about persons of interest. It gave the government the ability to track targeted individuals over time, giving an insight into their thoughts and probable intentions; ostensibly to gather data about 'dangerous' persons 'of interest'. It seems we are now all dangerous individuals. Dangerous no doubt to the unholy alliance that had been forged between systems of faith and systems of government.

                                              Zsoall Robi

How could I sleep, knowing even such scant general information as was available? Where does that knowledge put me if I decide to rebel and become a permanent Ghost, working actively against TC-S? I'm certain now that's why Ghosts existed … to fight the Gods, the Saints and all the Angels. Best to try and put it all out of the head for the time being. I want to see my brother again. I want to talk to my father; talk seriously to my father.

…

New game: Idur (long time chess companion), white to move. It's good to have some pleasant distractions from the daily pressures of uncertain existence.

e2-e4

…

Bed time ritual with Ikik and Valisy went smoothly and Kitty is lying beside me with purr functions fully operational. The book I have been reading; such a silly book really, is in my lap and my thoughts gradually return to a manageable level of disquietude. It's open on page two hundred and sixty-two, at the beginning of a new chapter, 'Roko refuses the cheese'. Roko is one of a pair of Siamese cats, whose human is a private detective. Their job is to discover clues humans are simply not equipped to recognise. Finding the clues is never a problem for the two feline sleuths. The problem is to communication them to the human. Even after years of training their human is still not quite clear about their sign language; such as the rigidly raised tail or the whiskers pointing fully to the front.

Faith

"MIAOW-Orrrrrr!"

Normally I wake up almost immediately when Valisy begins her lament. It took a while on Faith morning to become consciously aware my kitty wanted to be acknowledged, and not Roko admonishing me for being so stupid that I couldn't understand what she was trying to tell me about a most important breakthrough in her investigations.

As consciousness dawned on my drowsy senses, for I was sleeping much better since the SDD operation, I also heard tiny feet in the corridor drumming out the wake up alarm. I half imagined I'd even heard a tiny tentative knocking at my door. The urchins have disturbed me like that before. What could be going … Ah! I remembered. The ride on the motorbike. Those two never forget anything. Such a pity they have to go home on Pir. But I will need a break. I can feel the signs coming on already, and it has only been a few days.

If I were a motorcycle, there would be nothing more fun than having a three-year old grasshopper squeezing my fuel tank with her skinny legs and sounding my alarm system. As promised, we all got ready for the three wheeled dragon in anticipation of speeding around the property to loop around trees and obstacles.

Breakfast could wait. Kitty could wait. I was determined to drive my antique motorcycle into flights of ecstasy. The girls were ready; Pumpkin already had her helmet on, three sizes too big so if she swivelled her head suddenly the helmet would not change position and her nose would end up inside the helmet. But that is at it should be. Grasshopper started pulling the machine out if its garage … so what if those wide back wheels happened to flatten her a little itty bit. Grandad made sure that would not happen. Then it was a scramble to see who could get on the quickest.

d7-d6

Grasshopper knew where to put the key and which button to press to get the bike started. Obviously there was no real need for granddad to be there. They've been on many rides before and young girls never forget the important things in life.

"Can we go and visit Nethenk, granddad?" Although our destination was generally the same, there were many ways to get there.

"Granddad, over there - Over There!" Several big donuts and three circumnavigated trees later we were heading out the gate and speeding down the nature strip.

"Faster granddad!" It seems five kilometres per hour simply didn't do the trick for these two young speed freaks. They must have developed a need for speed from racing their billy cart down the slopes of the local park. I preferred to take them on the bike. It wasn't as exhausting as pulling a billy cart up the hill with two urchins on it. Uncle Nethenk wasn't home. So sad … not sad for long.

"Can we go home really fast granddad?" I don't recall which one of the speed demons asked me. They should have asked the bike because the speed didn't change … not until the last twenty meters! We drove into the garage so fast it made the girls squeal with delight. Of course we could not end the excursion without a final horn serenade.

Nb1-c3

Mummy and Nana Ulie had breakfast prepared for all of us. It was going to be a big day … a big decking day. Bearers and joists and lots of decking strips had to be cut. Progress is rapid at this stage of the construction and we pay little heed to all the off-cuts mounting up on the side of the patio. Those off-cuts are much more exciting than the lovely long straight bits. Just ask any grasshopper. Better still, just watch what the two of them can do with them. It was time for a break as lunch was getting close.

The architect in the family is definitely grasshopper. In the space of ten minutes she had constructed a tall tower of blocks stacked one on top of another. We could only marvel at her dexterity in being able to get it to a meter height. She looked towards us with bright eyes and a big grin to make sure we were watching.

"WHOP!" And the whole structure came tumbling down to the laughing sounds of the tower's creator. We adults can be so dumb! It was never about the building of it. It was all about the destruction! Pumpkin didn't take part in the several repeat performances, each of which got louder and louder. She was busy being 'creative'. Pumpkin had found a reasonably large block, and a long plank and was carefully trying to find the balance point of the plank on the block.

None of us could have foreseen the consequences of a malfunctioning see-saw. Pumpkin was perched on one end, up in the air and Grasshopper on the other end … bawling. She had her hands trapped between the plank and the deck surface. Decking lost a bit of its appeal for a day, at least until the pain in her hand had abated. May and I finished setting up the bearers and joists, ready for the final stage the following day.

Transition for the girls from waking to sleeping was smooth that night. Granddad didn't have to growl. Just as well, because my mind was both preoccupied and greatly disturbed by the information gleamed from last night's researches.

Ng8-f6

147

Zsoall Robi

I would have liked to have been able to share my thoughts with Ulie and May, but it wasn't possible. The idea that the rise of terrorism should bring about such extraordinarily comprehensive personal surveillance somehow didn't make sense to me. Why was that the only solution? Why was comprehensive education not a part of the equation? Perhaps I'm being cynical thinking that a multitude of educated people are harder to control. Better to keep everybody half ignorant and feed them fears - obviously the best way, for that is exactly what TC-S is doing. The State controls the levels of competency of our education system, and the Church continues to feed the fear of reprisals by the Deity if the people don't conform to religious dogma.

In any case, terrorism is now an efficiently organised campaign perpetuated by TC-S against the people they govern. To tell individuals their deaths have been pre-programmed, but not to supply them with the date … surely that is an act of terrorism.

Any counter-terrorism activity must assuredly be aimed exclusively at regaining personal freedom. But not so much freedom that under the cloak of anonymity undesirables could commit atrocities. Death should be random and unpredictable. I would go so far as to say that we, the people, should have the ability to freely choose our own time and method of dying. That attitude might be considered heretical. I would be immediately accused of heresy by our 'saints'. Is there a punishment for such a thing in our society? I don't know.

Bf1-c4

      Zsoall Robi

Sabt

The worst day of the week as far as I was concerned. Nothing could happen on Sabt. Work was not allowed on Sabt. So we played - not so bad. The day turned out to be quite hot, perfect for a pool day. First on the program was the 'urchin toss' in the pool, something like the caber toss, but with little children being propelled into the air as opposed to a tapered pole. It isn't for the faint hearted, especially for the parents of the child.

"One ... Two ... THREEEEEEE! With a sudden release of granddad's muscular potential energy, Pumpkin flies through the air in a graceful dolphin arc to plunge into deep waters several seconds later. Was that fun do you think?
"AGAIN!" She cried.

So granddad launched the pumpkin again and aging and again. "More?" What a silly question. Then granddad introduced a slight variation to the theme. At the next launch I put an extra little twist to her feet at the end of the launch resulting in a dolphin summersault!
"AGAIN!" She cried once more. Almost all of granddads reserves of potential energy had been transferred into kinetic within fifteen minutes. What can granddad possibly do next to amuse a waterlogged pumpkin and grasshopper? Crazy running jumps! Scoop up an unsuspecting grasshopper, hold her tight and do a monumental leap into the pool. Everybody screaming, everybody laughing! Next victim please – pumpkin tries to escape – May holds her tight and hands her over to the mad jumper. More laughing and screaming!

Loytar calls out "Let's hold hands!" First it is only the two of us. After the third jump we have Idda holding granddad's right hand while Loytar holds his left. Such a big splash that May gets drenched while trying to sunbathe on the pavers. Next jump there's four, then Ulie joins in. "Yeahhhhh!"

The day would not be complete without the dolphin dives. They are the best. Pumpkin is an expert and knows exactly how to control a granddad dolphin. Perhaps grasshopper is still a little young or she doesn't quite get the technique of diving under the water together and swimming as far as we can. So Loytar and I have the pool all to ourselves.

"On the count of three," I say. Pumpkin counts down, already on my back with legs clamped around my waist and arms around my neck.

"I can't breathe!" She takes no notice – Three!" She yells. I have to dive, air or no air! Breaststroke – stroke one, stroke two, stroke three, stroke four – choke – surface – cough. We will have to modify the technique.

g7-g6

"Hold me around my chest with your arms."
"Yes granddad."

We try again, and this time we dive from the edge of the pool not the second step. I can feel pumpkin starting to slide, but she clamps on tighter. We almost make it all the way to the other side.

"Mum! Mum! Did you see that?"
"AGAIN please granddad!"

Would I rather be in the pool with the urchins, or in the air with the eagles? A hard choice. Both offer such a great degree of freedom curtailed only by the tyranny of gravity. It makes me think of the kinds of freedoms still allowed us, and the kinds that have been denied us. I have the growing fear that the freedom to have our thoughts in private is in jeopardy. As our intent is often reflected in our body language, in our actions and in the words we use, we are already under considerable constraints to be circumspect. We can't trust the people around us, just as we cannot trust ourselves. Ignorance may be the better choice if one wants to live an unobstructed life, without fears of interference by the Peace Corps, the arm of TC-S best placed to protect it from losing power, losing control of the masses – and the bottom line, losing profits.

I'm a Ghost – I think. I want to be a Ghost – I think – no, I definitely want this. They have done the operation, now I must prove myself. They have said nothing to me, given me no help, no idea of what I should and shouldn't do. Perhaps that's part of the initial training. I will keep researching and learning, and I will do nothing to draw attention to myself.

Trembling little bodies and cold lips heralded the end of the day's fun by the pool. Granddad still had enough energy left to wrap the two urchins in fluffy warm towels and cuddle them until they complained.

 Zsoall Robi

Dominica
Nailing day

Surprising how quickly it progresses with a bit of prior planning, and a few helping hands. The girls have been keen to help again, the see-saw incident completely forgotten. Finding opportunities for little hands to get involved represents another layer of creativity that cannot be forecast until the moment the need arises. May and I cut the decking boards more or less to length and lay them out over the joists. For several meters we have to nail the boards in place by ourselves.

Bc4xf7+

The girls are beside themselves with anticipation because I promised they could help with the nailing. There is a primeval pleasure in clouting a nail on the head with such comprehensive force as to drive it home. There is no reason why urchins should not share in the pleasure. However, we must circumvent the pain that comes with hitting the finger holding the nail and not the nail itself.

So we start with a couple of light weight hammers, each urchin independently deciding the best way to hold the implement is to choke it with a death grip right near the head. No amount of persuasion could convince either one of them to hold the hammers further up the handles. Amen, wisdom will come with time. May tries to teach by example, but with no effect.

My job is to drill every, and I mean every, single location where there is to be a nail. Yes, it will prevent the composite decking from splitting. More importantly the holes give the nails a nest to hold them in place without having to put one's fingers in the danger zone whilst hammering.

Ke8xf7

May has begun putting a few nails in the holes and is driving them home. She says nothing to the girls. I stop and watch what they will do. I think Grasshopper will surely be an engineer. She takes the lead almost immediately and starts to copy the process. Pumpkin tries to copy her little sister's initiative. How many times does the nail have to be hit before it is flush with the deck? Only three times, that is if you are

Zsoall Robi

hitting the nail and not everything else around it. Taking aim is something the urchins must learn by themselves. But it kind of takes the fun out of nailing if after ten hits only one has scored a bull's eye.

May decides the girls might enjoy putting the nails in the holes more than wielding the hammer. Good decision. As soon as the new procedure is implemented we make famous progress. It becomes a race to see whether May or granddad can hammer faster, and if we can hammer fast enough to catch up with the girls as they put the nails in the holes ahead of us.

Repetitive processes tend to send my mind into the cavernous realms of introspection. Only two more months before my next appointment. It already feels like I'm getting ready for an assessment to be accepted into the ranks of the Ghosts, even without knowing what I'm supposed to be doing. At least I can take something with me to the session. I have learnt a few things about the NNET. It may only be its history and my conclusions may not be a hundred percent accurate, but at least I will be able to have an intelligent conversation. I haven't been idle.

Greeog hasn't been far from the surface of my thoughts either. What will I say to him if he decides to meet me? What does one say to a person risen from the dead? Will I even recognise him after all these years? I try to remember his face and it eludes me. Remembering the memory of someone is an unreliable source of information. All I can recall is what PDad told me many years ago. We never really spoke about Greeog after the Peace Corps stopped looking for him. The strangest thing that does come to mind is the look on our parents' faces when I mentioned his name. One would expect some pain to show, perhaps worry or remorse. Anything but disinterested neutrality. It didn't seem at all strange at the time, after all the harassment by the PC. But now, thinking back, it must have been because they knew he'd become a Ghost and they could not afford to give even the slightest indication of that knowledge.

h2-h3

I can understand now why they were so guarded about Greeog. They may not have been Ghosts themselves but they must have been using their positions with TC-S for spying and no doubt all manner of more dangerous activities. Greeog - the more I think about him the more I want to see him. A month and a half later I received a communication from the SDD Clinic.

"Werd here Zallo. You need to come in for a check-up. The adjustments we made require periodic inspection. They are required by law and also to maintain your continued healthy sleep patterns. Next week, Woden 9:30 pm."

He didn't wait for me to respond. It sounded much more like a directive than a request. Something must have happened, unless those kinds of check-ups are truly routine. I didn't know what to make of it. Ulie wasn't happy about it.

"Whatever it is you're doing I don't like it. I thought you said you've been sleeping without any problems. How many more times are they going to bother you?" She had a point. I would have to ask them, especially if the re-visits diverged from established patterns of SDD activity.

Greeog

The SDD Clinic
2172-12th September
Woden – 9:30pm

izard woman was obviously keeping up the deception when I arrived for the appointment. "Your code," she demanded. "2359599942APR252105ZALLO-LIOAN-CALI." I was careful not to smile at her or show any sign of recognition.

"Sit."

I'd brought a different book this time, one that I've already read but did it for the purpose of not breaking up the pattern. As it was a bit before my appointed time I had a chance to read, although my thoughts were on the questions I wanted to ask. They didn't let me speak much before, maybe this time I'll get a chance.

Nb8-c6

Eventually Werd appeared and we went to the sleep room. He was pleasant enough without being familiar. I made a mental note of that and did the same.

"Do you think there is a problem with the adjustment you made?"

"No. It's purely a formality we are required to adhere to. A report has to go to TC-S." It seemed only moments later that Sisi was urging me to wake. My immediate reaction was to notice she didn't have her hand on my wrist. I felt a twinge of disappointment.

"You are switched on," she said as soon as my eyes focused on her face.

"Hello Sisi," I ignored Werd and Dr.Peels.

"You did very well when you arrived. We are pleased you've followed our protocols so far," Sisi volunteered a smile for me, "We have a little more time than before."

Zsoall Robi

"Do you have any questions?" Dr.Peels asked while Werd attached some other monitors to my scalp, chest and wrist. I sat up and commented on the frequency of my visits and if there was anything unusual in that.

"We have been monitoring you since your last visit and the NITS implant."

For a moment an uneasy feeling surged to the surface of my mind. *Here we go again! Just another bunch of people watching my every move!* But then realised it was a different kind of surveillance. "We are aware of the research you have embarked upon, and the astuteness with which you realised some of the more critical aspects of our anonymity. But be aware we are not the only ones keeping an eye on you. If you continue your research with the same intensity, your activities will be flagged for closer scrutiny. In order to safeguard 'us' we will have to terminate you if that happens. There are no second chances for Ghosts."

d2-d3

I listened to Dr.Peels' words and turned my attention to Sisi. Her face was deadly serious. Werd just looked at me almost as if I had already ceased to exist. I got the message and looked back to Dr.Peels.

"Understand this Zallo, the deeper you become involved with us the more you will need to be on your guard against TC-S and against 'us'. Each Ghost, after an initiation period, is given the ability to terminate another if they believe that Ghost's anonymity has been compromised. You will effectively have three enemies, albeit for different reasons."

"Who is the third," I asked, although I already had my suspicions.

"You - Yourself, through any small lapse in concentration, in vigilance, in the slightest moment of hesitation when clear and decisive action is needed. In short, any small matter of carelessness can and will cut your new career path short." Dr.Peels was making it easy for me to understand the impermanence of being a Ghost.

"Do you want to continue?" Sisi smiled as she put the question. It became very clear to me that if I even hesitated with my answer to this simple direct question then life would immediately drastically change.

 Zsoall Robi

"Yes," I said quite plainly and without any show of undue enthusiasm. Werd was watching his instruments as I answered. Sisi and Dr.Peels were watching me, and Sisi had again put her hand on my wrist without my noticing it. Sisi looked at Dr.Peels and nodded, as did Werd when Dr.Peels raised questioning eyebrows at him. I seemed to have passed the test, perhaps not the only one to be administered.
Werd removed all the monitors and I even received a handshake from each of them.

d6-d5

"We know you are keen to meet with your brother," Werd informed me, "He's agreed to see you. Amongst the Ghost community there are those who are so deeply under cover they rarely meet with any individual, Ghosts or anyone else. So he's taking a considerable risk in exposing himself to you. From now on be prepared for the unexpected anytime, anywhere. He has been given the ability to switch on your NITS."

All I could do was to try and take in everything being said, realising I was indeed placing not only myself but many of those around me in great danger; Ulie, PDad and my mothers, these people at SDD and possibly Greeog.

"Yes," I said again, confirming my answer to the original question.

"Our time is almost up Zallo. Please follow these instructions. This isn't a request in case you are wondering. Spend more time with your parents. Particularly with your PFather. He has survived many years living in a most precarious position. I have spoken with him and he will instruct you. If you are sufficiently astute you will understand what he's telling you. Keep in mind he's not a Ghost. So anything he says or sees or hears, will be recorded by TC-S. Do not question him about your Death-Date-Code." Dr.Peels didn't elaborate on the last instruction. I guess this must have been my first lesson in trust. He continued after a brief pause and a glance at Werd.

"If you must go Tripping in the future I strongly advise you to seek out sequences on your History String unrelated to any of your previous Trips."

He's obviously telling me to avoid delving further into the details of my death certificate.

"There's nothing to be gained by going back to your birth event. The things you need to know will be revealed to you sometime in the future. There's also another danger you're not aware of and one TC-S doesn't freely publicize. They can and do manipulate data on History Strings: Enough said about *that* subject."

Qd1-f3

That much had already become pretty clear to me from my research. It was almost mandatory for a controlling force to do exactly that if they wanted to maintain a firm grip on the fate of the people they were using for their own benefit. No wonder Tripping was so readily and cheaply available.

Every time I came to the SDD Clinic I ended up with a great deal more on my mind than I had bargained for. Dr.Peels was relentless, and although Sisi didn't say much her steady unblinking stare definitely made me think of her more as a predator than as an ally.

"One last thing Zallo," Dr.Peels continued, "You will have a shadow for a while. Don't look for it, don't think about it, and if you think you have identified it … you haven't … and don't try to make contact with it under any circumstances. If it becomes necessary to terminate you, you will not even be aware of it as it will happen instantaneously – Do you clearly understand me?"

I nodded without hesitation. There were no longer any illusions, delusions or romantic ideas in my mind about where my life was heading. It didn't worry me. All I could think about was seeing my brother, and breaking the hold TC-S had on me, on us.

When I arrived home Ulie wasn't waiting for me by the front door. I expected her to be there with a few of her penetrating questions. She might still be in bed. Kitty was there, flag pole raised vertically and eyes giving me the 'feed-me' look. Although it was only Woden I was feeling particularly tired. No wonder. It was only a relatively short session at the SDD but it still interrupted my normal sleep pattern. Without bothering Ulie I fed the lioness and myself as quietly as I could.

D5xe4

The breakfast ritual always has a settling effect on my mind. It gave me a chance to think things through. I came to realise the more information SDD confided in me, the more I was drawn into the resistance group, and the greater the chances became for my life to be cut short. Wouldn't that put a kink in TC-S's plans for me if I died prematurely! I smiled at the idea in spite of the rather unwelcome repercussion for myself.

Customers were waiting for their orders to be completed. It was easy to forget the more mundane aspect of my life, for it had become mundane in relation to everything else going on. I even forgot to count the number of steps between the house and the studio. After a few hours of immersion in more creative activities I remembered about PDad.

"PDad, can we meet and talk?" He wasn't his usual circumspect self when I called. The only reason for that would be because Dr.Peels must already have contacted him.

"Does after lunch today suit you son? Say around three, at Restaurant Three Hundred in the main tower?"

I didn't know the place, but it couldn't be hard to find. There's generally only one restaurant per level from there to the top of the tower. It's the kind of place only people with the right kind of credit could hope to go to without being left destitute afterwards.

Ulie hadn't come out while I've been working, which was very odd. Surely she must have been awake by lunchtime. The house was very quiet, no sign of life at all. I found her still in the bedroom, just waking up.

"What's the matter Ulie? Aren't you well?" Her reply was a surprise, and I decided it would be best to deal with it after I've had the meeting with PDad.

"I've been up most of the night." She looked at me as if waiting for me to say something. I just raised my eyebrows. "It's a long drive to the SDD Clinic, and I couldn't stay and wait for you to come out."

I waited, not sure what I should be saying, if anything at all. If I thought my freedoms were curtailed before, it was now at a whole different level. What could I possibly say about what I was doing, or even demand to know why she decided to spy on me, for that matter.

                                              Zsoall Robi

Nc3xe4

"PDad is … that is … I have a meeting with him and I need to go." Ulie stayed in bed as I left her bedroom. Although much has changed in my life in a very short time there was no reason not to continue my simple renewable pleasures. One of those was riding the motorcycle. There is something cathartic about moving through the countryside at speed and sensing all the aromas of life, feeling the slightest variations of temperature, and moving to the rhythm of the winding roads. The mind relaxes and one's thoughts easily permeate through the helmet into the great freedom of the Cosmos.

Without even being fully aware of it, the motorcycle had brought me to my destination. How could one possible not be aware of a five hundred level tower complex? If you see it often enough, it almost ceases to exist to the senses. Like a painting that has been hanging on the wall for the last ten years. Only its sudden absence can proclaim it ever existed. As I get out of my gear I start thinking about how Ghosts can stay undetected if normal people can see and hear them. Perhaps it has something to do with their code and how they register on surveillance systems and peoples' NNETS.

I was a little early, but went up into the tower anyway. The feeling inside the lift is peculiar. It's strange because there is no sense of movement at all, not even when the lift stars to move. Those lifts can move vertically as well as horizontally, so you never really know where you are at any moment of time, until arriving at your destination. They move so fast they seem to defy the passage of time. Within just fifty seconds the door opened to the entry of the restaurant. All I needed to do was to give my code: "2359599942 …" I started.

"Just the last six characters."

"AN-CALI." PDad had obviously made the reservation and he was obviously well known there. The thing to notice here is that the last six characters of the code didn't entirely define me. It could just as easily have referred to my brother.

Nc6-d4

The receptionist moved aside to reveal a tastefully furnished sitting room, with discretely placed partitions to divide up the space into more intimate proportions. There were only four or five seating arrangements visible, and in front of us a ceiling to floor transparent force field revealed the landscape. Instead of using glass or clear aluminium the force field gave certain advantages. I'd heard of them, but never actually experienced one before. I was led to our table directly in front of the window and could immediately feel a slight breeze and a certain aroma to the air. The field could be adjusted to filter the outside air and let some of it into the restaurant. It felt as if one was sitting outside in the open air.

I knew that aroma, but couldn't immediately place it. At this height sometimes low clouds obscured the landscape, but today it was clear. One could observe everything stretching as far as the eyes could see. At first my attention was drawn to a meandering river as it reflected the light of the now slowly setting sun. Then a slight movement caught the periphery of my vision. Eagles, several of them, circling and rising. Suddenly it pierced my memory ... the aroma ... it was the same as what I had smelt when in the glider with PDad all those years ago. I became totally absorbed in watching those great birds manoeuvring and didn't hear PDad come up beside me.

"That's exactly why I like coming here, son. How long have you been waiting?"

"Just a few minutes, maybe five at the most."

"You have been staring out the window for the last twenty minutes. I've been watching you." He said and saw my face become incredulous with disbelief.

"This is one of the small pleasures of my life." He added.

I don't know if he noticed it, but my expression became even more surprised. He had never, never, actually said anything like that to me before. All I really knew about him was that he was my PDad with a highly trusted position in TC-S and now, that he had a clandestine life as well. I was beginning to remember the father I once had when I was still young and with whom I went flying.

We stood there for a little while longer, absorbed in a wonderful, shared experience. No one came to us when we were ready to order. PDad just spoke quietly, directly ahead of him and minutes later our refreshments were brought out.

                                              Zsoall Robi

Qf3-d1

"Did you have trouble finding the place?"

"Not at all. I've seen the tower so often it's almost like it wasn't there for my eyes to see at all, and I just stopped in front of it without thinking."

"Yes," he said, "sometimes when things become so familiar they no longer seem to be noticed." I waited for him to continue, but he didn't. He just looked at me as if expecting something from me. Then he asked,

"Did you have any trouble getting into the restaurant?"

"No, actually. They didn't even want my full code."

"Yes, I know. They are so used to seeing me here and knowing all the codes closely associated with me, they don't give it a second thought." Again he looked and waited, but not for long.

"Tell me about your sleeping. Is it any better since you've had the adjustment? Did you have to go back for a check-up?"

Sometimes I can be as thick as two short syn-planks! It just started to dawn on me about the 'not seeing the things that are so familiar' thing. PDad knew perfectly well I'd had several visits back to the Clinic, and he also knew about my NITS. He was testing me! - from the very first moment he arrived. These people just don't let up!

Nd4-c6

"Yes, a couple of times. They had to check the settings were right, and they had to do some kind of report for TC-S. Have you ever had any trouble sleeping Dad? Perhaps it was a question I should not have asked, but I had to find a way to know how far I could go with things.

"Now that I think about it, yes. Many years ago, when I was a lot younger than you. I started having nightmares about a flying incident that almost ended my life. After a while it became so serious I had no choice but to get some help. They are very good at the SDD don't you think?" He was doing it to me again.

"Exceptional. The technician had worked out my issues without my having to go into long winded explanations. He knew what to do, as did everyone there. The service was fantastic, and the attention to every little detail highly professional. They even gave me comprehensive

 Zsoall Robi

instructions on how to capitalise on the changes they had made." I thought myself to be pretty clever to have alluded to the 'secret' things, without actually talking about them directly.

"I'm pleased you are satisfied. If you had any further problems would you go back to them?"

"Without hesitation." I don't know what kinds of problems Dad could envisage, but I felt sure that whether they were related to my sleeping patterns or my Ghostly activities, SDD would help. To change the subject, I decided to ask him about his work. As soon as I had put my question I realised I'd overstepped the line, as did he. But he didn't react. Instead he ordered something else for himself and asked what I wanted, while at the same time recommending various delicacies I might like to try. I got the message.

"The same as usual," he said to the invisible servitor, then to me, "I've taken a little time off because your BMother has been unwell."

Then our conversation revolved around BMum's health issues, eventually coming to the conclusion it wasn't anything especially serious, but she still needed looking after by both himself and PMum. Then he resumed the topic of 'work' by asking me about what I was doing.

He seemed interested to know I'd been doing some important jobs, like the one for SDD and the unusual one for the special client. I even ventured to mention I was thinking about writing some fiction, and had started doing some research. At the mention of research, a cloud seemed to pass over his eyes. Again I became wary. It seems I had been flying too close to the wind with some of my probing questions and comments.

Ne4-g5+

"Was it because BMum is not well you suggested we meet here?" I brought that in as a logical place to go rather than to pursue the 'research' topic.

"Yes, son. I was quite worried about her for a while. But we didn't want to concern you until we were sure of what was going on. As it turns out the situation is nothing that can't be cured, so we decided not to tell you until now."

I had it my mind to talk to him about Greeog, but thought better of it. Perhaps another time. Anyway, I'm sure he knew exactly what was

Zsoall Robi

happening and that my brother had decided he wanted to meet with me. There was really no need for me to bring the matter out into the open. It would have showed my obvious lack of experience.

We sat opposite each other, parallel to the window and were both drawn to looking out into the sky. A light aircraft made its way across our field of vision. We could clearly hear its engine straining a little against what must have been a strong headwind, although in the sitting room we felt only the light breeze the force field allowed in. The sound and the smell of the burning fuel interrupted our discussion as we gave ourselves over to the experience. It was one of those very rare occasions when Dad and I shared a few moments of such delight.

All too soon the aircraft disappeared from view and our attention returned to the sitting room. We smiled at each other. I think that moment was the most rewarding and important of the entire meeting. In that moment we exchanged an understanding that the future would be very different for both of us. We knew the dangers that lay ahead if I was to embark on my clandestine activities, and I have no doubt we both felt the bond between us grow much stronger; not just because of the shared danger, but because of our joint experiences of the past and what we had just immersed ourselves in a few minutes before.

"When can I visit BMum?"

"Wait till the end of next week. She should be well enough by then to be out and about."

"Dad, there is just one other thing – Ulie – She's very worried about my health and I don't think she really trusts the people at the SDD Clinic. Could you speak with her please? You've had experience with them, and I thought that reassurances coming from you would settle her mind. I wouldn't want her to be doing something unhelpful that might make things more difficult for me."

Kf7-g7

He listened patiently, probably not thinking anything unusual about what I was asking. There was no reason for him to suspect Ulie had done a most remarkably dangerous thing by following me to the Clinic one night. I was definitely not in a position to explain anything to her, not unless she joined us. Now that I think of it, that might be the safest option. It would stop her from spying and drawing attention to us.

                                    Zsoall Robi

"How soon, son?"

"Before I get home. The sooner the better, anyway."

We left the restaurant together. What a remarkable place. I had no idea such places existed. Obviously there are many layers of existence that are not available to all and sundry. Not unless unusual circumstances broke down the barriers. Makes me wonder how the Saints and the Angels live. Are we out of touch with them, or are they completely out of touch with us? I think PDad made a deliberate attempt to introduce me to a small part of that other world. Not only had he taught me a few things already, but he's preparing the future path for me.

c2-c3

At home I was greeted with a somewhat cold reception. Not hostile, as I expected. It was difficult to tell if she'd spoken with PDad. Ulie announced she was going to visit May and the girls for a few days. There was nothing unusual in that. It was one of those little things she particularly enjoyed. The timing was a bit odd though. Normally she would leave early in the morning. The overnight bag was already at the door, and Tober had been freshly washed. Idda was going to be ecstatic to see her favourite little dog. They were the very best friends.

"When will you be coming home?" I thought it best not to bring up the difficult subject just then. She didn't smile, she wasn't angry.

"Two or three days. It'll give you a chance to get back to your normal sleep patterns."

So PDad did speak to her! I thought to my self, much relieved. Whatever he said must have worked, otherwise I would be getting a serious grilling right about now. I'll have time to go and visit BMum and catch up on a few things in the studio while she's away. The evening is ours to do with as we please, or as I'm directed by Kitty. Better to read in bed than to put the fire on. Anyway, that's best when Ulie and I can enjoy it together. Tober likes to stretch out in front of the wood heater, and even Valisy will come and join us. But both Dog and Ulie are gone, Kitty seems content to just to hang around and wash her whiskers and bottom. I make a light meal, as the food at the restaurant still made me feel replete; something simple just to get the ritual right. Ikik was happy to go to bed early and didn't make a big fuss when Valisy came into the bedroom we all shared.

Zsoall Robi

For a while I read with Kitty beside me, purring and being 'nice'. There was no lunge at my exposed arm to take a bite. She must have had a fulfilling day. The book, exploring the nature of Time, seemed appropriate in light of the research I'd been doing into History Strings. If space-time could in fact be bent or was actually bent, then it became entirely plausible to have History Strings that looped so their beginnings joined their endings. To make that an actual reality very little needed to be done. Simply determine the time of death of the individual, by bringing it about at the scheduled moment and the History String would be completed. My book quietly slid off the bed.

How would that work for creatures other than man? Can any living being die prematurely? If the creature had died and was resuscitated, how would it effect its History String? What if it happened to me? Would it be possible for me to go to Playback Inc. and ask to experience the sequence of my premature death?

h7-h6

I became unsettled in bed with those disturbing thoughts, and had the feeling Valisy had moved up onto my arm and was starting to shut off its blood supply. Moving the arm slightly seemed to make no difference to the pressure. I couldn't even feel the tingling sensation when the blood started rushing back into the arteries. Shaking myself awake I opened my eyes only to see a face bending over me. It didn't make sense. Kitty rarely did that. I felt my arm being squeezed and lightly shaken. There was a hand attached to it, the other end of which belonged to … belonged to … to a man. I sprang out of bed! Not fully awake, or fully alert but fully prepared to hit whoever it was that had woken me. I could see the clock out of the corner of my eye. It was two thirty-three in the morning. The man didn't move.

He said, "I have switched you on."

What an odd thing to say, but somewhere in the back of my mind it made sense. I'd been switched on before – the SDD! Realisation dawned quickly after that. The man must have seen the play of enlightenment on my face, for he spoke again.

Ng5-f3

"You know me," said the figure.

ℬy the bright moonlight I could just make out his features. No, I didn't know this man. He was a bit younger than myself, well groomed and appeared to be wearing expensive clothing. *He switched me on?* Ah! I couldn't believe it! He noticed me examining him so he moved a little more into the light of the moon. It couldn't possibly be the one I was suspecting. This man had such ordinary features; he could have been anybody and nobody at the same time.

"Greeog?" I whispered. He nodded. "But how …? You don't look like …"

"Cranial work."

ℐ couldn't accept any of this and decided it was one of those bad dreams I'd been having before the adjustments and moved towards the bed to lie down again.

"Do you remember the day I disappeared?" The question stopped me dead in my tracks. My mind flew as fast as it could through the forest of brother memories. The SDD came into focus.

"You'd been to the SDD …" I said.

"Then I didn't turn up at the Adjustment Institute …"

"Yes! And the …" I said.

"… Peace Corps hounded you for years looking for me." Greeog finished the sentence for me.

"It really is you!" I moved towards him to look more closely into his face. "It - really - is - you!"

𝔚e sat on the bed beside each other without turning the lights on. It was bright enough by the moonlight. Kitty ran and hid in the bathroom. Ikik let out a few little squawks and went back to sleep. I was told Greeog would make contact but I didn't expect it to be so soon. Everything was moving so quickly all of a sudden. We just looked at each other, silent, pensive. Without truly recognising his face it was almost impossible to have an emotional connection to this individual. He started talking about little inconsequential things from our common past; like the times we played silly pranks at the Adjustment Institute instead of following all the rules. He was truly a rebel, I only misbehaved. Greeog spoke about all the occasions when the other kids

Zsoall Robi

went out with their dads and we had to stay at home because our dad was always busy at work.

Little by little I began to feel the connection to this man who said he was my brother. He spoke like my brother. He had that cheeky tone to his voice like my brother. This was my brother! Impulsively I reached out and embraced him. Then the floodgates of my emotions opened up and words started gushing out almost incoherently. Greeog just sat there and listened. He listened to everything. I knew he listened to everything because his eyes spoke to me.

e7-e5

I told him about my bad dreams and my eventual visit to the SDD. He nodded.

"I know," he said.

I told him how I hated the whole concept of being spied on remorselessly through the TC-S implant. I explained about the people at SDD.

"I know," he kept saying.

There was really no point in my going on as he seemed to know everything, just like our PDad. But I persisted until I had completely unburdened my soul. There was never anyone I could talk to openly, not even Dr.Peels or the Lizard woman or even Werd.

"I've been following you, your shadow so to speak. I was in the restaurant when you met with our PFather. He knew I was there."

"But how can you go about like that in broad daylight? You're supposed to be a Ghost. Aren't you in danger of being recognised?"

"Not in the normal ordinary way you're thinking of. What I'm about to say is … well, it's one of those things that could end your life if you divulged it, shall we say 'unwisely'." I nodded, remembering what Dr.Peels had said, several times. "You already know about the cranial work. The alteration has been recorded at TC-S. You seem surprised. What did PDad say about not seeing the 'familiar'? However, the Peace Corp systems have been programmed with a 'does-not-exist' flag, and although they respond to my image they don't record having seen it."

"But what about your code? Everybody has a code. It's like having a heart beat."

"Ah, yes, the code. We all have one, just as we all have our NNETs. My code is always recognised, but never reacted to. The Saints

 Zsoall Robi

and Angels have their codes too. But they, like the Ghosts, are invisible to the TC-S and Peace Corps systems. Our NNETs operate like those of everyone else. When there are NNET integrity checks, ours show up as working normally. However, none of the data they transmit is recorded."

I listened in awe at everything he was telling me. So there was a way! The very same technology with which the Saints and Angels gave themselves freedom, denying it to us at the same time, could be used against them. My mind raced ahead, not hearing what else Greeog was saying. Was it possible the TC-S system could somehow be infiltrated at the highest levels of out global government?

Qd1-c2

"Zallo, Zallo! You're not listening to me. We have very little time. It's fortunate Ulie and Tober are not home, but our time together is not unlimited."

I snapped out of my distraction to focus on his face again. Greeog was looking extremely serious. I didn't want him to go yet. We had planning and plotting to do. His frown was telling me something different.

"You will not see me again until I initiate contact. There is only one thing you must, and I emphasise most strongly – must – do for the time being. Live your life as you have been doing. Don't get involved in anything out of character. Don't do anything to draw attention to yourself, and spend more time with our PFather."

I nodded, keeping my thoughts of insurrection to myself. He then gently motioned for me to lie down.

"Go to sleep now."

That was an impossibility. My mind was racing, I was fully alert and needed to act. Greeog pulled down the blinds to darken the room against the light of the moon. My eyes followed his every move. It was my brother – here with me – now – in my room – after all these years. He just stood there, saying nothing more, watching as I began to struggle against the weight of my eyelids.

There was so much more I wanted to say, so many questions I wanted to ask; like, when will I be like him at the same level of operation as a

Ghost, and as invisible as he was? When had my normal life ceased to exist? What about my family; Ulie, Bird, our naughty adorable poodle puppy, Kitty, Pumpkin and Grasshopper …"

"MIAOW-Orrrrrr! Mew, Purrrrrrrrrrrrrrrrrr…"

"Kitty, be quiet! It's too early." The room was still dark. The room was still dark? Peeking through half open eyelids I saw the drawn blinds … drawn blinds … Greeog! Suddenly I was wide awake. I hardly ever draw the blinds. Kitty jumped up on the bed and while I was stroking her the whole of the early morning's meeting came flooding back.

Live a normal life he said, be ordinary and uninteresting. Maybe I can do that – now I know Greeog is alive, that there is something we can do to fight the tyranny. Spend time with PDad – yes I can do that too. He's making the effort also. He wouldn't be doing that without a reason. After breakfast I made an appointment with Playback Inc. for another Trip. Perhaps this was going to be my last. At least it didn't break my recent pattern of Tripping. I though perhaps it would be best to do it while Ulie was away. It would only give her something else to worry about.

Bc1-f5

Trip five

Data corruption
2172
On the road with Nethenk

lie would not be getting home for another couple of days. It gave me time to do the Trip and if necessary, to recover from it. Although there wasn't much to be concerned about as I'd chosen a different location on my History String. My body was ready for pick up at the usual time. Amazing how accommodating Playback Inc. could be to 'regular' customers. I had only contacted them on Woden morning and by Faith evening I was on the way in their specialised vehicle. From my newly acquired perspective it almost seemed a little suspicious that Playback Inc. should be so accommodating. The unfortunate thing about the knockout potion was that it left the mind blank once the induced coma kicked in. So any ideas that might have begun to unravel along those lines simply ceased to exist.

Bc1-f4

Nethenk wasn't only a dedicated pilot but also a keen motorcycle enthusiast. We went on rides together reasonably frequently. Our respective preparation rituals were almost exactly the same. If you had any self respect as a serious rider your motorbike needed to be treated with tenderness and affection. Both of which could be lavished on it by maintaining it in top condition and as clean as a brand new machine. But perhaps that wasn't a universal law because the third member of our party, Rageme, seemed to have the opposite philosophy. If the bike didn't look like it was being used, then it probably wasn't. That entailed making sure dirt and mud were clearly visible in all the critical areas, indicating better than words that the machine and its rider had been 'off road' and into serious two-wheeled adventuring.

The ride today was sedate by some measures, entirely on made roads and with regular comfort stops. In other words, a civilized outing. Our destination, Tooloom Falls, was somewhere in the Yabbra State Forest about two hundred kilometres distant, with one major stop at a festival camp site set up for bikers. It was promising to be a good day.

All three of us had antique machines. One BMW, a Goldwing trike and Nethenk's Yamaha Boulevard. The BM was the only on/off road bike and Rageme must have recently had it off road. My Wing was immaculate when we met early in the morning, as was the Boulevard. Nethenk keeps his machine inside the house, on carpet. He probably didn't even need to bother cleaning it the day before, like I did. But then that's a pleasure in itself.

To get the maximum enjoyment out of it first you need to make the bike look chaotic. Lavishly lather onto it copious amounts of soapy water, making sure even the undercarriage and the exhaust pipes are well covered in swirls of suds. Then stand back and admire how good it is going to look after a hosing down with high pressure clean water. With any luck the bike will dry with dust spots, dust which would have got caught in the drops of water on all the surfaces while you took the bike out to dry in the wind as you raced it down the road.

Bf5xd3

Wax and polish. Rub the wax on in small dry sections, letting it set into a white powder on the surface. This isn't a laborious, onerous task. It is an opportunity to slip into a Zen-like state and begin to enjoy the forthcoming outing in its state of virtual reality already nestled in the mind. As each section is polished to sparkle it brings the reality of the ride a little closer.

I know this is only a playback, but even in the expectation of the known event there is more enjoyment to be harvested, unless I think too far ahead.

We meet at the studio just as the sun begins to rise. The weather forecast is worrying Nethenk. He would prefer a sunny, dry day. Rageme doesn't care. He's a hardened, all-weather rider. I would prefer overcast, cool, possibly with a slight rain. One of us is happy, another could be happier and Rageme didn't care as long as he was on the bike.

We all needed full tanks and tyre pressure checks. I arrived at the service station first, closely followed by Rageme. Nethenk took a while getting there, as usual. Not a good sign, I thought to myself. He must have had some very bad experiences in the past on wet roads, and must be taking extreme care around the corners. Either that or there's something else on his mind. The weather will probably clear up a bit later and we'll make good time. There's always a destination, but the ride isn't always about being there.

First stop, the Festival camp site about an hour out. Rageme took point, myself second. It had started to drizzle. Beautiful. Obviously the BM enjoyed those bends because Rageme cranked up the speed and I had to hustle to keep up. Fifteen minutes in I remember the Boulevard and glance into the rear vision mirror. It's not there. Now, here's the thing … when you're on the road you watch out for each other. You keep the bike in front and the bike behind both within sight. If there is a problem, then you can do something about it … that is, if you can see the bike.

If not …

But Nethenk wasn't there. I had to slow down and let Rageme disappear into the curves up ahead. Slowing down wasn't enough. I had to stop several times until I saw his headlight again, relieved. By this time Rageme must have been ten minutes ahead of us. No problem. As long as Nethenk was alright. I let him get nearer before pulling out onto the road again. I cranked my speed up, but he didn't seem to respond. I must have been daydreaming for a few minutes because the next time I checked the mirror he was right behind me. Ah, Good! We're on the way.

Qc2-d2

The road had decided to wind itself around the many hills in the valley, instead of cutting through them. That's what you want on a bike, curvaceous asphalt, come rain or shine. The Wing was just getting into a nice left-right-left rhythm when I remembered Nethenk again. Too many bends behind me and I couldn't see him, so had to slow down again. I found my mind concentrating on him to the exclusion of everything else, even our outing. I kept watching the road behind me more than the road in front.

In such a situation the most unlikely scenarios start going through the head. Injury, death, what to do, who to call etc. etc. etc. Nethenk, Nethenk, Nethenk. That was the only thing on my mind. By the time he came around the nearest bend I was almost on the verge of turning around and going back to look for him. He's completely relaxed, enjoying the ride. I should do the same. While the imaginary drama unfolded in my head the clouds had parted a little and the rain stopped. Perhaps now the road will dry and give us a better running surface.

Rageme had also stopped some way ahead. We were getting close to the Festival camp site, so the stop would give Nethenk a chance to catch up. Not that I blame him for being cautious. He's only had the bike for a little while and was probably still getting used to its handling dynamics. I would not even let Ulie pillion on our new bike until I had several hundred kilometres under the wheels. Probably not the best day anyway, to be out in the rain. At first we couldn't find the Festival camp site. Nethenk knew the area better and soon had us heading in the right direction.

Bike talk - Coffee and bike talk. Bikes of every shape and size, model and age were parked beside tents small and large. There is no end to bike talk, everything from the latest scandal, the latest horrific accident to the latest bit of new technology to make the ride even more complicated than it needed to be. It's known as progress. The stage was already set up for the evening's musical entertainment and over to the left of the stage, in a large flat paddock, a mass of dead scrub timber had been gathered for a bonfire. Unfortunate we couldn't stay.

e5xf4

Perhaps if there was a way to connect with another person's History String then the experience could have been shared. Playback Inc. had said it wasn't possible due to myriad complications arising out of cross referencing data. I couldn't quite understand what the implications were, but it didn't sound safe. It was comforting to know that TC-S had emphatically backed the safety of the system, reassuring the populace that the best possible Transmission Control Protocols had been put in place.

Zsoall Robi

Why should we worry about something so far removed from our ability to set right if something did go wrong? With only a couple of hours before our scheduled stop for lunch it was time to get going. Rageme again took the lead as he seemed to know the way. Nethenk brought up the rear. This leg of the journey was more relaxing for me as we kept pace with one another the rest of the way to Urbanville. Nevertheless, I continually scanned the mirror to make sure Nethenk was following. I was still completely preoccupied with keeping an eye on him, instead of fully immersing myself in the countryside and the experience.

The ramshackle country hotel didn't inspire confidence on first sight. Somewhat dilapidated, needing a new coat of paint, a refresh of its signage and perhaps a friendlier overall presentation. So it came as quite a surprise to be met with a most welcoming atmosphere upon entering into the main lounge. The open fire extended a warm inviting greeting, offering us comfortable lounges in front of itself for our cold weary bones. This second stage of the run had brought us along some difficult and rather poorly maintained roads. I was so fatigued from manoeuvring around the many potholes and keeping an eye out for Nethenk that the lounge seduced my tired body almost immediately.

0-0-0

The place was well patronised and most people were there for a meal, as well as the warmth. What can three men talk about, in public, after they had already exhausted their quota of bike talk for the day? The meaning of life perhaps? Much too dangerous a topic. Under normal circumstances it would be a much safer topic than say politics, or religion or even the fairer sex. So we spoke about our respective families, and we talked about food, the weather and the condition of the road and how we were going to get to Tooloom falls from Urbanville.

Bd3-e4

Anyway, it was time to move on after spending a goodly hour in front of the fire. Not easy when one is feeling replete, warm and thoroughly comfortable. As we were getting our riding gear on, my mind got entangled in finding a solution to help keep as together on the road. My head became full of Nethenk again and I didn't take part in the conversation between him and Rageme as we left the building.

                    Zsoall Robi

*

"Look at this," Mada, the Playback Inc. technician monitoring Zallo's Trip called to his supervisor. There was enough of a sense of urgency in the voice to make Veste take immediate notice. Variations to the brainwave activity of a Tripper outside acceptable parameters required immediate investigation. A slight variation was acceptable, even expected. The nature of Tripping was such that it allowed for new responses to the experience the Tripper was having. However, those could not be recorded because they didn't originate as new sensory inputs external to the cerebral environment.

There was a definite prominent spike in the EEG. Veste started recording the unusual activity. Although Playback Inc. could provide the sensory feedback to the Trippers, the technicians were not authorised to view the experiences themselves. That was reserved for the Saints and a select few of the Angels. So it was fortunate for Zallo at least that much privacy was afforded him. That may have been fortunate, but not what was actually happening in the playback sequence. Neither Mada nor Veste had the expertise to analyse the event, so they concentrated on recording the recurring spikes over several long seconds.

Qd2xf4

Just a few of those seconds were enough for what was taking place inside Zallo's neural network. What was supposed to be a straightforward one-way feed of personal data, made exclusive by the comprehensive unique code of the individual, turned into a two-way communication channel for just a few of seconds. What the people were told could not happen, had happened to Zallo. The data filters in the transmission system software were simply not adequately tested under the type of conditions that had just occurred. The software firewall had a small flaw.

"It's stopped now," Veste said, very much relieved. Mada continued monitoring Zallo's vital signs. "He's stable and I can't see any change in his condition." He said nervously.

These two technicians were people just like everyone else, living under the same stresses of life imposed by TC-S as everyone else. Perhaps a little more stress because of their specialist tasks, which from time to time involved highly unusual forms of data management. They were more than happy to let the incident slide without making an issue of it by writing up a report. After all, the man had suffered no ill effects, and the anomaly had not persisted. So the uncharacteristic event went unreported.

I must have been so distracted by my preoccupation with Nethenk that as I was pulling on the helmet, I found myself next to his bike about ready to hop on it.

"Whet are you doing Bro?" he asked. "Do you want to try it out?"

I think he was quite willing to let me ride his machine. Unlike myself, who would not have been comfortable with anyone trying to ride a trike without some prior experience. For a moment I became quite confused. I don't know what made me go to his bike instead of mine.

Bf8-d6

"Sorry, no, no, it's Ok. I was just distracted," I said as nonchalantly as I could. "I was thinking about which way to go to the falls. Did you look at the map?"

"No, did you?"

The tree of us looked at one another. None of us had bothered to check out the route, thinking one of the others would have done it. What a laugh.

"You had better take the lead Rageme, since it was your idea. Just don't get us lost." We all laughed. We were all supposed to be seasoned riders with many thousands of kilometres of road surface stuck to our wheels from that part of the world. As if Loki was in control; one of our 'unofficial' trickster Gods wanting to have a bit of fun, we headed off in the wrong direction. Even after finding a pedestrian who gave us directions we still got lost. It took twenty minutes of Gods awful road conditions and a complete absence of any signage for us to realise 'lost' was our operant status. Well, not completely as we knew the way home from where we were, but Tooloom Falls had to wait for another time.

The ride from the pub had been slow and cautious with Nethenk right behind me all the way so far. Yet I still kept checking every few minutes. I think some kind of paranoia must have set in, for it became a

                                    Zsoall Robi

compulsion to keep checking the rear vision mirror. As we wound our way out of the valley and back to the main artery between the local towns, the roads improved and so did our speeds. At least Rageme seemed to shoot ahead at an unnaturally fast pace. I thought I was going at a pretty fair speed. Not so. Unconsciously I had slowed to the same speed Nethenk generally rode at. Very odd.

At the next fuel stop we put Nethenk in the lead with me behind him. Rageme had resigned himself to 'limping' home at a snail pace. He will probably not want to ride with us again, which I can understand. Nethenk and I like to be much more relaxed out on the road.

Nethenk must have felt much better, for the rest of the way he kept up a good speed on the dried roads. We had agreed that from our local village we would each go our separate way home. As Nethenk and I peeled off to the left, Rageme gunned his machine and roared off straight ahead. No need to guess what he must have been thinking. For a guy who's always got everything right, getting us lost would not have put him in a good mood.

Qf4-e3

There wasn't anything unusual in my following Nethenk, for we lived on the same country road only a four houses apart. My place came up first. On every other occasion when we arrived home from a ride together I would slow and turn up our drive and he would continue on. There's nothing I could think of that could have explained why I didn't do so on that occasion but instead continued following him home. I even went so far as to go down the drive to his house.

Zsoall Robi

SDD Assignment

Sleep Disorder Doctor Clinic 2172
Pir – 9:30 pm

alisy called and called, Ikik squawked and squawked and both failed to rouse me in the morning. Although last nights Trip ride had originally taken place a couple of years ago, and although at the time I was considerably exhausted by the end of the day as I recall, the Trip last night felt no less draining. If anything it seemed more exhausting than the original real-live event. Playback Inc. had edited out very little of the experience and consequently it lasted for most of the night. They must have brought me home just before dawn.

In spite of all the good work the SDD had done for me, post Tripping disturbing dreams still prevented me from getting good rest. Several aspects leached from the Trip into the dreams. Part of it was an event sequence loop. We walked out of the hotel after the meal and I was putting on my helmet. Instead of going to my own bike, I went to over to Nethenk's. His questioning my action in doing the odd thing, reset the sequence of action to the moment of the exit from the hotel. The short sequence replayed over and over and over. Anything to break the looping would have been most welcome. The crazy thing was that during the course of the dream I was conscious of exactly what was happening, but could do nothing to stop it.

Qd8-g8

Then another looping sequence took its place. After the last fuel stop Nethenk rode out in front with myself behind. That arrangement didn't seem to satisfy the peculiar demands of dream protocols. So a strange little switch was made. In the dream Nethenk did stay in front, but I became his consciousness on my own bike riding behind him. Anxiety took hold as 'my body–Nethenk mind' became anxious about the road surface if it started to rain again. There was no sign of rain by then but that's what the mind does. The end result was the anxiety looped over and over on itself both for fear of taking corners hard in wet conditions, and loosing sight of the rider in front.

                                                        Zsoall Robi

Foraging animal noises during the night often woke me up. They became the focus of some considerably confronting cussing for having disturbed my sleep. I can only think those noises must have again interrupted my convoluted dreams. As often happens, dreams escape from the light of reality swiftly upon waking, but I do remember the last few minutes of the ride. And perhaps this small, seemingly insignificant event became the most worrying. I was just as keen to get home, have a shower and relax as Nethenk must have been. So why would I have followed him home to his place? I deliberately re-dreamt the sequence to see if there was a clue hidden in there to enlighten me. Sometimes it is possible to return to a dream either to continue it or to rerun it.

After what must have been several hours of tossing about in bed I finally woke to the sounds of a distressed Kitty begging to be let out of the bathroom. She must have identified with my own dissatisfied feelings and we comforted each other when I picked her up for big cuddles. Her purrs seemed to be much louder than usual. There was no option but to call the SDD for an emergency consultation. Something wasn't right.

b2-b3

The SDD Clinic had become unusually busy, and could not possibly accommodate me for at least another three weeks. What was going on? Did I do something I should not have? Like taking the last Trip? Were they letting me know in some subtle way they were not happy with me? Perhaps. The situation was getting confusing for me. In hindsight, perhaps I should have stayed away from Playback Inc. a bit longer.

"So, how have you been sleeping? Ulie asked almost as soon as she returned home. It was uncanny how she could zero in on the most sensitive things with unnerving accuracy. I hadn't even finished helping her get her bags into the house and already I was on the spot. What was I going to say that could possibly satisfy her?

"A really bad one a couple of nights ago," but hastened to add it was all much better now.

"You didn't go on another Trip, did you?" I just sighed. There was no way out for me. "Are you going back to the Clinic again?" Another sigh and an imperceptible nod of the head. It felt like I was

Zsoall Robi

placing it on the guillotine to receive the clean cut of absolution. I felt the need to take the offensive.

"Why did you follow me the last time I went to the Clinic?"

"I needed to know what is happening to you. I care about you. When I ask you about your problems, you say very little and I get anxious." Her response seemed genuine enough. Somehow my suspicion levels have been elevated since becoming a Ghost and understanding how precarious my life expectancy had become. For some strange reason that made me chuckle internally. How much more precarious could it become than to be told your death date had been decided, but you were not going to be told what it was?

"There is nothing more to it than something interfering with my normal life equilibrium, giving me a hard time when I'm trying to sleep. That's not unusual. So many people experience the same kind of problem that a world-wide business has sprung up to deal with it. That's why I go to the Sleep Disorder Doctor. In fact, I have another appointment with them in several weeks." I was feeling better after the little show of self-assertion.

Bd6-a3+

"How many more times?" It wasn't an emotionally charged question.

"As many as it takes." I said.

This thing had to be settled between us. Given her suspicious nature, or should I say inquisitive/caring nature, it could become a security issue in the future. Ulie seemed to relax a little. Perhaps now I could get on with some studio work. Live a normal life, Greeog said. Seems definitely easier to say than do.

The work was beginning to stack up. Several orders were waiting for production, a couple had to be packed and there was a bit of development work to be done on a new concept. Being a well organised person I began by planning out the rest of the day's activities and the priorities for the rest of the week. The length of the list was worrying. The time available seemed to be insufficient if I was also going to fit in my studies. It just didn't seem possible to rearrange the timetable so as to have time for my IFR training as well. IFR? Why the hell was I thinking about IFR training? I had nothing to do with it! Nethenk was the one right in the middle of the course. I'd only been with him for the first session, out of general interest. Sure, PDad has his pilots licence endorsed for many different aeroplanes, but I wasn't that interested in sitting on the back of a brick as it dragged itself though the air. This was weird. I made a mental note to tell Sisi and Werd, as well as about the other odd things relating to Nethenk.

By the time I shook off my disorientation there wasn't much of the day left to do anything productive, other than clean the bike perhaps. It might help to take my mind off things. It was particularly dirty after the recent ride in the rain, even though we didn't make it onto the unsealed road to Tooloom Falls. I kept thinking about how we managed to get lost as I reached for the handle of the garage door.

Suddenly I stopped. That ride was several years ago! Several years ago … several years ago … I kept reciting to myself.

The bike didn't get cleaned that afternoon. No more work got done in the studio either. I didn't even have dinner before going to bed early. Kitty and Ikik were served their meals by their disgruntled butler. There was no reason for them to get embroiled in the unravelling of my mind; maybe not unravelling but definitely having a few hiccups.

Kc1-d2

Must get back to routine, to the comfort of ritual. So I picked up the book about the Nature of Time. Kitty had already settled by my side. For a little while I concentrated on giving her tummy a massage. It worked well, starting up her purr machine almost immediately. I began to think about BMum and her condition. I really should go and visit.

 couple of days later we were on the way. Ulie came for the ride as well. We took the Goldwing in spite of an incredible urge I had to fly instead. It made no sense at all. The distance was too short to go by plane. What am I talking about! I never have the desire to fly as a means of commuting! No need for Ulie to know about my minor mental aberrations. She'll find out soon enough if my mind falls off its perch. All the way to PDad's place the recent strange events occupied my thoughts, successfully excluding conscious enjoyment of the ride. That was getting serious.

                                        Zsoall Robi

It was a relief to see BMum waiting for us as we arrived. She looked a little pale perhaps and maybe a little slower than usual as she came over to greet us. Other than that she seemed fine. I saw PDad watching from inside, as usual. I don't think he only wanted to stay out of the sun. Security and anonymity must be constantly in the back of his mind. Perhaps I should adopt the same strategy. We continued the greeting ritual indoors. PDad said nothing to me, choosing instead to greet Ulie first. My reward for the visit was much greater than usual. I received a handshake from him; a firm, full-handed, protracted handshake. What was that all about? I can't remember the last time he showed such a degree of intimacy towards me. Greeog! It had to have been something to do with Greeog. They must've talked about me and I must have done something right. At least I hoped that's what it was. This whole thing is so … so … so diffuse … so many things happening but so ethereally.

Ra8-f8

Fortunately, Ulie had come along and was able to spend time with my mothers while PDad and I retired to another room. Having satisfied myself BMum was well on the way to recovery from whatever mysterious illness she had; for they evaded all my questions about it, I could leave the ladies to talk about whatever women folk talked about.

"Dad, my nights don't seem to be getting a whole lot better." There was no point in small talk, he would've walked out of the room. He looked at me with eyes that could always work out what was going on in my head.

"Son, did you go on another Trip?" As soon as he asked I re-thought the reason for his 'firm' handshake. It was a 'warning grip'! I should not have done it.

"It was only to enjoy a bike run I had with Nethenk and Rageme some years ago. It had nothing to do with any of my recent Trips." He didn't comment. His head bobbing slightly backwards and forwards said it all. When our eyes met and his eyebrows raised themselves an almost imperceptible half a millimetre I knew he wanted details.

"Some things happened I couldn't explain. Nothing dramatic, only things out of character." PDad immediately became alert. "Do you have any endorsements on your flying licence, like IFR?" I asked.

"Yeeees," He drew it out not sure where I was going with the question.

"Did you ever take me along to any of your training courses?"

"Nooo." He was waiting for me to get to the point.

"I had this incredible sensation, in the studio a few days ago, that I had to make time in my schedule to attend an IFR training session. I became agitated as I couldn't finish the day's work to get there on time. Nethenk's the one who's been doing the training, not me."

Nf3-h4

Dad came over to the couch and sat down beside me, and didn't say anything for a minute or so, as was his way. "And – to come on this visit – I wanted to come by plane rather than on the bike." Suddenly his introspective face was replaced by a cheerful one and he said,

"If you want to fly so much, I'll teach you."

I don't know what I had expected to hear, but certainly not that. It was like the discussion in the restaurant. Without warning he just took a right hand turn in the conversation. OK – obviously it's not a subject I should pursue any further. What about the other things, during the Trip and in my dreams? Maybe I should save that for Werd at the SDD. I started getting lost in my thoughts when I felt him touch my arm.

"I said, when would you like to start?"

"Could we do something next week?" The brain can work things out in an infinitesimally short time when it has to.

I was told to spend more time with PDad – I needed to get to the bottom of this business about flying – and I needed to soak in some of his self-confidence, his … his … whatever it was that enabled to him to live the complex life of so many years.

Dad had arranged everything. All I had to do was to make time for the training. On the way to the airfield I kept having these flashbacks of PDad and I doing almost the same thing so many years ago. Again my memories got mixed up with one of my Trips and reality started getting a little surreal.

"Haven't we done this before, Dad?"

"No son, but I know what you mean. I can remember when we went flying together. But I wasn't teaching you then. We're not going to

Zsoall Robi

fly today. You have to know the instrument panel, as well as you know your left hand from your right hand."

It turned out to be one of the most relaxing days I've had for a very long time. Just being able to bring my full concentration to bear on a simple, uncomplicated exercise totally refreshed my mind. Being with PDad under such pleasant circumstances contributed enormously to the pleasure of the day's activity. I forgot about Ghosts and SDD and Nethenk and all those weird things that had been going on in my head.

When the day finally arrived for my appointment on Pir, October seventh at the SDD Clinic, I was no longer in a panic. Ulie seemed resigned to my regular visits and was pleasant enough when we left home. There was a minor problem with the bike, that's why she had to take me to the appointment. She came into the reception area to see what the place was like. Quite ordinary really. I think she was disappointed and left almost immediately.

Nf6-d5

The same routine started as soon as I stepped up to reception.

"Code?" Sisi was wearing a different outfit. It suited her dark complexion better.

"2359599942APR252105ZALLO-LIOAN-CALI." Resisting the urge to be friendly 'familiar' I said nothing else and sat to wait when commanded to do so. Five minutes later they were ready for me. Werd started the interview with questions about my latest activities, mostly work related. He waited until Sisi joined us before asking about the reason for my visit. We were all very conscious of our lack of privacy, so I tried to keep my comments general. As soon as I mentioned my latest Trip Werd and Sisi exchanged a look. Sisi sat beside me. Werd remained standing, his lips now set into a thin line and eyebrows drawn down towards the centre line of his nose.

"What was the episode about?"

s briefly as I could I explained the scenario, without undue emphasis on my preoccupation with Nethenk. At the mention of the first peculiar incident of going to his motorbike instead of mine, Sisi put her hand on my wrist. This prevented me from going into further detail; firstly because of the interruption and secondly because I was finding this lizard woman – what's the word? – disturbing! It was also Werd's cue to

                                                    Zsoall Robi

start attaching the usual sensors to my scalp. When I started telling them about the next peculiar event Werd stopped me rather abruptly.

Qe3-g3

"You don't need to say any more just yet. Let's get you set up and asleep so we can monitor your reactions. We'll introduce a few gentle stimuli and see what happens inside your head. I have an idea what could be causing a minor aberration. It's easy enough to sort out, but I need confirmation of the diagnosis."

I have to say I found the brevity of the consultation somewhat disappointing. Sleep came quickly as I was tired from a sleep deficit as well as the studio work.

"Your turned on," Sisi announced as she shook me awake. It was unexpected. I thought it would be a simple consultation and a few guidelines to help me over the current sleeplessness symptoms. Dr.Peels didn't look happy, nor did Sisi.

"We asked you not to go on anymore Trips." That's all he said and then waited – and waited. Excuses would not go down well here, that was plainly obvious. I was still trying to formulate an appropriate response when Sisi let out a big sigh and said,

"You will have to die."

"WHAT!"

It wasn't a threat. She wasn't emotional about it, or unduly businesslike. It was just a simple statement of fact. Fortunately, all the instruments monitoring my reactions had been turned off, no doubt because Werd knew my reaction would blow the lot of them. The statement physically jolted me off the sleeping platform, the blood completely draining from my face and my heartbeat – of which there wasn't one for several moments. They could all see my perplexed, uncomprehending distress. Having Greeog appear just at that moment only compounded my incredulity.

He took pity on me. "But not just yet," he said. "First we have to discuss what's been happening to you. Now tell us all the anomalies you've been experiencing."

Ba3-d6

Zsoall Robi

They all listened in silence as I went through all the different events in chronological order. Even to me it was getting clearer that somehow my connection with Nethenk had a close relationship to these interplays of my reality, both waking and sleeping. Werd was the expert on all things related to the NNETs, much more so than I initially though.

"Data corruption perhaps, but more like migration," he said, "but it's not serious. It would've been better if you had not made the last Trip. From what you say, there's been no interference with your History String. However, there has been some degree of cross-referencing during the data migration as you progressed through the event. It was a long Trip, with little or no time condensation?"

"Yes," I managed to dry whisper when my mouth finally responded to my brain's command to speak.

"You might experience a few other minor symptoms. As long as you're aware of what's happening, your neural bio-net will be able to cope with the distinctions between what data belongs to you and any other 'rogue' data."

"About you dying …" Greeog came into the conversation. Yes, the subject rather interested me. "We have an assignment for you. When it's completed you'll have to die. The question is, whether permanently or temporarily." They were all watching me intently. All I could do was to stare questions at my brother. He went on when he felt I'd absorbed the two alternatives. There were no others being offered.

"If the project is successful, then your demise will only be 'theatrical', shall we say." He didn't need to elaborate on the other possibility. My head already rattled without having something else thrown at it, yet that's exactly what Dr.Peels did.

"Has Ulie been sleeping well lately?" My head snapped around to the left to stare at him, to stare the question right back at him. *What has that got to do with anything?* I thought it, but could not say it. He must have read my mind.

Qg3-g4

"There's too much at stake. It's too big a risk to have you operating under cover while she's snooping around behind your back. She'll have to be implanted, and her continued existence will have to be synchronised with yours, whether she contributes to the project or not."

                                                   Zsoall Robi

The words were making their leisurely way from the speaker to my ears. They were even getting into the "I understand" reception desk of my brain. The reality switch was still off. One should never make decisions when that switch is off.

"We can end it all now if you want," Dr.Peels smiled benevolently as he delivered my 'exit clause'.

"No," I answered both for myself and Ulie. *I will wake up soon* – I willed myself to wake up. Sometimes it worked – not this time.

Sisi had not said much until then. "I'll sort things out with Ulie. You just carry on as normal." That was reassuring, as reassuring as being given rubber soled shoes to walk with on fresh lava.

Up to that point all of ten minutes must have ticked away from the life I had left to live. Any brotherly connection I may have felt towards Greeog was fast teetering on the verge of snapping. How could he be so detached, so devoid of any feeling towards me? Didn't it make any difference to him whether I lived or not? Perhaps I wasn't thinking the right things. Maybe my thoughts should've wanted details about the exact nature of this incredibly important mission.

"Zallo – ZALLO – focus!" Can they blame me for drifting? *How can I pursue my simple pleasures with so much shit being stirred into my life?* For a moment even the overt controls of TC-S seemed less malevolent than what was going down here.

"Zallo, stay with us." I heard Greeog's voice, not the voice of the man who was my brother; not the voice of the man who visited me in my bedroom. *Was this true reality?*

"We want you to help us expose a Saint. We have to show the people that the Saints are not pure, they are not all powerful. They don't deserve our respect, our loyalty or our obedience!"

Bd6-f4+

He became a lot more animated than the way I first saw him. His voice betrayed the extent of his commitment; the extent to which he was prepared to go with his own life, as well as the life of anyone who could contribute to the cause. To me it seemed hopeless. Whatever hope was kindled in me when I first learnt of the existence of Ghosts became very badly diluted in the face of the extremes which lay ahead of us. Obviously, in their minds, any concerns I may have had about my most

 Zsoall Robi

recent personal problems were overridden by their plans to put the project in motion. They seemed to be quite happy to let me cope on my own.

"Your involvement is minimal and presents no direct danger to yourself or Ulie," Dr.Peels seemed to want to sound reassuring.
Yeah, like that was working! "You will be contacted by an Angle about a special commission. Accept the job, and do the best you can. Make a point of doing a better job of that any anything else you've done in the past. That's all." The dismissal was as sudden as it was unexpected.

In the morning I was quite drowsy, more so than on other occasions, and pleased to have Ulie there to take me home. When she came into reception she and Sisi acknowledged one another, but didn't exchange a greeting.

Kd2-e1

I slept most of the way home, feeling a little more refreshed on arrival; almost in a jovial mood I asked Ulie, in a mock Kiwi accent,

"Heve you hed a good night's sleep?"

"What? Why are you talking to me like that?"

"Sorry." For some strange reason I just felt like being a bit silly and said the first thing that came to mind – the put on accent. It must have been a reaction to the extremely stressful discussion last night.

"As a matter of fact I didn't." She wasn't happy at all; restless sleep and then the long drive to the Clinic and back having their effect.

The days started flowing into one another with nothing out of the ordinary happening. Nothing, except every time I heard a light plane fly over the studio I rushed outside to see what it was. I couldn't seem to help myself. After a week or so of doing it, it almost felt normal, except I wasn't that interested in aeroplanes.

                    Zsoall Robi

The Commission

2172 – 7th November, Sabt – 10:25 am
An Angel comes to the studio

y mind continued being unsettled every day, as one week flowed seamlessly into the next. That was some pretty heavy stuff laid on me by SDD. Particularly the business with Ulie. Obviously there was no way I could bring up the subject with her. Then the imminent visit from Above, literally, because they all domiciled and worked at the highest levels of the tallest towers in all the capital cities. They actually spent most of their lives with their heads above the clouds. It was rare for any of them to make an appearance at ground level.

Although my dreaming pattern had settled, I didn't get much rest. The worry, the poor sleep, it all added up and I became short tempered and irritable with Ulie and even the animals. I noticed Ulie didn't appear to be well rested either after some nights. When I asked her about it, she denied any problems. But the circles under her eyes were getting darker. Every now and then I tried to make some light conversation, putting on my false Kiwi accent (which I found extremely amusing and satisfying) but it upset her so much I had to stop. Why in the world should I persist with that silliness, it was so out of character.

Rf8-e8

Then one day the communication came. I had to answer a series of odd questions, including giving my full code, the names of all our animals and how many Trips I had been on and their dates. The individual on the other end refused to identify himself even after I had answered all the questions – obviously correctly, for he didn't hang up.

"Sabt, 7th November, 10:25am sharp, be in your studio. Your wife should not be home."

"But Sabt is …" I started to say Sabt was a day on which work was forbidden, but was immediately cut off.

"Be alone, in your studio. Don't come out when we arrive." He hung up. I wasn't given a choice. The caller made it quite clear what was to happen. Besides, I was 'instructed' by Greeog to expect the

Zsoall Robi

contact. I could only assume it was the one he was talking about because ordinary people didn't communicate like that. I was in the studio at the time of the call, trying to enjoy my afternoon break with Valisy, difficult as it was with my head full of uncertainties.

"Ulie, you have to go away – wait, let me start that again, - sorry." A dark cloud had descended on her face as soon as I mentioned the words 'you have to'. They were not three words one should string together to Ulie if one wanted her to continue listening to one.

"The call was from – well, from someone in TC-S about a special commission." The darkish cumulonimbus cloud very quickly developed into an even darker cumulonimbus tower. They're sending someone to the studio on the seventh. I was instructed to stay indoors when they arrived, and for you to be away from the property."

Patchy frost started to form on Ulie's brow. I went over to her and embraced her. What could I say? I couldn't tell her about my 'assignment'. I certainly couldn't tell her the consequences of my making a mess of it.

"It's going to mean a lot of credits for us," she always liked to be in the black, well in the black as far our credits were concerned, "we'll be able to take a long holiday. What do you think?"

Ng1-e2

"What time?" It always surprised me how frugal she was with lavishing her words on my ears. Her good friend May never lacked in that respect from Ulie's generosity.

"10:25 am." I said.

"Could you be a bit more precise?" She responded smiling. That was a relief. I didn't need her dark clouds following me around until the hour of the event. The simple question seemed to ease the tension a little. Today was the fourth, so it didn't give me much time to prepare. What could I prepare anyway, except myself. Feeling in need of a diversion, like being in a comfort zone for a change, I immediately thought of going flying, not a ride on the motorbike, but a flight in Nethenk's Jabiru. Things seemed to be going from bad to worse! Those thoughts must have something to do with what Werd said about the data migration. I only wish my mind would sort the mess out, sooner rather than later. Tripping had lost its lustre as far I was concerned.

                                            Zsoall Robi

They descended from the air with a great deal of noise. There must have been at least two of them because I could hear one land, then the other continued making the noise before it also landed. I don't know what they were, because I wasn't even allowed to go outside. Why should there be so much security? I wasn't a terrorist. I had no weapons, or explosives or any intent to do anyone any physical harm … not yet anyway.

Three individuals entered through the side door. The first two immediately recognisable from their uniforms - Peace Corps personnel. Their faces were so alike and so featureless it would've been impossible to notice them in a room full of people. They walked into each of the studio rooms, quite casually, poked about behind a few things and generally didn't seem at all enthusiastic about their security check. I had no doubt however they were deadly serious. As soon as they returned to the side door, another individual entered.

Nc6-e5

What an absolute disappointment he was. After all the intrigue and all the stories one hears about these Angels, the mind creates fantastic phantasms, probably only for its own amusement, but the musings definitely had the added benefit of putting the mind on edge.

He, or perhaps she, it was difficult to tell which, just walked in almost as if the door they had just used was discovered by sheer accident. About the same height as myself, one hundred and seventy-four centimetres, and wearing the most extraordinary looking suit - It walked up to me within handshaking distance but didn't offer Its hand. As one would have suspected it was no ordinary suit, more like the surface of a computer screen before it focuses on all of its promised imagery. Funny how I looked at the suit before I looked at Its eyes. Maybe it was the symbol all politician-priests used instead of a cross that drew my attention. It looked like the yin-yang sign with slight variations; outlined in gold with an iron cross in each half of the design, exactly like the Templar Symbol of Prosperity. A Priest who no longer displayed the Christian cross, a symbol of suffering and torture - That could only be a good thing, right?

          Zsoall Robi

The creature turned Its eyes on me, with pale irises almost white and pupils just a minute point of black. Perhaps It had some ocular deformity, but I don't think so even though I'd never seen an Angel before - if that's what It was.

"Abaddon," he said in a silky smooth voice.

"Zallo."

"Yes, we know."

"Are you an A…?"

"Yes. Can you make it for us?"

Abaddon hadn't actually looked at any of my work, hadn't looked around the studio, and had not shown me what It wanted made. I know I keep calling him/her 'It' but that's the best my brain could do. Besides, It made me feel somehow – dirty – like I needed to go somewhere and confess to something terrible.

"Only if I know what it is you want."

I wasn't in the mood to play games. It'd got my back up the second I saw Abaddon's eyes. The face, that youngish smooth, unremarkable face other than for the eyes, turned towards me and half smiled, revealing some teeth. There was darkness in the gaps between the teeth, and a smell. My kitty has a litter box in the bathroom that has a memorable aroma just like that when kitty plants one in there on a hot day… I had trouble concentrating on what 'It' started to say.

c3-c4

The front of his suit lit up, an image formed of several intertwined naked bodies.

"I can do better," I said, thinking all they wanted was some cheap porn, or at least that's what it looked like on the first glance. "Do you have a brief for me?"

"Power, passion, out of control. Can you do it?"

"Budget?" I responded. I was really getting to dislike this being. It emboldened me to be cheeky, perhaps beyond acceptable limits.

"With you alive, or dead?"

Are there no other negotiating options available these days than to throw the ultimate bargaining chip on the table? They came to me, so I've got something they want. If the whole thing was set up by the

Ghosts somehow, then I figured I should not seem too keen to get the work.

"If there is a choice, let's make it alive."

"Enough so you'll not have to work again until your death-date-code matures."

That threw a spanner in the works. I might soon be dead at the hands of SDD if I mess this up. My death date might just be around the corner anyway, though probably not until the commission was completed. That's much too soon. I simply couldn't help myself and asked the obvious question.

"When might that be?"

Abaddon had had enough of the game. His pasty white face turned ever so slightly pinkish, the mouth tightened to a thin slit and the pupils of the eyes became even smaller. I had reached the limit of his patience. Ordinary people never get to meet an Angel face to face, let alone have a confrontational type conversation with one. I doubt if this one ventured out of its lair very often.

Ne5xg4

One thing was for sure; they definitely wanted me to do this job – a job destined for no ordinary Angel. The subject matter, and the extent to which I was able to stretch Abaddon's patience suggested to me there was a Saint involved. Possibly even President-Saint Sutsugua himself. I learnt from Greeog, after the job was well advanced, that it was indeed destined for our Supreme Guiding Star as decoration for his private offices at the Global Control Centre.

It was then that Greeog told me what the plan was. The nature of the job, a somewhat debauched sculptural expression of carnal knowledge in its fullest meaning, was perfect for what the Ghosts had in mind. They wanted to find a way to bring discredit upon the institution of Angels and Saints and the nature of the sculpture fitted their intention perfectly. Greeog was going to bury transmission devices within the structure of the sculptural group and effectively spy on our President-Saint. That was stage two. Getting the sculpture completed and installed was stage one. More than that I didn't know. Nevertheless, in my glee I let out an "Awesome Bro!" When he told me. That's not how I normally speak. Yea, my Kiwi mate Nethenk sure does, but not me. It was

                                                    Zsoall Robi

evident in Greeog's reaction that he noticed my deviation from normal speech, but he made no comment.

Eventually Abaddon and his minders moved to the door and they all slithered out. One of the PC officers turned his palm in my direction. I wasn't to follow them out to watch them leave. At the same time Abaddon said, "I'll be watching." He seemed to say this without opening his mouth. At least it prevented the moist kitty litter perfume to escape his lips.

Ulie arrived home much later in the day. "How much?"

Yeah, let's get to the point. Why worry about the intricacies of who I was dealing with, what I had to create, or what the arrangements were or any other insignificant detail.

f2-f3

"It didn't say exactly."

"It?" Oh, she's quick my Ulie.

"It was an Angel, Abaddon, and I couldn't work out if It was male or female."

"What exactly did 'It' say?" She wasn't smiling and didn't seem to be impressed by the nature of the apparition.

"That it would be enough so I wouldn't have to work again until my death-date-code matured." Oddly enough Ulie and I never really discussed our respective use-by-dates. What would've been the point?

"And – do you know when that is?" A perfectly good and logical question, the subject about which I was getting rather weary.

"How have you been sleeping?" I asked back.

"Rather badly actually. I don't know what it is, but if I don't get some decent sleep soon – well, I might even have to go and visit your friends at the SDD Clinic." Perhaps Sisi had been talking with Ulie already. Sometimes I just didn't know what was going on. The dark rings under her eyes were not improving and she was getting more irritable than usual.

"How soon do you have to start the job?"

"Immediately. I'll arrange for some models tomorrow."

"Models?"

"I can't tell you who the customer is – I don't actually know myself – but I have to create a sculptural bacchanalia group and I need some models." Her sleepless nights were only going to get worse after that bit of news. They need not have – on my account – because the only pleasure I was going to get from the experience was to satisfy the parameters of the commission brief, and of course the planned fallout.

Several months later I was only part way through the project. The dimensions I was given, three quarter life size figures, meant it wasn't going to be an excessively long process. Carrara marble was still available, more expensive than gold, but if credit was no object … the problem was the dust and the noise. The maquette had been approved and the carving only started a month or so ago. I spent a lot more time in the studio lately and didn't have any spare to go on bike rides, or play with kitty or indulge in any of the finer pleasures of the life I used to have; just continue with a bit of chess.

g6-g5

Ulie eventually followed her own advice and go to see Werd at SDD. Her sleeping pattern continued to deteriorate. As much as her sleep improved afterwards, her penchant to be so inquisitive diminished. We were given a code word, 'bugs', to use to talk about our respective neural enhancements. Like, "Don't let the bed bugs bite," silly nonsense. We each understood we had our NITS and one day would be able to discuss important matters in security. It wasn't possible for both of us to be at the Clinic at the same time. It would have aroused too much suspicion.

She remained interested in my project. one day remarking quite casually, "I hope the income is going to last till both our death-date-codes mature."

What a strange thing to say. That could only have come from one source. Dr.Peels must've told her about the tricky bits, should the project fail or succeed. She was now as much a Ghost as I was. We were not yet free, and in effect much more enslaved to the goals of the movement than we were to our Government. So we came to a mutual understanding. Whatever else was going to happen in the future, we needed to get something extra out of each day.

Zsoall Robi

Ulie made an effort to spend more time with Tober; take him for walks, playing in the garden and swimming with him. She devoted more time to other little activities she particularly enjoyed. Reading in bed was a favourite, and doing those thousand-piece jig-saw puzzles. I on the other hand, took regular breaks during the day's work to keep kitty's tummy well rubbed, always spent extra few moments with Ikik in the morning and every time I had to go in the house, and always took extra pleasure in the frequent visitations of Grasshopper and Pumpkin.

c4-d5

If the somewhat sinister undertones to our lives had not existed, I think we would have been quite happy with the pleasant rituals of our critters, friends and unusual family structure. Ulie even got used to my regular lapses into Kiwi-speak, which, although I had learnt to curb, still caused me considerable worry. On two separate occasions, which I had not told her about, I overshot our entrance on the way home from getting materials, and ended up at Nethenk's front gate. Sure, I get absent minded from time to time and go past my destinations. But to keep going directly where I didn't belong … that was most disconcerting.

                                                   Zsoall Robi

Death Dates

2173

redits started to flow into out account, a lot of credits. Greeog and the SDD Clinic had been silent for many months. There was one little odd thing though, about the sculpture group. The project was taking so long I had almost forgotten the primary reason behind the creation of it. Some minor details in the design had been changed when the group was about three quarters completed. Finishing the surface generally took the longest, and the process often highlighted the need for small modifications.

Be4xd5

Reviewing progress after a particularly deep sleep one night, which felt almost as if I'd been drugged, the changes were not immediately noticeable. Small dark areas appeared between some of the figures, which previously still had connecting marble elements. I didn't look too closely when I remembered what Greeog had said about hiding some transmission devices in the structure of the sculpture. I was going to mention it to Ulie over breakfast. Fortunately, by then I had come to my senses and realized the folly of having that conversation. Besides, Ulie looked about as worn out and drowsy as I felt.

The only thing I couldn't work out is how the Ghosts managed to drug us so we would not hear them in the studio during the night. For that was the only possible explanation. Are we, as a people, really so vulnerable to covert forces? It seems our lives are not our own, whether it was the Peace Corps or the Ghosts or the SDD interfering with us, it all amounted to the same thing in the end – loss of freedom. There were debates about Free Will centuries ago, as if it might actually have been a reality. We know now it was probably just a myth even then.

Ulie and I started using the extra income. Our life expectancy could not be counted in tens of years or even single years. It couldn't be defined at all under the present circumstances. PDad and I arranged to take my mothers and Ulie to Restaurant Three Hundred, at my expense. PDad seemed most surprised until I told him and my mothers about the special sculpture I'd been working on. Not the details of

                                    Zsoall Robi

course, just the fact that it was going to the Global Control Centre and it was financially very lucrative. PDad took it in his stride, rewarding me with a slight smile, probably just for appearances sake. He didn't seem surprised at all. PMum became worried. Why should she be?

Everyone enjoyed the restaurant environment, the service, the quality of the food and above all the degree of privacy. Restaurants on the ground floor were always so noisy and so crowded, even the very expensive ones. This one could not be considered expensive. It defied that description. What a pleasure it was to enjoy the sight of the birds and the clouds with Ulie, and the aromas of the sky coming through the force field window as it let in the light breeze. As we talked I suddenly remembered how odd it felt again not to have to give our full codes on arrival. Then it hit me. PMum works in Codes! That must mean she might have access to all sorts of codes, perhaps even death-date-codes. But why should it make her worry?

One thing Dr.Peels never mentioned was an orientation course for newly recruited Ghosts. If it was going to take so long for me to join the dots and figure out the connections between seemingly unrelated bits of information, then longevity of life was surely going to elude me. Of course PMum would get upset. It could only mean our demise was imminent. The closer the sculpture was to completion, the closer Ulie's and my step over the threshold of life became. How much longer did we have? Could I stall the completion? No, that wasn't an option. And there was nothing to be gained. We had made our choice, or at least I had, for both of us and that's all there was to it.

Nh4-f5+

It took a lot of self control not to engage PMum in a conversation that would inevitably lead to that sensitive area. If she was involved in any way she was in danger herself. I tried to put it out of my mind and concentrate on enjoying this very rare event with my parents in such opulent circumstances. It might only ever happen once in my lifetime.

The year 2173 started well for us. It brought the rewards of the best commission of my career as an artist, both in terms of remuneration and the degree of creative freedom I was permitted, no – actually expected – to use. Life in general flowed smoothly whilst I worked on the sculpture and there were no traumatic interruptions to our routine. After our sleeping disorders had been 'cured' and our future paths determined on our behalf, there was little to do except continue living as we always had – enjoying the simple renewable pleasures of everyday life. Except of course we knew for certain it was all coming to an end fairly soon. Rather than being depressed by that we both found heightened joy in our immediate family, our animal family and our extended family. Grasshopper and Pumpkin became more adorable than ever.

Amazing how some clients show so little interest in the work they commission. Maybe it's not a fair thing to say because I never actually got to meet them or him, or whoever it was. Even the loathsome, odoriferous Abaddon didn't make an appearance when the day of completion finally arrived. I suppose the fortune TC-S lavished on us must have meant very little to them. They didn't even bother to express thanks for a job well done. It was a superior work of art, the progress of which they were very well aware. If they had not been satisfied the transport vehicle would not have arrived on the appointed day. No doubt other things would have happened to me, of not altogether a pleasant nature.

Kg7-h7

What Abaddon had said about not having to work for the rest of my life was true. Ulie and I had just three weeks left, which we didn't know in advance. We had freedom, at least freedom from having to work to survive. Not only did we have abundance, we had wealth and the freedom to use it. But how does one use financial freedom, regardless of how it was gained? Urgency to indulge made that rhetorical question impossibly complicated. It was still not possible to sleep in more than one bed at any one time, or eat more food than there was room in the stomach or even be in more than one place at the same time.

But of course I was thinking with a mortal mind, the mind of an individual who had an unknown death-date-code and not with the mind of a Ghost. What did it matter if I was already a Ghost? Nothing of real significance had become my specific responsibility. Making the sculpture didn't feel like I was doing anything special. Ulie? How did she feel I wonder? No doubt just as lost as myself. And worst of all, we couldn't

                                                          Zsoall Robi

discuss any of the issues impacting so dramatically on our future. We haven't even had the opportunity to have our respective NITS switched on in each other's presence. So what value was freedom? Obviously the freedom 'from' had quite a different meaning than freedom 'to'.

As on many occasions in the past when the weather was fine, or there wasn't a lot of work, or we simply made time for it, the motorcycle became our escape 'from' as well as our escape 'to'. Was that our freedom? Has anything really changed? Where shall we go? A longer trip than usual might refresh our life energy. Destinations we could discuss without fear of repercussions. East would take us to the coast. We knew the coast well. We knew most of its towns and most of the pleasant places to visit. But there were always too many people, most of them not particularly friendly – too busy with enjoying their freedom or too busy learning how to use it, or just plain too busy, afraid to explore its boundaries.

North or South only took as to other familiar places. We needed something new, an adventure to take us out of ourselves. Someplace where we didn't know anybody, where we didn't know the roads; someplace where there were no great towers with a restaurant on the three hundredth level. Perhaps even a place so remote that we didn't have to use our codes and people would accept our names as 'legal tender'. PDad suggested we leave the motorbike and go on a cruise. It was much safer, he said, and now we had the credits there was no obstacle. Cruises can be nice enough, if there are not too many people on them. These days the ships are floating cities with little opportunity to actually enjoy the sea and all it offers. Mostly they are about manufactured entertainment for a mass of two thousand people, or more, floating somewhere on a big body of water. I became adamant about going away on the motorbike.

"Your mothers want to know where you intend going." PDad handed the comms to PMum. There were many irregularities creeping into my relationship with my parents since I became a novice Ghost; PMother wanting to speak to me was one of them, showing specially interest in such a mundane thing as a motorbike ride.

"We want to go somewhere isolated, away from everything. We need time to decide on a productive direction for our lives. Perhaps we might head out on the Gwydir Highway towards Lightning Ridge." I tried to reassure her we were experienced at touring and I knew how to prepare. She didn't seem at all convinced. I was surprised she didn't make a fuss about our intended direction. Outback Australia was well typified by that arid, remote unforgiving, environment, which no doubt lived up to its reputation to the unprepared traveller.

h3-g4

"Well, I want you both to be extra careful in that rugged country and don't take any chances - Good bye, son." She didn't need to say that, nevertheless it felt good she'd opened up a little. I'd become so used to her always being in the background of the family dynamic that it wouldn't have felt unusual if all she said was a vague farewell. To my recollection she had never before used the specific phrase, 'Goodbye Son'

*

PMum worked in Codes. I knew that. Not from anything she or PDad had said directly, but little bits of information that had filtered through over the years. The day after our conversation she was at work as usual. As a Senior Coder in the department PMum had primary responsible for the accuracy of all codes; Birth date codes, Driving permit codes, Communication codes and even Death-Date-Codes. Under special circumstances she had access to any individual's code string, particularly if she felt an operative had – let's say – made a mistake, or there was some extraordinary reason to modify it. My Birth date code was;

2359599942APR252105ZALLO-LIOAN-CALI. Attached to the end of that string was the following Death date code:

xxxxxxxxxxDEC112305ZALLO-LIOAN-CALI.

The only missing element being the specific time of day.

The actual time of my death had not been irrevocably pre-determined. President-Saint Sutsugua had instructed Angel Abaddon to extend my life expectancy. He was, I much later found out, most pleased with the debauchery implied and expressed in the Bacchanalia sculpture group, but not sufficiently so to bother letting me know, nor telling me about my 'bonus' payment.

PMum made the appropriate changes, introducing a minor error,

2400000000APR252173ZALLO-LIOAN-CALI, changing both the date and specific time of the event.

Zsoall Robi

*

We decide to go West. There are mountains and forests to cross out there and eventually deserts. All we needed was extra fuel. Touring remote places wasn't difficult for us. We had been to places like Van Diemen's Land and Kangaroo Island with its voluminous road kill and frequent bush fires. The decision to do something positive had an enervating effect on both of us.

Qg8-f8

Ulie wanted to go and see the urchins first, which meant at least two nights stay away from home. Pumpkin had her left arm in plaster for many weeks after a fall in the playground of her school. Both the radius and ulna were broken two centimetres above the ulnar notch, near the wrist. Fortunately, they were clean breaks and young bones always heal quickly. Two days after the cast was removed Pumpkin was already in the swimming pool. When Grasshopper heard Nana Ulie was going to visit, May could not cope with her. Little Idda had run upstairs and started packing her small overnight bag, thinking she was coming home with us to spend a few days with her Nana – a repeat event from only three weeks ago. What does time matter to a child? The quicker it passes the sooner a good experience can be repeated.

With Ulie away I had time to set up the bike. Our departure date was Dominica, 25th April. Coincidences always fascinated me. This journey could end up being the most important one of our lives, the beginning of a whole new existence. I was born on 25th April. This stuck in my mind and I resolved to tell Ulie. She enjoyed such synchronicity. Two days were more than enough time to lavish love and attention on our machine. One day for the local mechanic to check all the nuts, bolts, electronics and fluids. One day for a super good wash and a polish to a blinding sparkle. Deep maroon always looks best in full polish and without a single speck of dust.

Rd1-d5

Tober had the added pleasure of taking me for a long walk. "Come on little man, time for walkies!" Dogs have evolved beside humans over thousands of years and countless generations. Unlike us, their path didn't lead them to make bigger and better clubs to hurt one another

                                        Zsoall Robi

with; or to develop sophisticated surveillance equipment with which to control the masses of their species. They evolved sophisticated methods of communication with us, teaching us how to understand them and how to 'read' them.

Tober understood perfectly well what I'd said and what he needed to do. His head came up, back straightened and ears sharpened, focusing his eyes on mine. I nodded confirmation to his question. His lead and collar appeared in his mouth within a single minute, giving it to me with a grin so big I didn't think it was possible.

"Sit, handsome boy." Have you ever closely examined the eyes of your dog and what he's saying to you when he sits like that, with life's greatest promise before him? If you do, you'll understand the true meaning of the word "adoration". This little man did what he's always done, almost since the first time we put a collar on him and took him for his first walk. He picked up the other end of the lead in his mouth, and proceeded to lead me to the front gate and out onto the nature strip. The decision of left or right was always his. A dog needs to feel he can exercise his Free Will. Tober didn't always choose to go left. Ulie arrived soon after Tober and I had returned from our walk.

Our first day's destination, to be determined that evening by us only, proved we also had some freedom of choice, regardless of who was holding our leads. Lightning Ridge seemed like as good a place as any.

There were no witnesses to attest to our arrival at ground Zero on 25th April just before midnight, not until just after midnight; at least none who were prepared to come forward.

Early in the morning, very early at around three o'clock, the motorcycle rolled out the front gate with us on it. Our friends and neighbours, Nethenk and Eneri promised to look after our animals until our return. Not more than three weeks we told them. Tober wasn't happy to see us go, the cats continued sleeping though Kitty acknowledged us briefly and Ikik probably wasn't even aware we were on the way. The plan was to make a big push on the first day and get most of the hard riding out of the way early in the adventure. It seemed straight forward enough.

                    Zsoall Robi

"We'll head towards Texas from Lismore, follow Gwydir highway to Boggabilla then Moree. Plenty of places to fuel up before going on to Collarenebri," I told Nethenk, thinking it best somebody should know our rough plan.

Qf8-b4+

After about five hundred and eighty kilometres on the bike both of us were well and truly saddle sore.

Ulie gave me a nudge, "We'll have to stop. I'm worn out and dehydrated."

"Me too. I have to break through this road trance."

The condition isn't immediately obvious when one is in that state. It isn't the ideal mental or physical disposition for making decisions.

"I think we took a wrong turn somewhere."

Yes, we did study the map before leaving. Yes, it did look very easy, only two major roads, or at least B grade roads to travel. So what could be easier. We didn't need to take a map. Riding into the setting sun for several hours didn't make things easier. Then there was the frustration of keeping a constant look out for kangaroos at dusk and after sunset. Cattle were no longer farmed in that country. They produced too much methane, which was considered to be a major contributor to the global climate change problem. Kangaroo farming had mostly taken the place of cattle.

"That was the last of our water," Julie said, more annoyed than worried.

"I guess you're ready to eat as well." I needn't have said that. It only made the situation worse. Continuing on after just a brief stop I saw a road, the Burren Junction Collarenebri Road. It must surely lead to Collarenebri so we turned left onto it. Within fifteen minutes we saw nothing but flat country by the light of the moon. Absolutely flat. Not a tree, a boulder or a distant hill. The horizon surrounded us completely.

"We are definitely lost," I was loath to admit. It had become so disorienting we had to stop, and pulled right off the road onto the dry verge strewn with small gibbers.

"Should we be stopping right here with all those loose stones? What if a road train came roaring through here? Those stones could turn into lethal projectiles." Ulie became extremely worried, I might even say distressed.

It was almost midnight, in ten minutes it would be tomorrow.

"Yes, we are lost. What are we going to do?"

As we discussed the limited possibilities, faint lights appeared behind us from the direction we had just come. We watched them approaching. On a dead straight road you can't tell how many vehicles are behind one another, not until they're right on top of you.

"Zallo! Those lights – they're coming straight at us!"

"Run – Over there, to the fence!" We ran off to the side and put about ten meters between us and the bike. There was simply not enough time to get back on the bike and outrun the lights.

Kel-dl

Everything happened very quickly as we looked back towards the bike. It was indeed a road train, with four trailers. As it sped by, a piece of large heavy bulldozer came off the back of the last trailer, landing directly onto our motorcycle.

"The bastard didn't even stop!" I screamed after the shock of it and went over to the bike.

"Here he comes now," Julie pulled me away from the bike to warn me.

"Hey, what do you think you're doing?" I yelled at him as he started loading the bulldozer part back onto the last trailer. He took no notice of me – didn't even stop to look at me.

Several other things happened before he finished loading, but we only remembered seeing the approach of another vehicle. It was the escort, as the truck was carrying an exceptionally wide load. We learnt later that the truck driver and the escort vehicle personnel were all fully qualified Ghosts. They were the Invisible Ghosts, not like Ulie and myself who were only novices.

We were still watching the truck disappearing into the distance when two of the escort vehicle people stole up behind us and drugged us with something fast acting. We were told several days later, by a Ghost unknown to us, that at precisely midnight, or as close as it is possible to read the time on an analogue clock, a bulldozer part fell from a road-train trailer and killed two people on their motorcycle when they stopped by the side of the road in Outback Australia. Photographs taken by the escort vehicle personnel confirmed they were Zallo and Ulie Bori. The evidence was corroborated by the sensory input of all the individuals who attended the scene of the accident.

"Right, you got all that?" Greeog asked. "Hello Ulie. Sorry not to introduce myself, but you don't need to know. Here's what happened – A couple of our people drugged you both and took you over to the bike. After a bit of makeup and appropriate arrangement of your bodies under the bike, we took some photos and let the NNETS send the backup sensory evidence." He stopped and waited for us to understand. "You are both officially dead now' a minor event in the greater scheme of things." Ulie just gave me a blank stare. I hate to think what must have been on the tip of her tongue.

The data gathered at the scene was sufficiently convincing that the Peace Corps didn't need to get involved beyond the routine logging of the information and the images for verification. We were dead - alive, yet dead. So where's the freedom in that, I asked myself. The shock of the whole incident caused considerable consternation. Ulie coped with it better than myself I think. Too many other things had been happening to me in a short space of time. It all started with the Tripping. Then the Sleep Disorder Clinic, being recruited as a Ghost, getting killed but staying alive and – and not forgetting all those minor problems with the data corruption after the last Trip that seemed to send my mind loopy. All these events occurring on the same timeline conspired to put my mind into overlapping realities.

Re8-d8

Needless to say, we could not be seen or heard in public, or anywhere else other than by Ghosts whose NITS had been activated, as ours had been continually since the accident. There are always those little details written into the fine print of a contract nobody bothers to read and nobody bothers to tell you about. Nethenk and Eneri inherited our animal family. We were not allowed to go anywhere near them, or our parents.

"Good bye son," PMum had said. Now I understand.

                    Zsoall Robi

Our status as Ghosts was elevated from novice to Invisible through that rather dramatic initiation ceremony.

"What does it actually mean to be an Invisible Ghost?" I asked Greeog, as he was one of them.

"It means you each have to live an entirely new life with totally new identities. It also means you have to live differently and learn to interact with people and organisations almost as if you were an alien from another planet."

I didn't like the sound of that too much, especially the idea of having new identities. Somehow it made me feel particularly uncomfortable. He reassured us we need not be concerned about surviving financially, as the Ghosts organisation had ensured that from the income of my special Commission.

Rh1xh6+

"How will we achieve this miraculous transformation into a new life," I asked with not a little scepticism. Greeog's persona had taken on a diminished lustre for me since learning of his readiness to sacrifice his own brother to the cause.

"Cranial reconstruction to start with, then plastic surgery, then bone augmentations to change your heights and finally new codes with special software links."

"Do I get a say in what I'm going to look like?" Ulie appeared to grasp our new incarnation at its fundamentally most important aspects.

"No." Greeog's answer was as brief as it deserved to be for the question.

"Ah, let's get back to codes again. I was hoping death would bring some relief."

He just laughed and continued, "It's not the codes that are the key element here, but the associated reprogramming of the central computer surveillance system at TC-S headquarters, with its links to all Peace Corps data on you. What I'm about to tell you is such sensitive information that if you weren't already dead, I would have to kill you. Which I may still have to do if there is any danger of a leak or even the faintest suspicion of a leak."

 Zsoall Robi

"Deader than we already are?" Again Ulie jumped in with her peculiar sense of humour. Again she was ignored.

"The reprogramming is already completed. That's why I can talk to you about these things. Although your NNETS is picking all this up and transmitting it, the receptors at TC-S have been programmed to ignore the ingoing data. In other words, you're still transmitting, but they are not recording it. When ordinary people see you or hear you, the same thing happens. Their sensory input about you is transmitted, but the data isn't recorded. So effectively you have both become invisible."

"Awesome, Bro!" What a reaction. It even surprised me hearing it from my own mouth. Greeog raised an eyebrow and Ulie stared at me. I was back to my old habit of mimicking Kiwi slang.

"You don't get all this for free. You will both have some new responsibilities. For the present you have time to reorientate your thoughts before the reconstruction surgeries begin."

Was that an instruction, a threat or just a little kindness?

New recruit for TC/s

July – 2176

wo years seems like a lifetime when preparing to be resurrected from the dead. The Ghosts had created entirely new identities for us, complete with new birth dates and death-date-code certificates. Our medical science had leapt forward in the last few hundred years, taking great strides in surgical procedures. Yet our bodies still had to follow the same old timelines in recovering from those procedures. New bone structures had to strengthen, extended muscles needed time for tempering and the post-operative bruising and swelling still took nature's well established timespan to heal.

Kh7-g8

Two years of constant operations, recoveries, more operations and more pain. Most of all, inactivity and too much time for thinking. Having too much time to ruminate creates monsters in the mind. The imaginary ghouls of uncertainties and fears can quickly become pseudo realities; not unlike all those strange little aberrations of my character resulting from the strange data migration event during my fifth Trip. I asked Greeog more about that, because Werd's expertise was no longer available to us.

"All I can tell you," he said, sounding circumspect even before I'd uttered a full question, "is that sometimes your recorded experiences can be corrupted due to your brain finding a path to someone else's data sets within their History String. Any key word can trigger such an event if the key becomes too strongly concentrated on the surface of the Tripper's thoughts during a playback event and goes viral, searching for its connections."

It kind of made sense, but I was still not fully grasping the implications, although I knew some of the symptoms rather well.

"The greater concern is the feedback loop. Having found its origins, the key can then trigger a memory dump back into the neural network of the Tripper. Do you understand what I'm getting at?"

Zsoall Robi

"Are you trying to tell me that it's entirely possible I'll start thinking I'm actually someone else. But isn't that what you are trying to achieve with years of surgery and software manipulation?"

"Yes and no. In your case the fifth Trip has left some residue of another person in your mind. It's like a memory, but more than just a memory. We think it's quite a weak residue and hope it will dissipate with time."

Rd5xd8+

Greeog didn't appear to realise how much more complicated it was in my case. I think the coming together of memories and re-experiences of events with my PDad as well as with Nethenk, and my personal interest in flying, came together in a unique way and mixed things up in my mind somewhat comprehensibly. There had already been many outbreaks of symptoms pointing directly at the problem. I could only hope Greeog was right about the healing effects of time.

*

Ulie and I had a new home now, with new neighbours and new animal children. We lived in an apartment of a tower just above the commercial floors. In spite of all the rehabilitation, new location and new everything, I still didn't quite feel alive. I often asked myself, '*What simple pleasures are left for me to enjoy now that I'm dead?*' At least I can finish my chess game. That was one very small spark of continuity in my life. I always liked playing the ancient game. It might be more than two thousand years old and out of favour in our advanced civilization, but my friend Idur and I have always enjoyed playing.

For years we played at each other's homes when we lived close to one another. We continued playing via the Global Net when I moved to another part of Australia. We played when I was going through my sleep disorder problem, after recruitment as a Ghost and even now we play. It's a slender thread of sanity I'm most reluctant to surrender. It is one small pleasure in my life of no value to anyone else, so I hope they leave me in peace with it. PDad taught me to play. One day I actually beat him. After that we didn't play so much. In the last two years there's been no contact with my family at all. Undoubtedly they know about us. I knew only what Greeog has been telling me. It wasn't enough. I needed to see them and be close to them.

Kg8-f7

The motorbike was gone and a new one has not taken its place. It had died a true death. Ulie and I had to find another form of recreation for our leisure hours. Fate, or through the cruel machinations of the Gods, I have acquired a pilot's licence during the long convalescence periods; only for light planes and so far without any special endorsements, but I can take Ulie with me. During the course of the last two years many aspects of our lives have changed. We don't just look like different people; we have become different people with new interests in life - all made possible by the almost unlimited credits available to us. Our internal world has remained the same, with all our idiosyncrasies, our needs, our private problems.

It's been difficult to learn to live with this new 'freedom', which has yet to be tested. In the back of my mind there still lurked the urge to try another Trip. I knew it was impossible now. It would put us in serious danger of dying again if I tried. My History String had been terminated upon my death and stored permanently. My beginning had joined with my adjusted predetermined ending. Any request from me to Playback Inc. would only result in us being discovered. Which code should I give them? My new one or my old one. Either would end in disaster. Yet I so wanted to relive some good times.

"Absolutely no way!" Greeog advised against it vehemently. Normally he was a very even tempered Ghost with exemplary self-control. Just the mention of the idea brought an unnatural colour to his cheeks and clenching fists.

"OK, Ok," I said to him, "I only wanted your opinion. It's not as if I was seriously thinking about it." He didn't seem reassured. I tried to convince him as much as I was trying to convince myself. A bad, bad idea.

Rh6xh8

Yet once the rogue thought had made itself comfortable inside my head it became impossible to dislodge. What event would I want to re-visit anyway? It became an obsession. In the absence of any meaningful challenges in my life what else was I supposed to do? Like a slow motion movie, memories of my past life played themselves out as the two years slowly merged into three. Where were those special responsibilities

Zsoall Robi

Greeog had mentioned? What were they waiting for? I had to do something, anything!

Night dreaming became daydreaming. Sometimes they merged into hallucinations. Like my first Trip for instance. Remembering the event became so real, it was almost like a playback session. Was it really only an hours struggle from the womb down the birth canal into the unwelcome light of day? How could anyone forget the face of the man, that sadistic idiot with the bloodshot tired eyes of a basset hound? I recalled the bulbous red nose, the blotches of discoloured reddish skin from drooping jowls to patches of baldness on his scalp, and was again revolted by the very thought of him.

More and more details came flooding back as restful sleep became a thing of great unattainable desire. Worst of all, the last Trip, when I went on the motorbike ride with Nethenk and Rageme, kept replaying itself over and over. Going to bed became a thing to dread. My purring kitty was gone, Bird was gone. What did I have to look forward to except more anguish. The SDD couldn't help me anymore. I was a dead man, and my new identity was too fresh to expose openly to public scrutiny. The Peace Corps was just as likely to be doing a flash security check while I was out and about.

One morning in July I thought I awoke without any memory of dreaming. No dreams? I was expecting to have to agonise over another unsatisfying night. Lying there in silence – Kitty didn't call, nor did Bird – Oh – I remembered – it all seemed very odd.

Kf7-g6

Something wasn't right. Even the bed was wrong, it felt just a little strange. I went to get out of the strange bed and banged against the wall. It was the wrong side! I'd tried getting up on the wrong side of the bed! The impact of the wall sent me falling back onto the mattress. Lying there, trying to work out what had just happened, my arms spread out over the surface of the … as if searching for something. I was taken aback - I was lying in a single bed. It should have been a double bed!

That utterly strange idea propelled me to a standing position, on the other side. I stood there uncomprehending. It felt too early. It was only five thirty, not my normal eight o'clock. While still pondering yet

another anomaly I found myself in the shower, and immediately turned the water off. Evenings! Evening showers! That's my routine.
I never shower in the mornings, only in the evenings! A quick towelling off before putting on my clothes.

Perhaps it was all just part of a very weird dream, and I had only just woken up. That's what it was. The more I thought about it, the more convinced I became. I walked over to Ulie's bedroom. She was still in bed, apparently asleep. There was something very strange about having to walk over to her bedroom. Why wasn't she in my bed?

"Hey, whet are youse doing still in bed?" I asked quietly.

She grumbled and mumbled something at me.

"Whet did you sey, hon? I asked

She looked at her clock. "It's not even six o'clock! What are you doing up already!"

I always get up around five. Why would she say that? I walked away from her door and made my way to the balcony.

Rh8-h6+

Nine thirty came and went before I heard Ulie having her morning shower. It had time to think. Out on the balcony, looking over the countryside, which had become familiar over the last couple of years, it all began to come back into focus.

*

Zallo decided he'd spent the night in the wrong place. He didn't care why he did that – it was too weird. He shouldn't have been there. He knew exactly where he should have been – at home, not at his friend, Zallo's place. Zallo left before Ulie got out of the shower.

He knew Ulie of course. He and Eneri had been friends with Ulie and Zallo for many years. He could even remember how the friendship had come about, down to the last detail. Millie, an old Blue Healer kangaroo dog they found wandering along the country road and rescued. He could remember many other things as well. Like the numerous motorcycle rides he and Eneri shared with Zallo and Ulie.

 Zsoall Robi

They were always good times, some great shared adventures. Sometimes I felt a little – what's the word? – when a group of bikes sped ahead and I was always at the back - left behind – that's it. I wasn't trying to catch up - just having a relaxed ride my own way. There was nothing wrong with taking a little extra care around corners on a wet road. You were more likely not to die prematurely before your death-date-code matured. There was one particular ride, not all that long ago, with Zallo and Rageme when we got lost looking for Tooloom Falls. Zallo had stopped several times to wait for me. It's always a good idea to keep one another in sight, but other than that there was really no need for Zallo to be doing it. I did appreciate though.

About four end a half hours later I was finally getting close to home. I could still not fethom why I should heve spent the night so far awey at Zallo's place. End enother thing, he started doing some really strenge things efter thet ride; even during the ride. Like when he ceme over to get on my bike instead of his. Whet about thet business of turning up uninvited a few times at my plece? Not thet I minded.

The garage door was down and all the doors were locked.

"Demn! Where's my key?" He searched every pocket. Not there. He looked at the secret hiding place. There was no house key there either. '*Bedroom window! Eneri alweys leaves thet open.*' Inside the house nothing was out of place. He half expected something out of the ordinary.

The person who had just climbed in through the bathroom window, and who looked like the 'renovated' Zallo found everything to be exactly where it should have been according to his Nethenk mind. He reached into the third cupboard on the left in the kitchen to get a tea bag, and into the second cupboard on the right for the sugar. Everything was in its place. Eneri always put the jug back in the cupboard, right where he just retrieved it from. Water from the water filter, and five minutes later the Zallo look-alike sat at the kitchen table reading the local paper. He was starting to feel much better; he was at home, in familiar surroundings – Yea bro – much better.

*

                                        Zsoall Robi

"He's been gone for hours! What am I going to do? He didn't say where he was going, just took off before I even got out of the shower." Ulie confided in Greeog.

"Just try to relax Ulie, we'll find him. Was there anything out of the ordinary in his behaviour? Did he do or say anything strange?"

"Well, yes. He was up too early. Much earlier than he usually gets up – and – and he was talking strange. He sounded like a Kiwi again. A lot like Nethenk, now I come to think of it."

"Don't go anywhere. Stay exactly where you are. I'll send someone around to pick you up." Greeog tried to keep his voice as calm as he could under the circumstances. This was an emergency. If the Peace Corps found Zallo before he did, the consequences could be disastrous.

Within fifteen minutes a moving van had appeared with a group of men in their Company uniforms going up to Zallo's apartment. In another thirty minutes the apartment was completely empty. No furniture, no animals, no Ulie, not even finger prints anywhere. There was absolutely no sign anyone had ever been there – scrubbed clean.

Soon afterwards Aabharana, also known as Ulie to the Invisible Ghosts, found herself living in India, looking like a dark brown, unmarried Indian woman. It was Ulie's third incarnation, without her partner this time.

Greeog had a strong suspicion where Zallo had gone. After his brother's fifth Trip and his descriptions of strange symptoms, he knew exactly what had happened to Zallo. He also knew what the most probable outcome would be after the data migration. Nevertheless, the Ghosts took the chance and carried out all the necessary steps to change both Zallo and Ulie in the hope Zallo's mind would not flip. That's why they waited so long before giving him an assignment. They had to be sure he was going to remain as Zallo, and not become Nethenk in his mind.

Kg6-f7

As well as getting Ulie out of sight, Greeog immediately alerted his organisation and arranged for his parents to be informed. His PMother had to make some more urgent changes on behalf of Ulie.

…

 Zsoall Robi

𝔐eanwhile, and unfortunately, the Peace Corps squad which arrived first on the scene of the disturbance, wasn't the one with the Ghost members. The real Nethenk and Eneri arrived home to find their garage door open. Nethenk was sure he'd locked it before they went away. They walked around the outside of the house, finding some crates stacked up under the bathroom window. They lived in a quiet neighbourhood. Thefts and break-ins were rare. It took great desperation for any individual to break the law, given the incredibly tight surveillance system under which the population had to live. Eneri didn't doubt they had a dangerous intruder and immediately called the nearest Peace Corps facility.

"I'm going in there to see whet is happening," said Nethenk.

𝔈neri was against it. These individuals who break into other peoples' homes only do it if they are literally out of their minds. They could be extremely violent.

"I don't want hem wrecking our home! I'm going in. You go to the gate and meet the PCs."

𝔑ethenk was in law enforcement himself once. He knew how to look after himself and he was a courageous, clear thinking man. As he walked into the garage, built as an extension of the house, and about to enter into the kitchen he mentally prepared himself for the encounter. He stopped for a moment to listen.

Rd8-d7+

𝔄ll was quiet – except for – he couldn't believe it. He was sure he could hear sipping; like someone sipping a cup of tea. It was just not possible! His mind refused to entertain the thought, so when he pushed open the kitchen door and saw Zallo, or at least someone who reminded him of Zsoal sitting at the table … the visual image sent to his brain could not immediately find a comfortable resting place. The stranger certainly looked at home with his tea and newspaper – that was clear enough to Nethenk, and unacceptable!

𝔷allo felt the scrutiny and raised his head - the two men regarded each other. Zallo was as surprised as Nethenk, but for an entirely different reason. Standing before him was himself. At least that's what Zallo's brain told him, and what his eyes told him. But he knew instantly it

                    Zsoall Robi

wasn't possible. He jumped up out of the chair and yelled at the man before him,

"Who the heell are you, mate! Whet you doin' in me house?"

Without bothering to wait for an answer Zallo lunged at the intruder. It infuriated him that some stranger should just walk into his home, and was trying to impersonate him! Nethenk, quick on his feet, side-stepped the lunge and pushed the man head first into the wall. Dazed, Zallo staggered towards the kitchen door leading out into the garage. Nethenk took a hold of him by the collar and his trouser belt intending to shove him outside. Zallo twisted himself around and landed a fist hard against Nethenk's temple, dropping Nethenk to the floor. Zallo was getting ready to kick the prostrate man's head just as the Peace Corps arrived - two separate teams of them rushing into the garage.

Kf7-g8

Each team though the other was a back-up, the Ghost PCs being the second team through the door.

"Thet guy looked so much like Zallo I ken't get over it," Nethenk said to Eneri after receiving some medical attention, "and why was he speeking with thet strenge Kiwi eccent?"

Nethenk and Eneri were mystified by the whole incident. As should have been expected the PCs gave them no information at all. Standard PC practice. Nethenk heard no more about the affair - from anyone. After several weeks it seemed to them they must have imagined the whole thing.

As for the Ghosts – they went to ground. The SDD, Greeog and his family all took the evasive actions prescribed in case of an emergency threatening to expose them. All covert projects were postponed and all personnel went out of circulation. The SDD Clinic received an influx of clients; all of whom were 'sleepers' waiting for just such an event to ensure all SDD clinics appeared to have business as usual. Zallo's sculpture for President-Saint Sutsugua had the implanted transmitters immediately deactivated by the Ghosts, so no outgoing signals would be generated.

Zallo's surgical changes were good - good enough to fool anyone in the general public. But not good enough to get past a forensic inspection by the Peace Corps. Their initial scans revealed a close enough cranial match between the man they had apprehended and another individual in their records (who had been terminated about two years ago, as defined by his death date code), to warrant a more comprehensive examination. They couldn't get any sensible information from the man himself during the first interrogation.

When asked his identity Zallo said he was Nethenk Lobasht, the man who lived at the premises where he was apprehended. He even knew his full (Nethenk) code. Clearly he wasn't that man. The detectors indicated that as far as the individual was concerned, he was telling the absolute truth. To the interrogating officers, Zallo's raving about eagles and flying and motorcycles made no sense at all.

Rd7-g7+

X-rays revealed he'd had cranial modifications, as well as leg length implants. The information prompted the PC's to contact their superiors, who in turn informed a certain Angel by the name of Abaddon. Because Zallo's alterations matched the characteristics of a particular artist who had, several years ago, completed a commission for TC-S, everyone in the Peace Corps became particularly nervous. Hence the need to bring Abaddon into the picture.

Zallo's sculpture was removed from its pride of place and totally deconstructed, wrecked systematically in other words, and the transmission devices discovered. Several aspects of the case excited Abaddon's imagination. Firstly, here he had an individual who was supposed to have died, exactly according to his death-date-code. Yet he was still alive. Clever, very clever.

> "This man could not have been operating on his own," he said to himself.

Abaddon next reviewed the data collected during the production of the sculpture. There was nothing there to indicate this man Zallo had a hand in planting the devices into the sculpture. Though he wasn't directly involved, he obviously had something to do with it. Under normal circumstances a rogue citizen would be terminated expediently, without any undue fuss. However, this was a special case. This individual was either incredibly clever, or had a whole subversive organisation behind him - or both.

                                    Zsoall Robi

"His putting on a good act, but I just don't buy it." Abaddon didn't for an instant think the man may have gone loopy.

Kg8-f8

"He should be considered a potential asset, not a threat!" Abaddon was quite convinced about that, so Zallo's personal History String became his exclusive preoccupation. He examined every minute detail along the entire closed loop, as well as the as yet open ended History String of the man's new identity.

"I'm going to enjoy this enormously," he announced to himself at the end of the long investigation after he'd decided on the best course of action. Everything was there for him to see, even a few inconspicuous lines in the algorithm he didn't pick up on. He wasn't a code cutter, so he didn't know what to look for or how to interpret certain pattern changes. That's the only reason the SDD, Zallo's parents, Greeog and others were safe. Those little hidden strings of programming ensured all reference to the existence of any 'unusual' connection between themselves and Zallo would never get recorded.

Under Abaddon's instructions Zallo's History String underwent some major theatrical modifications.

"I want him to see us as his friends," he ordered the programmers.

Whole segments of his life were changed to orient him towards a friendly disposition to TC-S. An entire new theatrical script, because it involved the hand of a master script writer, movie director and a range of actors. Abaddon had embarked on a previously untried experiment to rewrite a man's life, feed it back into his brain and get him to believe it.

"If I could do that, and retain the man's innate genius – well – what an asset this rogue could turn out to be."

With the help of this individual he, Abaddon, might be able to uncover the identity of the organisation that had attempted to infiltrate his master's inner sanctum, and at the same time reap some nice rewards for himself.

'It would be nice – if I could become a Saint!' He thought to himself as he smiled, revealing the rotting teeth and releasing a breath of putrid odour.

Rh6-h8≠

Zallo wasn't tortured. On the contrary they looked after him very well; made sure he became accustomed to luxuries that would not have been a part of his previous life. They even let him enjoy a few simple pleasures, like reading in bed and playing chess. In the afternoons, at intervals of a few days, he was prepared for Tripping and gradually taken on excursions into his newly scripted life. At nights, when he was supposed to be sleeping peacefully, his EEG was closely monitored. If he showed any signs of disturbed sleep, automatic impulses adjusted his theta brainwaves to reduce any anxiety and provide the most restful sleep possible.

Several months into the experiment, Zallo was subjected to tests to see how his perceptions of himself and his 'new' past life-map were being absorbed. Abaddon wasn't encouraged by the results. Zallo still had a very confused comprehension of his past. Abaddon's manipulations only made matters worse. Effectively he wasn't making any progress at all. Zallo's loyalties had not changed; and he still babbled on about having multiple experiences as Zallo, as Nethenk and as some other new identity - the artificial one Abaddon had created for him.

Abaddon could modify the History String, but he could not manipulate Zallo's own internal neural network. As much as their technology had learnt about the human brain, it still remained largely a mystery. Whenever their scientists though they had conclusively defined its behaviour, its characteristics and above all its capabilities, those theories became unstuck. Unfortunately for Abaddon and TC-S, and fortunately for Zallo, his neural data cloud was so comprehensively corrupted during those few seconds of his fifth Trip that no amount of external interference could unravel the chaos.

If only the technicians at Playback Inc. had the experience, expertise and the good sense to immediately take corrective action, then all this would have worked in Abaddon's favour. But as it was, Zallo was safeguarded by the negligence of the very organisation that now wanted to take complete control of his mind.

Zsoall Robi

That evening he finished a chess game he'd been playing with his friend Idur for some time.

"Checkmate!"

"Another game?" Zallo asked eagerly.

----------------------------- * -----------------------

Principal characters

Aabharana – An alternative name for Ulie for her third reincarnation.

Abaddon – An Angel (a Priest-Politician). Ranked as the highest administrative aid to President-Saint Sutsugua, who is the supreme ruler on Earth.

Tober – Zallo and Ulie's miniature black poodle.

Cali Bori – Zallo's PFather (Provider father and Biological father)

Dr.Peels – Manager of the local Sleep Disorder Doctor Clinic.

Eneri – First wife of Nethenk. His second wife died in an aeroplane crash.

Greeog – Zallo's brother who was recruited by the Ghosts, an organisation dedicated to the overthrow of the World political/religious system of government.

Idda – Zallo's younger granddaughter. Nickname - Grasshopper

Idur – Zallo's chess playing friend.

Ikik – Zallo and Ulie's Sun Conure parrot, Nicknamed – Bird.

Loytar – Zallo's older granddaughter. Nickname - Pumpkin.

Lioan Bori – Zallo's birth mother

Ulie Bori – Zallo's wife. He wasn't required by the Church-State to have two wives, or two children.

Mada – Technician at Playback Inc.

May – Idda and Loytar's mother.

Nethenk – Long tome friend of Zallo, and aeroplane pilot.

Rageme – Motorcycle riding friend of Zallo and Nethenk.

Siila Bori – Zallo's PMother (Provider mother. She went to work to earn credits, while BMother remained at home to raise the two children).

Sisi – Receptionist at The Sleep Disorder Clinic, and clandestine member of the Ghosts.

Valisy – Zallo and Ulie's kitten, a three legged Tonkinese who likes to bite into Zallo's arm as well as show other, less drastic forms of affection.

Veste – Technician at Playback Inc.

Werd – Technician at The Sleep Disorder Clinic, also clandestine member of the Ghosts.

Zallo Bori – Principal character, an artist who is eventually recruited into the organisation of Ghosts.

                    Zsoall Robi

Abbreviations

EEG – Electroencephalographic measure of brain wave activity
IFR – Instrument Flight Rules
NITS - Neural Interference System
NNET – Neural Network Transmitter
PC – Peace Corps. The official peace enforcement arm of TC-S
SDD - Sleep Disorder Doctor
TC-S - The Church State

Organisations

TC-S – The Church-State – The Catholic Church had formed a coalition with the World Government to rule the planet.

Playback Inc. – A surveillance branch of TC-S. Its secondary function was to make available to the public reruns of their previous experiences.

SDD - Sleep Disorder Doctor – Addictions to Playback episodes has created major sleep disorders; mixing dreams, experience reruns and reality.

PC -   Peace Corps – The Police Force enforcing the rule of TC-S with little regard for individuals' freedom.

AI -   Adjustment Institute – Each child is required to attend this 'school'. Its primary function is to habituate children to accepting the rule of TC-S and the neural implants they receive prior to birth.

Caveat

'librorum prohibitorum' – The Church-State examines all literature. If not completely banned they still may be published for general consumption but with their seal of disapproval. This is not open for negotiation.

                          Zsoall Robi

Zsoall, born in Hungary, was brought to Australia by his parents after the 1956 uprising in Hungary.

He currently lives a creative life with his wife and animal family in the Northern Rivers, New South Wales, Australia.

His life has changed direction a number of times. Starting as a Secondary Teacher then becoming an Administrative Officer. Neither offered much in the way of creative involvement. That began when he embarked on a career as a Computer programmer. Whilst in that profession his continuing compulsion to create made it inevitable that his life would change again. Completely giving up programming he immersed himself in creativity as a Sculptor and Painter. Much of his time is now spent creating glass paintings and sculptures and in writing Science Fiction.

www.ingramcontent.com/pod-product-compliance
Lightning Source LLC
Chambersburg PA
CBHW030424120726
47903CB00003B/793